JUSTINA SZILÁGYI

*Princess of Transylvania
and Dracula's True Love*

Petronella Pearson

CONTENTS

PROLOGUE

This is the story of a strong noblewoman in times when women were not allowed many fears, desires, and victories, despite life's many twists and turns. A symbol of strength and the nobility of womanhood, she fought through it all and left her marks in the sand of time.

Sunsets were gorgeous in Transylvania. The spectacular view, as the bright orange fiery ball of warmth blended with the dark clouds of the evening sky in a synchronous harmony that cast an eerie, serene yet beautiful shadow on every element of nature, could only be described as breathtaking. Yet, as beautiful as the sunset was, Transylvania could boast of another beauty, one hidden in time and submerged under the ruins of history, subject to the cruel hands of fate but still a conqueror and survivor, a woman who decided against the many odds arrayed against her by fate, to walk her path for as long as she could and keep her head high through every trial when life threw her off balance. She was the one true love of the infamous villain, Dracula, yet her story didn't begin here. It started a long, long time before she met with the Voivode. She was a woman of strength and grit. She was Justina Szilagyi.

Justina's background is as mysterious as she is. Born in the late fifteenth century, around 1455, history has many controversies about who her father was. However, it is on record that she was the daughter of Osvat Szilagyi. Whatever the contradictions may be, the undeniable fact is that Justina was born of royal blood, and she was a noblewoman and cousin to one of the most remarkable kings of Hungary, King Matthias Corvinus.

She lived for only about forty-two years, between 1455-1497. Yet, caught between fulfilling the wishes of her cousin, King Matthias, and satisfying the needs of her husbands, she kept her head high and her pride intact, doing what was necessary and required of her, but not to the detriment of her happiness.

CHAPTER ONE

HUNGARY, 1472 KING MATTHIAS CORVINUS' CASTLE

The tall fortress of the castle loomed magnificently high in the distance. The smooth, hard exterior belied the weariness of age and time. The castle had been

there longer than King Matthias, longer than the king before him and kings before that one, yet it stood high and tall, cold and unwavering as a somewhat metaphorical representation of what the chief occupant was like.

King Matthias Corvinus became king of Hungary, younger than most of the kings in his lineage. He had lived a tough life and perhaps that explains his paranoid outlook on life. As a young child, he watched his father, John Hunyadi, die an inexplicable death as the regent of Hungary and was imprisoned alongside his brother shortly after the demise of their father for ridiculous charges labeled against them. His brother was executed one year later while he watched, leaving him as the only surviving son in his bloodline. King Matthias learned at a young age how cruel and lonely life can be. He learned to protect himself and not trust others; that was how he made it this far after all he had been through. He learned to strike first and act fast if he suspected anyone before they even got the chance to hurt him, and that method, that paranoia, has kept him alive all these years and he would not let go now. Two years after the death of his father, his uncle convinced the royal court, also known as estates, to enthrone fourteen-year-old King Matthias as king in a secret ceremony. He ruled as king under his uncle's guardianship for two weeks, after which he began his direct rule. Since then, fourteen years ago, he has ruled as a strong and fair monarch, doing what he deemed best for himself and his kingdom, even if it means hurting a few people along the way.

King Matthias snapped out of his reverie as he heard footsteps approach in the distance. Out of instinct and because of years and years of military training, his hands went to his sword immediately and his ears perked up. He sat up on the edge of his seat and waited, every muscle in his body alert and ready to strike. The door opened slowly, making a loud squeaking noise as the hinges moved reluctantly to support the door. The figure stood still as they waited to be granted permission to enter. The courtroom was dimly lit, so it was difficult to see who it was, but King Matthias could already guess who, judging from the silhouette. He relaxed a bit and let the sword lie limply in his hand.

"Come in!" His voice sounded dry and grumpy.

The figure approached gracefully, gathering as much of her garment around her as she could while the rest trailed beautifully behind her. Her skin was fair and clear, which is something she has in common with her maternal cousin, the king. She had long, glorious dark hair, and she let it cascade freely down her back in warm, curly waves. Her bright green eyes glowed and glimmered whenever she was excited, but they twinkled now because of the covering of darkness around the courtroom. King Matthias watched with a sense of pride as she approached. It was useless to deny that his cousin was a beautiful woman. He had gotten several compliments on her behalf and won many political favors because of her, although she was unaware of this. He used her beauty to his advantage politically whenever it was necessary, which was all the time. Her delicate, fragile looks mask the strength and grit hidden within her; that was another trait they had in common. Despite her looks, she is one lady who doesn't tolerate just anything; rather than listen and obey like the others, she would talk back and voice her opinions. Growing up she was a girl who would throw tantrums just because she isn't allowed to play with swords with the boys and would run around walking into places her fellow girls wouldn't dare go. He had watched that strength play out frequently while she was growing, and though he would never admit it to her, he admired that quality. He did not like it, but he respected it. She was the only woman in the castle who was both brave and hot headed enough to defy him; because of their strong personalities, they often had clashes and disagreed on many things, but she would not hesitate to let him know if she disagreed with him. In the end, she might have to succumb to his bidding and do his will as king, but she was not easily swayed.

Matthias eyed her as she came to a halt a few feet away from him. He could read the defiance and distrust in her eyes and knew that what he was about to do would not be easy. He could tell she would not like what he was about to tell her, but he was just as stubborn as she was, so he said it anyway.

Before he was King, it wasn't too hard to disobey him.

As a young boy, King Matthias had always been tough. He loved the power he had, especially over women.

King Matthias trained himself hard while growing up.

At eighteen, he was already a skilled swordsman. He knew he was the successor, but wanted to live up to it. He was going to protect his people, even at the cost of a human's head.

5

His little cousin wasn't given that much space though. He always had a way of saying that he was in charge, and there was nothing she could do but obey. He was King Matthias, with an emphasis on "King".

Of course, this made her furious, but she had to obey. "You're getting married!" he said without warning.

She stood glued to the spot, doing everything she could to ignore him and what he had just said. She was behaving like he was not talking to her. King Matthias watched her throat bob up and down as she swallowed back; aside from that, she stood as still as a statue before him. He sighed, running his hands through his hair.

"Justina?" he called. Perhaps if he tried a softer approach, he would get her to agree quickly.

She raised her head and looked him directly in the eye. She was furious, and he could see it in her eyes. She opened her mouth to speak several times, but no words came out; she couldn't get the words to form. It was like she knew nothing she could say could change his mind. He was not asking her permission or suggesting to her. He was telling her what he had already decided.

Her eyes narrowed as she flared through her nose; angry at how he never seemed to care about her feelings or ask for her consent. Who was she fooling? Consent is not needed in the affairs of politics, nor is it demanded.

King Matthias wasn't bothered; although he noticed her countenance, there was nothing he could do. It was for their good. His own good.

Justina felt a rush in her blood. In irritation? Anger? She couldn't say which to pick. Her eyes stung, but she had to fight back the tears. It would make her look weak if she cried. "His name is Wenceslas Pongrac of Szentmiklós. I've invited him to dinner a week from now;

You'll meet with him then." He took a sip of the wine that was on the table before him, gulping it down noisily. "Don't look so sad. I bet you would like him, and this… it's for your good. He's good for you!"

"And you, too," Justina said quietly. Her voice was choked with sobs. She felt furious and helpless at the same time. How dare he decide her fate like she was some puppet to be anchored? She was sick and tired of having to carry out the king's will every time he asked, but worse still, she knew that no matter how sick and tired she was, she would still end up obeying his commands. A countless number of times, she has wished she could leave the castle and live her life freely and independently, away from King Matthias's probing eyes and selfish interest. Maybe, just maybe, this was an opportunity in disguise.

"What?" King Matthias said, even though he heard her.

That this marriage could be her long-awaited chance to escape her cousin seemed tantalizing to Justina, but she was careful not to look relieved in front of the king. It would seem odd that she gave in to his will just like that, and he would suspect that she was up to something. King Matthias doesn't react calmly to suspicions, regardless of whomever they may be. He would crack down hard on it until he found out what he needed to know, and she couldn't have that now, not when she was so close to her long-awaited freedom.

"You heard me, my lord," she said mockingly, with a dis- dainful smile playing at the edge of her lips. "What is in it for you? I'm sure he's good for you, too, otherwise, you wouldn't have made this arrangement. Lands? Military might? More kingdoms? What's the deal, my lord?"

"Justina, you will not speak to me like that. I am your king!" He clenched his fist around his goblet and slammed it hard on the table, causing her to jump from the shock as the impact resounded all around the courtroom.

She bowed her head to apologize.

King Matthias was silent for a while, then he finally spoke. His voice was calm and gentle. "Join me, have some fruit."

"I regret declining your kind request, my lord, but I have no appetite."

King Matthias nodded and waved his hand to dismiss her. He could see the tears running down her face and knew she was waiting to leave his presence before she gave in and let the floodgates open. He couldn't bear to see tears. It annoyed and irritated him, so he let her go.

Justina bowed slightly and gathered her cloth around her as she turned to leave. She was grateful for the tears that ran freely down her face and made no attempt to stop them from flowing. Her chest was heavy and tight as she walked. She felt weak, like she was suffocating and had to lean on the wall for support; breathing was a chore, her vision was blinded by the tears, and her throat was clumped with pain, anger, and frustration. The only thing that came easily to her at the moment was to cry her eyes out, and she did it passionately. Her maids found her crumpled on the floor on the way to her chambers and helped her the rest of the way. Locked in the safe confines of her chamber, she wailed and thrashed, and screamed into the pillow. She was happy that she would escape the king but the fact that it isn't on her terms and she would have to leave the palace where she has found comfort still made her sad.

The night passed in a blur, but the memories lingered for years to come.

CHAPTER TWO

HUNGARY KING MATTHIAS'S CASTLE 1473

King Matthias's castle was abuzz with activity and talks among the servants as the king's commander returned to the palace with a hostage, and shortly after, an emissary entered the castle gates with Lady Justina's maidservant. She was not locked behind iron bars like the prisoner Lord Sebastian returned with, but she looked scared and the servants knew something might have happened because she was not with Lady Justina.

King Matthias was informed of lord Sebastian's return, and he requested Lord Sebastian come straight to him with his prisoner. Not long after, the huge mahogany doors of the courtroom opened and Lord Sebastian walked in, flanked by two other knights of the Black Army on both sides. Behind them, two royal guards escorted a prisoner with bound hands and feet—the chains were loose enough to allow him to walk—to the center of the room. They left him there, saluted the king, and walked back to their post.

"Your Majesty." Lord Sebastian greeted him with a bow, and the two soldiers with him followed suit.

"Thank you, Sebastian!" the king said with a wave of his hand. The soldiers straightened and moved to the side of the room, leaving the king and his prisoner alone in the middle. "Vlad Tepes!" the king said, drawing out his words with spite and anger. The addressed prisoner remained with his head bowed. "Tell me, traitor, why did you betray me? It does not make any difference, but I still want to know. What could have been more valuable than your own life?"

Vlad Tepes raised his head and stared straight into the king's eyes. "I did not betray you, my lord. I would never do that."

"Liar!" King Matthias roared.

"Why would I betray you, Your Majesty? It makes no sense. We both fight for the same cause, to help me keep my throne, so why would I jeopardize that by betraying you?"

"You ask the same questions I just asked you, and only you can provide answers to that, Vlad. You beseeched me for help when the Ottoman Sultan Mehmed II invaded Wallachia, and I marched with my army to support you. So, tell me, Your Highness, why do I have a letter with your seal in it addressed to the Ottoman sultan? You dare pledge your support to that barbarian?"

"Your Majesty, you are a smart and intelligent king. The tales of your conquests are told all over the kingdom, and everyone knows how fearsome you are. But you, my king, did not achieve all that just with brute strength. Your intelligence is unmatched, and you think strategically before you jump into any battle. That has kept you this far. So, I ask, Your Majesty, that you think critically about this before you make a rash decision. I detest the ottomans as much as you do, and do you think that all that disgust towards those barbarians would go away in a flash? What have they to offer me that I would pledge them my support? And if I may, Your Majesty, may I see the letter?"

The king scoffed. "Why would you request to see a letter that you wrote with your own hands? Do you think you can make a fool of me?"

"Not at all, Your Majesty, but I did not write the letter of which you now accuse me. I do not know having sent out such a letter, but in the light of all this, there is an easy solution to this."

"What is that? Your head on a pole? That will happen eventually, but I assure you that if I find out you wrote this letter, you will experience the most excruciating pain, so much that you will beg for death."

Vlad maintained eye contact with the king, undaunted by the threatening words the king uttered. "I had quite a different solution in mind, Your Majesty, and that would be to bring the scrolls written by my own hands and compare them to the writing on this letter that you hold within your possession. That should provide the answers we both need."

"I shall oblige you, and I hope for your sake you are telling the truth, but until I am certain you are not a traitor, I cannot welcome you as a guest in my castle. I shall have a room prepared for you in the dungeon. I trust you will be comfortable there until I have this clarified."

Vlad Tepes bowed his head without another word, and the king gestured for him to be taken away.

CHAPTER THREE

The rest of the week went by quickly for the rest of the castle except Justina. She was awfully aware of every passing minute until the day she was to be introduced to her betrothed. The entire castle was a beehive of festivities in preparation for the announcement of the engagement between the king's ward and a nobleman. King Matthias was not one to do things in halves regardless of what it was, and he certainly would not do less than expected with his cousin's wedding. Not with one that will be profitable to him. He spared no expense in announcing to the royal court, the whole of Transylvania, the surrounding villages, and every land under his monarchy that he was a powerful and affluent ruler.

Justina often accuses him of doing things for himself and his gain. Although he denies that accusation to her face, it would seem her words were close to the truth. There was no one happier in the castle about the impending wedding than the monarch of Transylvania himself. Justina spent most of her day scooped up in her chamber, brooding over the impending engagement. All she could think of was her freedom slipping away from her. She declined all the dinner invitations from the king just to get back at him. She ate very little and barely spoke to the surrounding people in the days leading up to the engagement, but of all the people in the castle, she hardly had an encounter with the king. She knew he would be concerned for her, and the only way she could get back at him for forcing her into marriage without her consent was to ignore him openly. She was careful not to push her luck too far, but the door opened and her maidservant entered with a tray full of olives, grapes, bread, and milk. She walked in quietly, bowing her head slightly when Justina looked in her direction before moving to keep the tray on the table.

"Aargh! Please, Esme, close the windows," Justina said when her maidservant threw the curtains open to let in sunlight.

"My lady," Esme began, "you have been cooped up in here for days. You should go out and get some air." She lowered her voice and looked around the room cautiously. "You will need your strength for the days to come."

Justina's head came up sharply at her maidservant's words. "What do you mean?" Her voice was weak and raspy from crying for so long.

Esme moved closer to her and slowly untied her hair as she got ready to brush it. She oiled the length of the hair, running her fingers through it softly to disentangle the curls. When she was done, she warmed up some more oil with her palm, rubbing her hands rapidly together, and then she massaged it into Justina's scalp gently. It was an age-long remedy between them, she has seen Justina in similar situations before now, and every time, a gentle scalp massage has helped calm her down. Justina relaxed beneath her touch as Esme moved from the scalp to the nape down to her shoulders.

"I've seen no one so tense," Esme muttered under her breath.

Despite herself, Justina chuckled. "You say that every single time."

Esme clicked her tongue. "Maybe because it's true. I don't know how you do it. You become tenser every time."

13

"It's so that I can get free massages from you," Justina said and winked.

Esme saw her wink in the mirror and smiled. "I'm happy to be of help to you, my lady, anytime!"

Justina placed a hand on Esme's, halting the massage, then looked into her green eyes directly. "I'm glad to have you, Esme. You're more than a friend to me. You are family, better than that gruff cousin of mine that's ruling the kingdom," she added with a snort.

Esme gasped loudly and backed away, looking nervously to see if anyone heard Justina's words. "Please, my lady, do not say such words. You'll have me killed. The king might spare you, but me, he will show no mercy."

Justina's eyes softened, and she smiled to reassure her maid. "Don't bother with the hair. I don't care how I look. I won't be leaving my chambers at all today either, so you should just let it be. Give your hands a rest."

"It's not a bother, my lady. You have such beautiful hair... and I'm not just doing it for you. Tending to you helps me relax."

Justina scoffed, knowing Esme was only saying that for her sake. She has known Esme for as long as she can remember, and Esme has been her maid for that long. She was the kindest, gentlest, selfless soul ever, so not that she didn't believe Esme meant what she said. She just wished she could do more for her maidservant.

"But, my lady," Esme started, but stopped, waiting for permission to finish up her sentence.

"Speak, Esme! You know you can always talk to me."

Esme swallowed. "Are you going to keep avoiding the king? I no longer know what to say when he asks me about you. I think you should see him, just once, at least."

"Don't worry about me, Esme. I'll be fine!"

Justina stopped talking and angled her ear towards the hallway. Esme noticed and did the same. They heard footsteps in the hallway moving toward Justina's chambers, and at once, instinctively, they both knew who it was before the herald announced his presence.

"Announcing the king…" the herald began, but was cut short as the king opened the door to Justina's chambers and barged in.

"What a surprise visit, my Lord. Forgive me. If I had known you were coming, I would have fixed myself up a bit," Justina said dramatically.

Esme bowed slightly and scurried out of the room as soon as the king stepped in. King Matthias looked around the room like he was seeing it for the first time, which might not be far from the truth, as he hadn't been in there for a long time. Placing both hands behind his back in the way royals do, he strolled around the room, coming to sit on the edge of her lavender-themed canopy bed. Justina remained standing in the same spot. She had stood to courtesy when he walked in, and she did not want to sit and encourage a prolonged visit.

King Matthias paid no heed to her subtle suggestion, making himself as comfortable as he could be in her chambers. He flung the trailing end of his robe on the bed behind him as he sat, leaning on the edge of the bedding furniture in a relaxed pose. He examined his cousin with careful, experienced eyes.

"I was worried about you," he said after a while.

"Of course, my lord, I…" Justina swallowed back the hun- dred different versions of sarcastic answers that she could have replied with. Instead, she bowed her head and said, "I needed some time to take in what you said to me, and I didn't mean to cause you any trouble, my lord."

King Matthias was surprised at her reply. It was unlike her to reply calmly in a situation like this. If she had replied in her usual way, he would have known what to say to her, but now he was at a loss for words. So, he got up, patted her gently on her back, and walked out of the room. He stopped at the door and turned back towards her. "Dine with me tonight!"

She nodded, and he left.

Esme had been standing just outside Justina's chamber with the king's guards and herald, and she walked back in as soon as the king left. She rushed forward to Justina excitedly. "Will you be dining with his majesty? What will you wear? Not to worry, my lady, I have a few dresses in mind. I'll lay them out for you…"

"Esme!" Justina called. "Yes, my lady!"

"I have a headache. Will you be so kind as to inform the king that I cannot make it to dinner this evening?"

Esme gasped. "Oh, no! No! No! No! No! My lady, the king will have my head. Please, I can't do that, couldn't you…" She stopped talking and threw herself at Justina's feet. "Please, my lady."

Justina was shocked at Esme's gesture and yelped in surprise. She bent quickly to help lift her back up to her feet. "Never do that to me again, Esme. Never throw yourself at my feet again!"

Esme nodded and bowed her head.

Justina relaxed her tone. "I'm sorry. You're right. I shouldn't drag you into this. I will tell the king myself."

Esme's eyes popped from their sockets, and her head came up immediately. "What?" she asked before she could stop herself. Justina looked at her questioningly and she continued, "Please, my lady, five minutes. Stay in there with him for five minutes, and you can excuse yourself to go back to your chamber. Please…!"

Thoughts were running through Justina's head. She knew exactly what to do. The king would not have a hold on her for too long. She smiled at the thought that crossed her mind, it was a good one, and she couldn't wait for it to happen already. Her plan was simple and easy. She wouldn't be confined to the king's demands for long.

"Thank you, Esme, for your sound advice," Justina said with a smile.

CHAPTER FOUR

The weather was exceptionally clear on the day they introduced Justina to her fiancé-to-be. It was as though every element of nature was trying to egg her on and let her know she had support. That morning, she woke up to the beautiful sound of birds singing by her window. By the time Esme came in with her pretty dresses, glass bottles of fragrances, and an array of royal attendants to help groom the king's ward for her big day, she found the ward seated by the window, leaning out with both hands in front of her, palms up and filled with sunflower seeds for the birds to peck. It was wonderful sightseeing as it took an army to get her out of bed in the days leading up to this one.

Justina looked so peaceful and radiantly beautiful with the wind whispering in her hair. The sun cast a radiant glow on her face, making it shine with heartwarming brilliance. She was so at peace and carefree, listening to the birds and feeding them seeds. She did not realize she had company. Esme observed her quietly, hushing the other maidservants that came to attend to Justina with her as they dragged in the local cosmetics they needed for their job. She wanted Justina to enjoy the peaceful solitude for as long as she could, but sadly, it wasn't very long. A small jar filled with fragrant powder fell off the cart and bounced around a bit before settling at the edge of the stool where Justina was sitting. Justina looked up quickly, but she was even more surprised to find out she had an audience.

"Esme?"

"Yes, my lady!"

Justina chuckled softly. "How long have you been standing there? Come in."

"I'm sorry, my lady, you looked so peaceful I didn't want to interrupt. I haven't seen you do that in a while."

"Do what?" Justina asked, although she knew very well what her maidservant was talking about.

"Look so calm and well-rested sitting by the window with such calmness feeding birds and listening to them sing," Esme replied.

"I guess that's because the birds have not been coming to sing either. Why did you come in with this many people this morning? Is there something else you need to do?"

"No! My lady," Esme replied, head bowed. "They're here to help you get ready for today."

Justina laughed quietly under her breath, then turning to the extra help Esme had gained, she said, "Thank you all very much. I appreciate your help, but I'm fine. It will make me feel a lot better if you channel your energy towards something else and not bother about me. Esme and I can handle ourselves."

She bowed her head slightly, and the maids curtsied and left her chamber.

"My lady," Esme began.

Justina knew what she was about to say, so she said some- thing first. "We're having lovely weather today, don't you think?"

"Yes, my lady, but you know what I was going to say," Esme said accusingly.

"I do, and I think it's unnecessary. I do not need that many people to get dressed. I'm not getting wedded today, Esme; it's still a long way away."

Esme opened her mouth, but one look and she snapped her mouth shut. "Yes, my lady," Esme replied with a smile around her eyes.

Justina smiled back, too, and they broke out in laughter. After the giggles died down, Esme stared at Justina for a while with a puzzled look on her face.

"What is it?" Justina asked.

She shook her head in response as if to dismiss the thought, but after a short while, she sighed and spoke up. "You look happy, my lady!"

"And why does that worry you so much?" Justina asked, "You say I look happy, yet you say it like it's a burden that's weighing you down."

Esme paled at Justina's words, and she gasped. "Oh no, my lady! That's not what I mean. God forbid that your happiness would be a burden. That's not what I mean at all. I'm glad you're happy I'm... I'm just worried that perhaps you might not really be."

"Hmm, do you think so?"

"What I mean is, I'm worried you might be putting on a brave face, my lady, just to get through the day."

Justina chuckled. "Oh Esme, you worry too much about me. Of course, I'm trying to get through the day with a smile, but I am happy. I mean, I've done all I could, and it made little difference." She paused. "It changed nothing, Esme, so the best I can do for myself right now is to be happy and at peace."

"You are an amazing woman," Esme said. "Don't look at me like that."

"Like how, my lady?"

"Like you feel bad for me. I'm okay. I can handle myself." She placed her hands on Esme's shoulders. "Stop worrying so much about others, about me. I'll be okay."

Esme nodded and smiled at her. "Time to get dressed, my lady." She lets out an exaggerated sigh, and both ladies laughed off.

~ ∞ ~

"Introducing Lady Justina of the house of Szilagyi, cousin of his royal majesty, King Matthias of Hungary," the royal herald announced, just as Lady Justina walked in, looking beautifully regal in her choice outfit comprising an emerald green dress, supported by layers of fabric underneath and its outer layer a ravishing silk material that sparkled in the light. The bodice of the dress clung fiercely to her chest, giving a little peek of the creamy white flesh of her supple chest to the outside world. The dress emphasized her slim waist in a tight fit, supported by a corset, while the rest of the dress trailed downwards, forming a huge balloon from her waist down. Her hair was held up in a princess-like ponytail that formed a bun with the rest while letting the hair around the nape and the baby hairs in the front fall in luxurious, wavy curls. She completed the deep green and boldness of her dress with bright red local-made cosmetics Hungarian women used for their lips and topped it all up by wearing her mom's emerald- green necklace. Justina was aware of how beautifully radiant she looked, but the stare and sighs that followed her entrance into the ballroom hall were a confirmation of the effect her beauty had on others.

As she had expected, the hall was packed full of faces she neither knew nor recognized. She could only identify about a handful of people in the room; the rest were King Matthias's guests. She drew in a long breath, gathering up enough courage and strength within herself to get through the night. As she exhaled, she fixed a smile on her face and wore that smile throughout the rest of the night as she moved between the small group scattered around the hall, huddled together in discussion or laughter. She stopped briefly with each group to exchange pleasantries and moved on almost as quickly as she stopped.

"My dear Justina, you look amazing tonight," King Matthias said in a loud voice, more for the sake of the surrounding people than for the person whom he was complimenting. Justina broadened her smile and curtsied down to greet the king.

The king responded to her curtsey by extending a hand to help her up. "It's good to see you out and about. How's your headache?"

"I'm all better, my lord," Justina replied.

King Matthias sized her up and down with a smile. "You look much better. I'm rather thinking I might have been hasty in setting up a marital arrangement for you."

She realized the king was making a joke when he laughed out loud at his own words. She smiled at him, unable to get herself to fully appreciate the joke.

The king noticed her forced smile and said, "Don't worry, my dear cousin, I made a good choice for you. I'm sure you will come to appreciate it once you have a better understanding." Justina recognized her betrothed even before she was introduced to him. Although they had only heard about each other and had not seen the other person before she could tell instantly that he was the one the moment she saw him across the hall before he walked up to her and her cousin. He was not a fiercely handsome young man, the kind that has ladies swooning over heels when he walks into a room but, he had a certain beauty around him. He had a quiet strength and a compassionate, kind gaze in his eyes. He was an intelligent man, the kind that would read a book rather than pick up a sword. She was impressed by him; her cousin did make a good choice for her. She was not in love with him, but she was attracted to his gentlemanly nature.

"Aha!" King Matthias said suddenly when her betrothed walked up to them. "Time for some introduction. Wenceslas Pongrac, I would like to introduce you to my beautiful cousin, Lady Justina. Justina, this is Wenceslas, your betrothed."

Lady Justina curtsied to the young man that was now standing in front of her, and he bowed in response to the greeting. "My lady!"

Without another word, King Matthias took his leave, leaving them alone to figure out how to make the best use of their time together. Justina noticed Wenceslas blush lightly when they were alone, and she almost laughed at him. She had noticed how men reacted around her; they either tried to impress her or act shy around her. She guessed that her betrothed fell in with the latter group, and she found it endearing. At least, it would be awkward for both of them, but that was a good place to start.

"Would you like to take a walk, my lady?" he asked suddenly, cutting into her thoughts.

She looked up and blinked. It surprised her he had spoken so soon, but better still, she was more shocked at his request. He hadn't asked for a dance, but a walk. She nodded, and he extended his arm towards her, which she took graciously, and they made their way out of the ballroom. A palace guard noticed them leave and with the way he looked them over and turned to leave, she knew he was going to report to the king. "Ah! Finally, some air!" he sighed as they came out to the balcony. Despite herself, Justina threw her head back and laughed. Wenceslas smiled as though he was impressed with himself.

"I take it you're not a crowd person. It's okay. I do not care for these elaborate parties, either." Justina said. So far, Wenceslas was nothing like what she had expected her betrothed to look like. Maybe this was why her cousin kept insisting he was making a good choice for her, and she would be happy. In some ways, she was impressed with his decision, but she knew her cousin too well to know this was not all that the arrangement entailed. He had his own agenda in mind, something that would profit himself and his kingdom. She was almost sure of that. But contrarily, she didn't presume that Wenceslas would be that way.

"I guess you could say so," Wenceslas said. "Although I always think of it as I am a friend of nature, rather than humans. I like to enjoy the beauty and serenity of nature around me, to inhale the sticky sweet smell of flowers and listen to the birds singing and feel the warm evening breeze on my skin." He paused when he noticed Justina staring at him.

"I'm sorry, my lady. I must have put you off with my blabbering."

"What?" Justina said, shocked. "Are you kidding? You did not put me off. I was just thinking that I was right."

"Excuse me?" he said.

"I had an impression of you when I saw you in the hall. I thought you had a certain air of strength and confidence. It wasn't the brash kind that comes from glorying in war victories. It was a quiet, refined kind, and it turns out I was right. You did not put me off. I was simply delighted in how easily you shared your thoughts and confidently admitted to the things that society would term inferior and weak." Wenceslas blushed lightly and smiled. "You're quite an eloquent one too, my lady. I'm glad, you are even more beautiful than I imagined and you hold a good conversation. This marriage will not be boring."

Justina's eyes dropped as he said those words.

"I'm sorry, my lady. Did I say something to upset you?"

She was about to reply when the king's guard came out to meet them and request their presence back in the hall by order of the king.

The king wanted to formally announce their engagement to the guests, and he wanted both of them back in the hall.

Wenceslas kissed her hand and bowed slightly to her before going back to the hall. Justina's hands fell limply to her sides when he let go. She couldn't squash the feeling of disappointment that overcame her when he kissed her hand. She had expected her insides to burst out in a harmonious chorus and to swoon with pleasure at the feel of his lips on her skin, but instead, she felt a dull numbness.

The rest of the night, she smiled and laughed and responded to the conversations going on around her, but all the while, in her head, she was agreeing with Wenceslas. Their marriage would not be a boring one, but it wouldn't be a fun one, either. No passion. No spark. No fire, just gentle affection, and mutual companionship. That might be good enough for others, but not for her. She wanted more.

Justina sighed. She had tried to see a silver lining with this marriage, hoping it would bring the freedom she desired. But she didn't feel free. She felt trapped.

CHAPTER FIVE

Emperor Frederick III was the Holy Roman Emperor and ruler of the Ottoman Empire. The emperor conquered the kingdoms of Serbia and Bosnia, ending the zone of buffer states along the southern frontiers of the kingdom of Hungary, and laid claim on it, but was met with strong opposition from King Matthias. The two monarchs clashed heads, but King Matthias held strong, refusing to defer his kingdom to the emperor. In the aftermath, the emperor captured the holy crown of Hungary, which was to be used in crowning King Matthias as royal monarch, refusing to promote him and allow him as king over that region. The monarchs later agreed after the intervention of Pope Pius II, who mediated the peace treaty between the Emperor and King Matthias.

The envoys of King Matthias and Emperor Frederick agreed on a peace treaty in April 1462. The agreement was that the emperor would return the holy crown of Hungary for eighty thousand golden florins and that both monarchs would keep the rights to be addressed as king of Hungary. The emperor and King Matthias signed the treaty with the pope's blessing, and the duo, who had once been at loggerheads, created a peaceful alliance that gave way to a more cordial and amiable relationship between them. Following the treaty signed between the two rulers, the emperor adopted King Matthias. The adoption granted the emperor the right to succeed his son as an heir if the son dies without an heir. Soon after that, Jiskra's army, which had been waging war with King Matthias, conceded and retreated, seeing that he now had the help of the emperor.

The alliance between the king and the emperor was mutually beneficial, such that both monarchs sought help from the other in case there was an attack against either of the kingdoms. During the invasion of Victor of Podebrady in Austria, some years after the treaty of alliance between the king and Emperor Frederick, the emperor appealed to King Matthias for help in subduing Victor's troops. As a reward, the emperor hinted at the possible crowning of King Matthias as King of the Romans. King Matthias went to great lengths to subdue Victor and his allies, going to the extent of expelling his then father-in-law's troop from Silesia. Which in turn caused strain between himself and his father-in-law, George of Podebrady, but instead of receiving the promised reward; the emperor accused King Matthias of allowing the ottomans to march through Slavonia when raiding the emperor's realms. The petty accusation by the emperor against King Matthias annoyed him and caused a strain on their relationship. Thereafter, the emperor and King Matthias allied with whoever was favorable to their political cause and agenda.

CHAPTER SIX

HUNGARY KING MATTHIAS'S CASTLE

Esme paced back and forth in front of Lady Justina's chamber, dreading the next few minutes. Lady Justina had been so cheerful these past days when the king

had not been around. The news around the castle had it that the king went to fight a war in Silesia and to curb it before it spread, while some others amongst the palace servants were assured that the king went instead to pay a visit to the emperor. About the reason for the king's visit to the emperor, different speculations arose. Prominent amongst them all was the speculation that the king was probably warming up to the emperor and wanted to invite him to his cousin's wedding. Nothing could have been farther from the truth than this.

But none of this was Esme's concern. She cared very little for palace gossip except, of course, if it involved anything relating to her mistress. And now it did! She had just received the most disturbing news, and she didn't know how to handle it. Not that the news itself was bad, it was the many complicated situations, and the people involved she worried about. She drew in a deep breath and rehearsed her lines repeatedly. She hated to be the one to bring the news to her mistress, but she would rather her than that annoyingly straightforward and utterly emotionless messenger. The messenger had recited the message from the king like it was a hymn and had departed as soon as it was delivered, leaving those who heard it to deal with the consequence.

"Dear lord," she said under her breath, still pacing and rubbing her palms together furiously. She ran her sweaty palms down the length of her gown and continued rubbing them both together. "Oh, dear! Oh, dear! Oh, dear!"

These past few days had been the best for her, and she could safely say for her mistress, too. Lady Justina had been so cheerful, taking her evening strolls under the moonlight and gently tending to the flowers. Esme told her about a nightly get-together that the servants were having, and she paid a surprise visit. She laughed and danced throughout the night, much to everyone's delight. Perhaps she knew she was only stalling the inevitable, so she lived in the moment and enjoy each moment to its fullness.

Esme sighed. "If only we could stall a little longer…" She could hear footsteps echoing in the hallway and coming in her direction. She couldn't stand in front of Lady Justina's door forever, so she summoned up courage and knocked.

There was no response, so she knocked again and pushed the door open gently. "My lady," she called as she went in. The door hinges creaked quietly as she pushed it aside to make room for her to step in.

Lady Justina was stepping out of the bath, and she smiled broadly when she saw Esme. "Good morning to you," she greeted with a cheerful smile.

Esme bowed her head quickly, apologizing for coming in at such a time. "I'm sorry, my lady, I didn't mean to intrude. I knocked…. There was no response, so I thought… I thought… to check. I'm sorry, my lady."

"It's okay. Now you're here, you can help me get dressed." "Huh?" Esme's head came up sharply, and then she realized that was her job, and she blushed and apologized again. Her head was in the clouds, worrying about Lady Justina. She tried to help the young woman pin a button on her dress, but she kept pricking herself with it.

"Are you alright?" Lady Justina asked, taking the pin from her and buckling it on by herself. Esme bowed her head apologetically. Justina turned around to face her and asked her to sit across from her, with her head raised so she could look her in the face.

"Esme, look at me."

Esme hesitated, but Lady Justina insisted, so finally, she sat and looked at her in the face. It took all her willpower to do that, and her hands trembled as she did. She tried to hide her hands in her lap, but Lady Justina had seen her hands trembling.

"Take a deep breath and tell me what this is about," Lady Justina said in a calm, soothing voice.

"I'm sorry, my lady, I shouldn't have come in here so early with such news, but I wanted to be the one to tell you myself before you hear about it from anyone else. News like this is fodder for gossip, and it is bound to spread within minutes, and I couldn't bear for you to hear about your wedding casually from a palace gossip on your way out to the garden in…"

"WHAT?"

Esme jumped, and the shock made her hiccup. She placed her hand over her mouth and bowed her head again. She had just carelessly spilled the information she had spent hours trying to prepare and fine tune.

The look on Lady Justina's face was heart breaking. It was the look she had been trying to prevent. Lady Justina's eyes drooped, her face looked paler, and her lips curved down. The hours of preparation and pacing dissolved with the wind and Esme was at a loss for words. The lines she had so carefully rehearsed escaped her and she was speechless.

Lady Justina found her voice before Esme. "What did you say? What do you mean?"

"A messenger from the king arrived this morning with news that he is on his way back to the kingdom. He wanted preparations for your wedding to begin, as you are to be wedded by the end of the week."

"End of the week? Wow! Then I suppose we have no more time to waste or linger around. Will you be so kind as to help me pack my things? Of course, I could not leave with everything at once." Lady Justina chuckled. "But I'm sure my dear cousin, the king, would be kind enough to do his newly wedded cousin a favor and help me send the rest over with a carriage. So, what do you say?"

Esme stared at Lady Justina with her mouth wide open; the hiccup was now gone. The shock was enough to stop her heart, which might explain why the hiccup left quickly. This reaction from Lady Justina was scarier than anything she had expected. Never in her wildest dreams would she have expected this. She was so calm and normal.

Yeah, that was the problem, the normalcy! How could Lady Justina act so ordinary, like she had not just been told to pack up her life and go somewhere else? She was acting like she was preparing to go on a vacation rather than get married like this was something she had planned, and now the day was finally approaching. Could that be it? Could it be that she had become fascinated by the future groom and she had braced herself for wifehood? Was that it?

"Oh, dear!" Esme muttered.

"What did you say?" Lady Justina asked. Esme shook her head. "You haven't given me a reply to my request."

"Huh? My lady did… did you… did you mean what you said?"

"Why, of course, I do." She dropped her voice down to a whisper and said, "I know we're getting married and all, but I can't exactly walk into his house naked. That would be scandalous, don't you think?" She giggled, but Esme was too shocked to move her face.

"Come on, Esme, don't look so disheartened. I'm fine! I am, trust me. What, did you think that I didn't know this was going to happen? I know my cousin, and I know him well enough that he would never call off the marriage except if something miraculous happened. These past few days were borrowed time. I knew that, and I did my best to have as much fun as I could. I am glad I had those times to myself. I could determine what happened in my life and do what I wanted. I have no regrets. I'm okay! Now, please, for the umpteenth time, will you help me pack?"

Esme replied with a nod. "And please," Lady Justina said, "Wipe that look off your face. I'm getting married, not dying. Why do you look so sad?"

Despite herself, a smile broke out on Esme's face. A sob, and another and another quickly followed it, until she was weeping profusely, her shoulders heaving. Lady Justina drew her in, patting her gently on the back until she was done.

Esme was going to apologize again for being such a messy crybaby that morning, but Lady Justina stopped her.

"It's alright, Esme, don't apologize. We're humans, and part of our humanity is the ability to feel. I'm glad that you care this much about me. I appreciate it, so do not apologize for having such a kind and caring heart."

Esme nodded.

"Take some time to get yourself together. I guess I'll just have to pack my stuff myself. You're such a big crybaby, whew!"

Esme giggled and insisted that she would join in. They spent most of the day in Lady Justina's chamber, sorting through her things and packing the essentials for her new home before the king sent the rest of the things to her. While they worked, they made small talk to keep their minds busy and away from thinking about the implication of what they were doing. Esme kept observing Lady Justina throughout, but she tried not to be too obvious about it.

Towards evening, Lady Justina dismissed her maidservant, asking her to get some rest. After Esme left, she walked casually around her chamber, and the change registered with her. The empty spaces that had once been filled with candles and books were now packed up in boxes. She had been putting up a strong front with Esme because she knew her maidservant would be worried to death for her, but she wasn't feeling as confident as she had made Esme believe. Even though she knew this day was bound to come, nothing could have prepared her for the shock she had felt when she found out that by the end of the week, she would be shackled to a man whom she had met just once in her life. With Esme gone, she dropped to the floor beside her bed and poured out her emotions into the atmosphere. By the time she was done, she felt lighter and relieved that she fell asleep almost immediately.

~ ∞ ~

The king arrived in Hungary two days later with much ado. Justina heard the noise from her chamber and knew before she went to the window to check the king was back. The villagers welcomed him with loud cheers and songs of victory; like the palace servants, they had heard the rumors that the king went to fight an uprising war in Silesia, and he won the war before it could escalate. He might not be the best king, and his taxes were incredibly high and almost suffocating, but they were assured of one thing. He would always keep them safe. As long as it was within his power, he would do everything he could to fight for his kingdom and his people. The villagers sang his praises until they got to the castle. After that, the royal guards dispersed the crowd and shut the castle gates.

A light knock on the door startled Lady Justina and drew her attention away from the window. She adjusted her dress, straightening out invisible creases. Come in."

The door opened to reveal Esme, as graceful and petite as ever. She bowed when she came in and said, "My lady, the king is back."

"I know. I heard the ruckus when he stepped into town. The showoff.

Esme giggled quietly, but it died down immediately as she put up a serious face lowering her head in shy embarrassment. "He asked after you and requested to see you, my lady."

"Really? He could not wait a few minutes before he torments me with his plans and decisions, could he?"

Esme did not have a reply, so she kept her lips sealed. "You want me to go, don't you?" Lady Justina did not wait for an answer. She already knew what it would be. "It's fine! I might as well have this last encounter with him before I leave for my new estate as a married woman. I will be with the king shortly."

Esme smiled at her, "Okay, my lady," she said and departed. Justina went to see the king a few minutes later. For someone who had been on the road for the past month, he was roguishly handsome and clean. Perhaps he had freshened up before she came in. His face was tired, however, and it was expected. She bet he had only had a few hours of sleep in the last few days. He needed to rest, and she was going to tell him. "You just had to see me," she began, "would it kill you to get some rest before you jump back into your political affairs?"

She would tell him to get some rest, but she didn't say that she would be nice about it.

The king chuckled. "Such a rare, wonderful sight of my cousin worrying about me. I've missed that. Thank you for your concern, Justina. I will get some rest now."

Lady Justina scoffed.

"Did you get my message when I was away?" he asked. "Yes, I did, and I cannot tell you how thrilled I am to be marrying the man that you have chosen for me."

The king was in a pretty good mood, and he just laughed at all of Justina's jabs and smart comments. "I see you have been doing well. I was worried about you, but it turns out there was no need. You're as feisty and snarky as always."

"I wouldn't say snarky."

"Hmm," the king replied amidst a mouthful of juicy grapes.

After he had chewed and swallowed, he asked her, "So what would you say?"

Justina moved her shoulders back and forth in a girly manner and enunciated the word as she said, "Sassy!"

The king threw his head back in laughter, and she joined in, too. They quieted after a minute, then the king must have remembered the other thing that he had to say to her. "Wenceslas has requested to come to see you today. He should stop by around noon. You look good in anything, but I would suggest you dress up a bit."

Justina arched her brows at him. Her cousin infuriated her every chance he got, sometimes intentionally, and at other times, he was cluelessly dumb. Like right now, he was telling her that her betrothed asked permission from him to come to see her, and he didn't see anything wrong with that. Instead, he told her to dress up pretty to welcome their guest.

She closed her eyes and let out a loud sigh. "And the wedding?" she asked, "Should we have the wedding today since he's coming around?" she meant that sarcastically but... "Wonderful! Perfect! Justina, I didn't think about that. Why did it not occur to me? I mean, it is a splendid idea. Why waste any more time? Let's just get it over with at once. I was going to have the wedding tomorrow, but what difference does it make?"

He stood up and walked over to Justina, then kissed her lightly on the forehead. "You are one amazing, smart, and beautiful woman, my dear cousin. I will inform the court at once, and we can get ready." With that said, he walked out.

Justina sat glued to the same spot, unblinking for several minutes as the realization slowly dawned on her that she was going to get married later that day due to a sarcastic comment her cousin couldn't interpret. She groaned and leaned her head forward on the table. After a few minutes, she braced herself and got up. It was just like her cousin had said. There was no need to delay things further. She might as well just get it all over with.

By morning the next day, she would be married. The thought chilled and excited her at the same time.

CHAPTER SEVEN

"You are the most beautiful bride I've ever seen, my lady," Esme said as she put the finishing touches to her lady's look and outfit. It was a long white dress with flowers adorning the tips and precious stones all over the tightly held corset. The dress had long lace sleeves that covered her hands and its neck was round, revealing an impressive amount of cleavage.

Lady Justina had a broad and cheerful smile on her face. Never mind the circumstances of her impending marriage, she was getting married, and she looked gorgeous in her outfit. To her, that mattered more, and it was enough reason to smile. Esme smiled, too. She looked happy and proud to be standing beside such a beautiful bride. Somehow, in less than twelve hours, the king had gotten the palace chef to prepare a palatable feast for the occasion. He had informed the church and invited a priest over to officiate the wedding. He had gotten Wenceslas to agree to get married that evening instead of the next day, but Justina doubted it would have taken much to get him to agree. It was undeniable that Wenceslas was smitten by her. He had stopped by to see her when he got to the castle before she began dressing up to be wedded, and he had gotten her a gift. A beautiful golden bracelet now graced her hand in complement to her other accessories. He was just as sweet and kind as she remembered, but just like the last time, he did not spark up any fire in her, not even when he made a brave move and kissed her on the lips before he left. It was a light kiss, like a feathery brush, but still, her heart did not skip or anything. It just felt good, not magical. And she wanted to feel that magic. She craved it.

"My lady," Esme said, interrupting her thoughts. "The priest is here; the ceremony will begin shortly. Are you ready?"

"What do you think?" Justina asked.

Esme nodded and smiled. "I think you are, my lady."

"Yes, I think so, too."

Esme escorted her lady towards the entrance of the church, where the Priest stood on the cobblestone floor. The minstrels' procession had begun, with the sonorous sounds of the bagpipes and flutes flowing through the air. Wenceslas was standing right next to the Priest, beaming radiantly with joy like a child that had just been told he could have all the fruits that he wanted. They exchanged smiles before she took her position at his left side, just as God had with Eve. She stood a few feet away from him, facing him only when she had the courage to. In a symphony, both parties knelt in front of the priest before the altar. The Priest began the ceremony and after they both said their vows to each other and consented to the marriage, the Priest pronounced them man and wife.

It was time for the kiss of peace.

The Priest kissed Wenceslas gently on the cheek, her husband's brown eyes bright as he turned towards her once more.

"You may kiss the bride," the Priest said amidst cheers from the crowd. It was a small crowd, given the spontaneity that came with the wedding, but it didn't matter to her.

Wenceslas moved closer to his bride, unveiled her, and claimed her lips in a passionate kiss that was nothing like the other light, timid kisses he had given her so far. When he let go, she was breathless and her face filled with heat.

The hymns were sung before the merriment began.

The celebration lasted the rest of the night. There was lots of food and wine to keep the party lasting for a week. She smiled and danced as soon as the music began, but despite the many activities going on around her, she couldn't get that kiss off her mind. It was different, and it felt so good. After their dance, Wenceslas walked around the hall with her hand around his arm to greet their guests. When he suggested they retire for the night, she was more than happy to oblige because, although she knew it was their wedding night, she was exhausted. She had been standing for most of the day, and she doubted her legs could keep supporting her weight at this point. She was relieved to give them a break.

The king had requested a bigger chamber to be prepared for them, and it was to that chamber Wenceslas led her. As soon as she got into the room, she threw her shoes off and flung herself onto the bed, too tired to be bothered about anything else; that it was their wedding night that didn't occur to her. Wenceslas got in bed beside her, and she jerked up. She was so used to being in bed alone she reacted subconsciously.

"I'm sorry," she said and leaned back into the bed. Every muscle in her body tensed and tightened as she lay back.

Wenceslas chuckled lightly. "It's alright. This is new for me, too, and I'm just as nervous. Get some rest. Goodnight!" He kissed her forehead. He picked up a pillow from the bed and walked toward the adjoining room.

"Wenceslas!" Justina called, and he stopped. "It's okay. I'll have to get used to it at some point, so why delay it further? Please, come and sleep in bed with me."

He opened his mouth to say something, and she snapped before he could get the words out. "Will you please stop being a gentleman and just come here?"

His mouth shut in shock. She blushed. Once again, her mouth had developed a mind of its own and given her away on their first night. Without another word, he came back and climbed into bed with her. She moved to make room for him, and he lay stiffly and quietly beside her. They slept with their backs to each other.

~ ∞ ~

Wenceslas was awake long before Lady Justina. Lady Justina must not be a morning person, he concluded. After freshening up and getting ready for the day, Wenceslas thought he would wake his new wife up with a kiss and bent over her to do just that, but he hesitated. He was not feeling as confident as a few minutes earlier now he was so close to her face. He felt her warm breath on his skin.

She looked so beautiful and peaceful while she slept that he couldn't take his eyes off her. He watched her sleeping instead, and as he did, from the corner of his eyes, he caught her chest rising and falling steadily with each breath. He looked down at her chest and gasped at the creamy white skin that was exposed under her nightdress. One of her buttons had come off while she slept, and his eyes were exposed to the full curve of her cleavage. Her skin looked so silky and soft that he became curious and felt compelled to touch her.

He raised his hand slowly and cupped the exposed breast. The contact felt so good that it sent electrifying sensations throughout his body, and he released a soft moan. Without thinking, he squeezed lightly and delicately. Her skin yielded under his hands and melted into his touch, and he grew warm all over. His engorgement throbbed as it filled with blood and became stiff. In a cruel twist of fate, Justina's eyes opened. She must have been consciously awake for some time, because she sounded calm.

"Not quite the gentleman, eh, I see!"

Wenceslas' hand was still as he left it, and she looked down at it. His eyes followed the direction of hers, and he jerked his hands off her as if she burned him. His face turned crimson with embarrassment. He stuttered as he tried to apologize and explain.

"I'm sorry! It's… I… I was just… I didn't mean to…to…touch without your consent… I was… I'm sorry."

Justina sat up and snapped the loose button back in place. Perhaps if her skin was no longer exposed, he could look her in the face, or chest, without feeling flushed and embarrassed. "It's alright. Don't look so ashamed. We're married, after all…" He stuttered a 'yes', but she was not done. "Next time, just…" She paused and thought about her words. Just what? Don't do it while I'm sleeping. Don't do it without my knowledge. What is the right word to use here? She rolled her eyes and decided to wing it. "Next time, don't start the party without me."

"Of course," he said, rising to his feet.

Justina saw the bulging flesh between his legs and raised her eyes towards his face with a smile in a bid not to embarrass him further. He disappeared behind a door, and she knew he would be there for a long time. She sighed and leaned her head back after the top railing of the bed. She had been awake as soon as his hands touched her skin. She wasn't for sure a deep sleeper that she wouldn't notice such trespass, but she had been curious and excited to find out what would happen. His touch felt warm and sent a fuzzy feeling through her, and she wanted more. She had hoped he would be brave enough to take hold of the other soft mold of her chest and lose himself in it, but as she thought of that, he held tighter to the flesh under his hand and squeezed. Against herself, she gasped and opened her eyes. She would have snapped them shut if he hadn't seen her, but he did. She'd willed him to go on in her mind, to become wild and carefree and do what he wanted at that moment without thinking about how she would react or try to be the gentleman. But one look at his crimson face, and she knew it would not happen. He was a gentleman, and he felt embarrassed for touching his wife while she slept. She would have told him to go on or started the rest of the act herself, but her pride would not let her.

Justina rolled her eyes and got out of bed. She needed to get ready for the day's journey ahead, so she set out her clothing and accessories while she waited for Wenceslas to emerged from the bathroom. He walked out a few minutes later with his chin high and his shoulders straight and Justina suspected he might have given himself a pep talk in there. She wondered how long he could pull off this charade and what it would take to shatter his defenses. She was feeling defiant and daring, so she messed with him a little. She maintained eye contact with him to make sure he was looking at her; when it was certain she had his attention, she loosened the rope that was tied behind her dress and undid each button one after the other. Wenceslas stood transfixed to a spot, and his eyes bulged as he watched her. She let go of the dress and it slid smoothly down the length of her body, bringing her full chest to exposure before sliding down to reveal the rest of her silky, smooth skin. Wenceslas shut his eyes before the dress slid down her waist to reveal her nakedness.

Justina cupped her mouth with her hands as she laughed. His reaction was even better than she had expected. He looked so still and stiff, and he kept his eyes tightly closed; perhaps he was afraid that they might open of their own accord. She was still feeling audacious, so she walked past him to the bathroom, naked, stopping to pat him on the shoulder as she went.

"I'll be out in a minute." He stiffened further under her touch, like she was afraid that he might break a bone if she did it any harder. This time, she couldn't help herself, and she laughed out loud. By the time she came out of the bathroom, Wenceslas was nowhere in sight. Instead, Esme stood with her hands folded and her head bowed as she waited for her mistress to come out of the bathroom.

"Ah! It's you," Justina said with a mischievous smile playing on her lips. "May I ask where my husband went?" She looked around the room.

Esme smiled broadly. "You look so happy, my lady. You're smiling so wide; it's blinding. That's good, huh? Just one night, and you already look for him when he's not in the room."

Justina cackled. She couldn't hold back anymore. She couldn't tell Esme the reason for the beaming smile and happy laughter that came from teasing her husband, not spending the night with him. It would take a long explanation for Esme to understand, and she didn't want to make Wenceslas look bad, so she said nothing and enjoyed the private joke by herself. It was her newfound guilty pleasure, and she intended to savor it alone.

Wenceslas was downstairs by their travel carriage when she came out. It amused her to think he didn't want to be anywhere within the circumference of their chamber that he had to come down here. He looked a lot calmer and better now, unlike the forced air of confidence he had when he came out of the bathroom earlier. This time, he looked relaxed and confident. Maybe it was the air and the feel of nature around him. Wenceslas had informed her the first time they met he was an absolute lover of nature, and nature made him feel at peace. She could see for herself now that his words were true. He was definitely at peace. He smiled when he saw her and walked over.

"My lady," he said with a slight bow, and kissed her hand before leading her toward the carriage.

Lady Justina had requested that the king sent the rest of her belongings to her as they would not all fit into the carriage. She had also requested her maidservant. The king agreed to her request without hesitation. Perhaps she should have asked for more. Esme was waiting for her by the carriage, having helped her pack her things in it beforehand. She wanted to give her final goodbye wishes, even though she would see her again by the next week. Her cousin did not come out of the castle with her to say goodbye. He had said all he had to say earlier when they bargained about what she wanted, and he granted them to her. His parting words to her were that he knew she could take care of herself, and he wanted her to do just that.

"Seriously?" Justina had replied, feigning affront. "Is that all that you have to say to me?"

He was unfazed by her display of anger. "What else do you want me to say? Promise I will write to you weekly or ask that you do the same for me?"

Justina rolled her eyes. "Please, no! I'd rather not."

"That's what I thought. So take care, cousin, and enjoy your marriage." He said that last part with a wink. Justina understood the implication and smiled. He was family, and he cared about her, but he showed it in strangely annoying ways. She caught him off guard and gave him a peck on his cheek before she strolled out of the courtroom. That was the easier part of her sendoff. The more emotional part was walking to the carriage.

Wenceslas let go of her hand when she got close to Esme and gave them space to say their goodbyes. Esme kept wiping her eyes with the backs of her hands to stop the tears from spilling, but it was a futile effort. The tears poured out regardless. Lady Justina drew her maidservant into a warm hug and teased her about being such a cry baby. "I'm not going away forever, Esme. You'll be at the estate with me in a week, so brace up and get yourself together. You have the week to yourself without having to deal with my tiring needs and orders. Enjoy it!"

She kissed her goodbye on the cheeks and got into the carriage beside her husband to begin the next phase of her life. Her stomach tightened with anticipation and excitement as the horseman hitched the reins, leading the horses down the path that was to bring her to this new life without the watchful eyes and influence of King Matthias Corvinus.

CHAPTER EIGHT

The journey down to her new home was a long one. It was the first time that Justina had traveled that far from home and away from her cousin. He was the only family she had known for as long as she could remember, and it felt strange being away from him for the first time and for that long. Wenceslas was a darling, and he tried to make her as comfortable as he could throughout the journey.

"Where are we going?" she asked.

"Transylvania, my love." He said, then turned away to cough into a handkerchief. She noticed he did that a lot but paid no attention to it.

His last word resounded in her ears and she tried not to cringe. Wenceslas was good company, and she had adapted to being comfortable with him. He was easy to be with and fun to talk to. He was a patient listener, and he always had something thoughtful and wise to say whenever they had discussions. But despite all that, it still felt strange hearing him call her "love." Their relationship so far was cordial, but the one crack that they needed to fix was the physical relationship between them. The tension was still there, and several days of being cooped up together in a carriage and forced on each other with every gallop on the way did not help ease it out. Sparks flew whenever their bodies met, and every time that happened, Justina willed him in her mind to do something about it and not just retreat, but that was the exact thing he did. Wenceslas would coil back and apologize.

"The last I heard, you had an estate in Slovakia, so why are we not going there instead of Transylvania?"

Wenceslas lowered his eyes, and his voice dropped to a whisper. "They forced me to deny my ownership of that land for another in Transylvania."

He had more to say. There was more, and Justina could tell. She could also tell he was refusing to speak for her sake, and she realized the reason he would hesitate to tell her was probably that her cousin had something to do with it.

"It's okay! You don't have to say it. I know my cousin. I lived with him for more than a decade. I think that's enough time to get to know someone." She reached out and took his hand.

Wenceslas looked up at her with a smile and said, "Thank you!" He was about to lean in and kiss her on the cheek, but the cough came again and he turned aside. She brushed his trousers with her finger lightly. It was unintentional, but the feeling it elicited in him was quick and vibrant. He jerked at the impact of her touch, and unfortunately, in the series of awkward events happening at the wrong time, the carriage bounced up and down the bumpy road, and he fell forward towards Justina. His head fell against her chest every time the carriage bounced. By the time they were out of there and on a stable road, his face had turned completely red. Justina looked away from him because if she did not, she might end up laughing at the tomato-red hue of his face, which would only embarrass him further. Aside from his awkwardness with being with a woman, Wenceslas was a terrific young man. And Justina's earnest desires were that he would get a grip of himself and snap out of feeling so cautious and damn gentlemanly every single time.

"How much farther are we from Transylvania?" Lady Justina asked the carriage rider.

"About a day's ride, my lady."

Wenceslas found his voice. "It's getting late. Find us a safe spot to camp for the night or stop at an inn if we do come across one."

"There are no inns along this road, my lord," the carriage rider replied. "We passed them a long way back, but not to worry. We are within King Matthias's territory, and this place is safe from robbers and thieves. We can spend the night anywhere without worries."

"Very well, then. Have us stop for the night somewhere around here. Do you think we might come across a stream on the way?"

"Yes, my lord. There's one just ahead." "Excellent. Have us stop there for the night." "Yes, my lord!"

"Thank you!" Wenceslas said, much to Justina's delight.

She had heard him say that about a hundred times during their journey to the carriage rider and the servants that attended to them on the way. He said thank you to the inn owner after paying for the night. He was polite and proper to the core. She prided herself on respecting all humans and treating them right, but besides her husband, her propriety was dwarfed completely. It did not matter that she heard him say thank you to everyone throughout their ride to this point; no matter how many times she heard it, she couldn't get used to it. She was impressed with this young man. He was nothing at all like her cousin.

The carriage came to a stop by the stream the rider had mentioned earlier. Wenceslas got off first and came around the side to help her down. It was exactly a week since they had been married, and they were yet to consummate their matrimony. She could tell that all the tension and abstinence were eating him up. She knew that because she felt the same way. The heat had been building up between them and they let it burn them out instead of putting it off. She thought about the fact that it must be painful for him to have to douse his arousal every time he felt it, which, to the best of her knowledge, was every time he was around her.

She watched him come around towards her side of the carriage to help her down, and all she could think about was how he had handled himself so far. She knew for certain that her cousin would not be this patient or exercise this level of self-control with any woman, less so his wife. He had been married twice, and each time it did not take more than a night for him to lay claim to his bride. The sounds of their passionate consummation had kept her up on many such nights, and she wondered what exactly he did to them to make them emit such noise. The next morning, the king's new bride would grin from ear to ear and glow with a superhuman brilliance that radiated from deep within. Justina dreaded breakfast on such mornings, as it made her feel like an invisible spectator to their erotic escapades. The bride could not keep her hands off Justina's cousin, and she often wondered what was so good about him that made them so smitten. It would appear that marriage did not bring answers, as she was yet to experience that level of sensual chaos with Wenceslas.

She stood as he approached her, and he put his arm around her waist to help her down. He did not blush or react with the usual clumsiness he exhibited whenever he got in close contact with her.

"I requested we stop by a stream so you can freshen up. I know it must have been a long and hard journey for you. I apologize for the discomfort. I assure you we will arrive at the estate in no time, and once we get home, you will forget all about the stress of the journey."

"Home, huh?" Justina said. She mouthed the word over and over, feeling the way it sounded and the emotion it stirred up in her. It felt strange to refer to somewhere other than the castle as home.

"Will you also be having a bath?" she asked Wenceslas.

"What?" he asked, stunned.

"You have been traveling, too. You have been on the road as long as I have, and I can bet you feel uncomfortable from all the dirt and grime of the road. I assume you love to feel clean and fresh and must be itching for a good bath now."

He snickered. "You have me pegged, my lady. I will have a bath too, right after you."

"Why not together? I was asking if you wanted to bathe with me."

Justina could not explain where that came from, but the deed had been done. She might as well just go with it. Wenceslas choked and coughed at her words. Adam's apple bobbed as he swallowed and his eyes teared up from the choking and coughing. She waited for him to come to himself. She would not let him off the hook this time. When he had calmed down, he muttered something about going to help her get soap, bowed his head, and escaped.

Justina noticed him putting her clothes together and swam toward the edge of the stream. When she came out, he was gone, and there was a bar of soap by her clothes. She laughed silently as she picked up the soap and went back into the water for a late-night bath under the moon. She lathered her body and lingered in the water for a while longer, savoring the silky feel of the water. When she was done, she walked out of the stream, picked up her clothes, and went in search of Wenceslas. She found him in a blink. He was not so far from the stream; he had kept a good distance between them, but he wanted to be close enough to watch over her or hear her if she cried out for help. His excuse sounded ridiculous, even to himself, but he held on to it, anyway.

His heart stopped for a minute when he saw Justina standing naked a few feet away from him. She held her clothes but did not cover herself with them. Her full body was within view and his heart raced like crazy at the sight of her.

"What are you doing?" he whispered.

"I grew up in a palace, Wenceslas. I've had servants taking care of me and dressing me up since I was young, so I'm quite comfortable in my skin."

"Yeah, but… but… that doesn't mean other people are comfortable seeing you."

"Do I make you uncomfortable?"

"No! Of course not!" he cried, aghast at her words. Of course, she knew what he meant, but she wanted him to spell it out. She was done playing this endurance game with him. He might exercise superhuman self-control, but she was human, and she was at her limit. She moved closer to him, and he staggered backward and turned his face away.

"What's the problem?" she asked in a sultry tone. "Someone might see you," he whispered.

"We're well away from the camp. The only person here is you, and I don't mind that at all, husband!" She emphasized the last word to get the message through to him. But just in case that wasn't enough to communicate what she wanted, she leaned in closer to him and breathed her words in his ears while her nipples brushed against his chest.

He put his hands on her to push her away and put some space between them, but his hands followed another course of action the minute they contacted Justina's wet skin. His hands slid down her back and trailed an invisible line around her buttocks. He had been curious about what it would feel like to hold the roundness of her backside in his hands, and now that he had that liberty, he explored it to his heart's content. He grabbed, rubbed, massaged, and squeezed her, but it wasn't enough for him. He wanted to taste her, to feel her with his tongue and lips and bring her in direct contact with his masculine organ, but his clothes created a barrier between them. As if in synch, Justina reached down for his pants and slid her hands underneath them. She was just as curious as he was.

He drew in a sharp breath when she took him into her hands. Her hands were soft and warm, and the feel of her hands on his testicles filled his shaft with blood. It shot forward, standing erect. He broke free from her and put some distance between them. He was panting, and he bowed his head as he tried to catch his breath.

Justina did not understand what was happening to him, but she did not wait to find out. She picked her clothes up from the ground and stomped towards the camp. His need was huge, judging by what she felt. When she stomped out, she was going to get some privacy and nurse her wounds for being so stupid to start any form of intimacy with someone who was practically a eunuch. She berated herself as tons of uninvited thoughts flooded her mind. This was an arranged marriage and, for all she knew, he was taking her as collateral of some sort against her cousin rather than a wife. It was a ludicrous thought, but she entertained it along with many others of that nature. Wenceslas followed immediately, hot on her heels, but she did not slow down or stop for a second to look at him. When they got to the tent, he caught up to her, but she refused to acknowledge his presence.

"Justina! Justina, please, please listen to me. I'm sorry, I have a good explanation. Please hear me out—"

"Oh, it better be a good one, and you cannot tell me you are impotent or not aroused, because I felt it."

"No! Not at all. It's just… I wanted it to be special," he blurted out. "It's going to be the first time that I will be with a woman, and I wanted it to be a memorable one for me, but I didn't consider how you felt about it. And by God, this has been the hardest thing I have had to do. I couldn't even keep up the charade. You are a special woman and I… I… Just… I wanted it to go right."

She paused and turned to face him, but she was still naked, so he grabbed a piece of cloth and tossed it to her. He wasn't concerned about what he was giving her; he just wanted her covered.

"I'm sorry, I didn't mean to hurt your feelings, and I apologize because I did just that. It was selfish and thoughtless of me to not consider how you would feel about this. I did not want to remember your cousin's castle as the place where I consummated my marriage to the woman I love. Or an unmarked stream along the paths between Transylvania and Hungary. I know that this might sound sentimental, but I wanted it to be done in our new home."

He paused and stretched his hands out to raise her face towards his so he could look her directly in the eye as he spoke. "I want to take you as my wife within the walls of our new estate and stamp the rite of our matrimony there, not in an unknown, nameless piece of land. I know you might need some time to grow to love me, but I don't need that. I've loved you ever since I first met you, and that is why it is important to me to do it right. You are a gorgeous woman and I want you. Let me prove it to you…" He drew her close and devoured her lips in a fierce kiss. By the time he let go, they were both panting for breath. The throbbing bulge between his legs was yet to relax, and he caught Justina looking at it.

"There, you see!" he said, pointing at it. "More proof that I cannot resist you." He kissed her on both cheeks and excused himself to have a bath.

Justina stared at him as he walked away. She had felt embarrassed and annoyed when he pulled away from her after fondling her backside like it was a puzzle he needed to solve. She had seen his desire, felt it with her hands, so there was no doubt at all he wanted her.

But now Wenceslas had given his explanation, her feelings had changed. She was speechless and embarrassed in a different way. She felt she had been too forward, and that hurt her pride. All the while Wenceslas gave his explanation and apology, she knew she had to say something in response but couldn't get the words to form on her lips. Instead, she felt so aware of her nakedness like she had never felt before and was grateful when he tossed her a garment to put on. His words reassured her, but they could not take away the humiliation she felt at being rejected. Never in a thousand years could she have ever envisioned a man would turn her down, much more her husband. She did the turning down. She had graced a few of her cousin's court meetings, and she was aware of how much she affected the men around her, how they undressed her with their eyes and wished she would agree to a relationship with them, and now this?

She held her head in her hands and groaned as the scene replayed in her head repeatedly. Wenceslas was done with his bath, and she could hear his footsteps approaching the tent. Quickly, she laid out the bedding and lay on it, pretending to be asleep. She could not face him just yet; she couldn't bear to look him in the eye and have him look at her like she was a delicious snack to be savored after what just happened between them. She turned on her side to make room for him, but also because she wanted to hide her face.

"My lady?" He called when he came in. He smelled clean and fresh, like a mixture of roses and fresh spring. He must have used a different soap than the one he gave her. What she used had a softer, feminine allure to it, like a collection of different scented flowers.

Somehow, in the last few minutes, the tables had turned between them, and he became the daring, irresistible one while she took on the vacant role of being embarrassed and shy. He got down to lie beside her, and her nostrils filled with his rich, masculine scent. While she was fully dressed, he seemed to have worn only short breeches and nothing else.

This time, he did not lie with his back to her. He lay facing her back and spooned her into the curve of his body. It was more than Justina could take. She was undeniably aware of his body, and she had to fight the urge to want to see or touch what she was feeling. His male organ pierced through the thin fabric of his hose and nestled comfortably against her buttocks. Against her will, she felt her butt tighten against it, and she let out an embarrassed sigh. She concluded he was giving her payback for having teased him earlier on in her cousin's castle.

Wenceslas dozed off the minute his head hit the pillow beside her. She heard his breathing become more relaxed and steadier and knew he was fast asleep. Quietly, she turned around to face him so she could get more comfortable, but facing him proved to be more uncomfortable than turning her back to him. His nose and lips were only an inch away from her and, true to her suspicion, he was naked from the waist up. It surprised her he hid muscles underneath the pristine outfits that he wore all the time. He didn't seem like one who would have them, but he wasn't as thin as she had imagined. "Oh, dear Lord," she groaned. How did she ever get to this point? The abstinence between them had been bearable when she thought she had control of the flow. Right now, getting intimate with him was all she could think of. She wanted to feel him, every bit of him, and quench the hunger that was threatening to swallow her whole. She closed her eyes, took a deep breath, and turned away from him. It was better not to look; that way, she could imagine something less attractive and be sane. It was just one day. She could handle it.

Dawn broke out slowly, but Justina was grateful for it. She got up before the first light for the first time ever and went to bathe in the stream. She lounged in the water, letting it wash over her and take away all the frustration from the previous night. By the time she was done, she felt more relaxed and ready to face her day and her irresistibly attractive husband.

* * *

Wenceslas was up when she got back to the tent, and he greeted her with a bright smile and a kiss on her cheek, to which she responded with nothing. Thinking she must still be angry from the previous night, he excused himself to go for a bath. When he got back, Justina was nowhere to be seen, and panic rose in his chest. He dressed up quickly to go after her because he thought she might not have gone far and he could bring her back. He rushed out of the tent to the carriage and found her seated quietly at the other end, looking out the window. His heart slowed to a steady pace, and he sighed, relieved.

"I thought you left."

She turned to face him with a blank expression. "No. I came to wait in the carriage. I wanted to give you some space."

Her words brought back a déjà vu feeling, and he remem- bered when he had done the same thing back at her cousin's castle. He got into the carriage with her and waited for the servants to unpack the tent before they continued their journey. Throughout the rest of the ride to their new estate, the couple said very little to each other. The air between them became even tenser than it was before. Justina was wrapped up in her feeling of embarrassment and felt content to stare out the carriage window than striking up a conversation with her travel companion. While on the other side, Wenceslas was lost in thought, wondering what could have made his bride so sulky and quiet. It was unlike her usual self, but he couldn't decide if she was feeling embarrassed or annoyed. He decided that his best bet would be to respect her wishes and keep quiet for the rest of their journey.

The journey seemed to drag on forever because of the tense atmosphere in the carriage, so it was a great relief when they arrived.

Subconsciously, both of them breathed a sigh of relief simultaneously, and they laughed at the other person's reaction. Wenceslas went around to help her down from the carriage, and she thanked him. As she got down, she stood for a minute to examine the magnificent edifice that was to be her new home.

It was huge. The Pongrac estate spanned several acres of land and loomed high above the ground on a hill. Tall trees and lush surrounded it, trimmed green grass. Justina angled her head, and the musical gurgle of cascading water reached her ears. There must have been a brook nearby. A yellow songbird flew above her head, and she followed the trail with her eyes to a tree where there were several others nestled in a nest. Their melody made her face light up with her smile. A soft draft of wind blew past her, blowing her hair. She stood on her toes, hands outstretched to get more of the wind in her face. She opened her eyes to find Wenceslas staring at her with a longing gaze and forced herself to smile.

"Come, let me show you the rest of the house." He stretched his hand out ahead of him, showing for her to go first. He walked closely behind her, showing her as much of the mansion as he could with what little light came in from the evening sky. The house was huge, with several wings and turns that would take a while to get used to. He led her up to the second floor and came to a stop in front of her room. "This would be your chamber, my lady," he said. "I hope you find it comfortable. We can always work on it later if you feel we need to. My chamber is right beside yours." He went inside ahead of her and opened an adjoining door that connected both rooms. "I'll be in here if you need me. Get some rest. I'll have the servants bring you dinner upstairs and a fresh set of towels."

He bowed and disappeared behind the adjoining door before she could have time to reply. She looked around the room and was touched that he made her feel comfortable. He replicated the same furniture, bedding, and curtain materials she had in her previous chamber at the castle. She appreciated the thought, but she would have preferred to see something different.

She reclined on the bed and leaned back, lying down with her legs dangling off the edge. She felt a numbing feeling of disappointment as she stared up at the ceiling. She had been looking forward to the end of that tedious journey, hoping that upon their arrival at the mansion, Wenceslas would let go of his shield of discipline and melt her brain to mush with rounds after rounds of passionate intercourse. She had looked forward to it throughout the rest of their journey. It was not enough that he kept telling her how much he wanted her, his actions were the only proof she needed and so far, his actions did not back up his words.

Separate rooms? She scoffed.

A knock on the door jerked her back into a sitting position. She waited for the knock to come again, as she could not tell which of the doors the sound was coming from. The knock came a second time, and she asked whoever it was to come in. The door opened and two maidservants about the same middle age as Esme came in with a tray of food, a fresh set of towels, and sweet-smelling oils. Seeing them brought back memories of Esme, and she realized how much she missed her maidservant. She would not be feeling this lonely if Esme was here.

She thanked the servants, and they excused themselves with a bow. The meal looked palatable, with lots of fruits and meat, with a jar of fresh milk to top it off, but she could not work up an appetite for it. A maid returned with a lit candle a short while after, as darkness was slowly enveloping the mansion.

After a few minutes of being restless and indecisive about what to do, she got up and went in search of the brook she had heard earlier. Maybe a late-night swim under the moon would help her relax. She found the brook behind the house, tucked behind a wall of flowers, with a garden on both sides. It was a spectacular view to behold.

She filled her nose with the sweet scent of the flowers, taking in the view of the calm waters before her. She smelled a familiar fragrance, and it brought back memories with it, uncomfortable memories that made her face fill with heat. Slowly, she got rid of her clothing and walked into the calm embrace of the water, surprised to find it warm. She felt relaxed already and realized that might be exactly why the flowers were there. It was like bathing in a large bowl filled with scented oils and petals. Where she had planned to swim, she now lay quietly in the water with her eyes closed, savoring the feel of nature around her. She purred softly as the water caressed her skin. Her blissful experience was cut short when a rustling noise made her open her eyes. She found Wenceslas standing at the edge of the water, devoid of any clothing at all. He was bare and open for her to see, and she feasted her eyes on him. She couldn't look away even if she wanted to.

What Justina did not know when she took a swim was that the landowner, who was her husband, had been detailed in the structuring of this mansion. He wanted to be as close to nature as he could, so he had his window placed directly in front of the brook. One looked out of the window and he would see the gardens and the peaceful flow of waters. He had been on edge, too, and stared out the window for some peaceful, soothing sights. But the scene that he stumbled on was far from peaceful.

He looked out just in time to see Justina take off her clothes to enter the water, and his brain brought back memories of what it felt like to hold her in his hands. As if in a trance, he made his way downstairs and to the brook. Now that he was standing here, seeing her curvy figure floating in the water, he could not think of anything else but the throbbing ache between his thighs. He gravitated towards her, drawn by her allure and the hunger that darkened her eyes.

"I wanted you to get some rest because I thought you might be tired from the journey," he said when he was standing a few feet away from her. "But I saw you standing here from my window and... I couldn't think of anything else. All my courtesy and manners went with the wind, and I'm here."

"Finally!" Justina exclaimed. "About time—"

He drowned the rest of her words with an intense kiss, ravaging her lips with all the desire he had locked up inside for so long. Justina answered his intensity with hers, matching his hunger and fire with equal measure. They had starved themselves for so long that they now devoured each other with ferocious intensity. He pulled her closer to him, so he felt every inch of her skin against his. They fitted perfectly together like a glove. It wasn't enough. The heat from their bodies consumed them, yet they clung tighter to each other. Justina raised her legs to his hips and wrapped them tightly around his waist, drawing him into the soft curves of her body. She had her chest pressed up against him and the feel of her naked breasts on his chest made him forget how to breathe. He was excited, and he became long and hard. Justina felt his erection against her, and she opened like a runny tap, wet and eager. The soft mold of flesh between her legs throbbed with desire, and her knees got weak. She wanted to take him in and wrap tightly around his organ, squeezing tight, then let him go and have him back in there again.

Consumed by the scent and feel of her, Wenceslas' hands wandered down her back to find themselves against her rounded backside. He grabbed on with both hands and squeezed tightly, unintentionally pushing her closer to his stiff erection as he did. Justina savored the feel of his raw, hard flesh against her thigh and she slid downwards on him to get it closer. She moved back and forth against the bulging appendage, rubbing it with the hot flesh between her legs.

Wenceslas pushed back against a door to give way into the room and laid her down on the bed. With the way her eyes looked around, Justina must have not noticed that they were no longer in the brook until her back touched the bed. Wenceslas climbed on after her, and still exploring the curvy complexities of her body with his hands, he bent his head down to one of her nipples. Justina grabbed onto his hair and held tight as she laid herself open for him to explore. He sucked hard on her nipple until she was gasping and panting, then he went for the other breast. By the time he spread her legs open to thrust into her, she was ready. The bed was damp and when he entered her, it was a smooth slide.

She constricted around him in a strong claim of ownership. She leaned towards him and pulled his waist closer to her to have all of him inside of her. Wenceslas set a steady rhythm for the thrust, being gentle and kind with her. He placed his hands on both sides of the bed to support his weight as he entered her, but Justina took them off and brought them to rest on her bust. She knew he enjoyed fondling her breasts, and she guided his hands toward them and showed him how she wanted to be touched.

Wenceslas let out a throaty groan and lost himself in her. He increased the tempo of his thrusts, consumed by his lust, and Justina rode high with him, matching him thrust for thrust even with the slight pain, now and then, a soft moan would escape her lips, much to Wenceslas' delight. They danced to the rhythm they created, their bodies merged, rising together with the tempo until finally, together, they climaxed and burst forth into harmonious ecstasy.

The last thing Justina remembered was snuggling closer to Wenceslas, legs wrapped around him, until the darkness swooped down and claimed her.

CHAPTER NINE

Life at the Pongrac manor was almost everything Justina thought it would be: Boring, monotonous, and insanely lonely. Although she was married, she felt more alone than before she got yoked together with Wenceslas. Her only consolation was Esme; bless her heart! Esme was her companion, confidante, and play partner, all the things that Wenceslas was supposed to be to her. Not to be mistaken, he treated her well, and he was every inch the gentleman that he had always been, even better, but it would seem this was the problem. Wenceslas enjoyed the company of nature and books much more than he preferred to sit with Justina or take a walk in the garden around the house. The only connection of intimacy they had between them was sex, and even that had to be scheduled to Wenceslas' timing. He was not a believer in spontaneity, and as expected, his rules fashioned his sex life and habits. Justina tired of having to wait for a prearranged time, place, and setting to get down on the sheets with her conjugal partner. Soon enough, even sex with him lost its appeal as it became monotonous and tedious. Not to mention the constant coughing. She also noticed that he was becoming leaner by the day. It was to be expected, her husband was one to skip meals for endless hours of monotonous study.

Much as it irked her to admit, she missed the toned, muscular man that has come for her back in Transylvania. Now, Wenceslas was all bones and flesh, held up by an insatiable hunger for knowledge.

She picked up interest in the books he so engrossed himself in after a year of being married to him. The first year was a long, unending period that she liked to think of as a trial stage. It was difficult because she had yet to understand him and the reason for his robust passion for literature and nature. After several long months of frustration and an unbalanced rhythm, they came to a place of mutual understanding. Justina no longer concerned herself with how many hours he spent cooped up in his study, and he, in return, did not bother with whatever she did with her day. Wenceslas omitted wanting a child, and neither did she, she had a feeling he cared little about things like that. It was a mutually beneficial, cordial relationship, and they maintained that synergy for the latter part of the year.

However, at the start of the second year of their being married, they began a tradition of sitting out together in the evening to discuss literature. There were tons of other things that Justina would have loved to hear or learn about, but Wenceslas only knew about books and only ever discussed what he knew about and had a burning passion for. It was during those nights Justina gradually developed an interest in literature. She would sit and listen to him talk for hours and hours about a puzzling concept that, after they retired to their separate chambers at night, the thoughts would remain with her until she fell asleep. The next morning, she would go to his study and ask to borrow a book so she could muse on it and satisfy her curiosity. One book turned into two, and then it became a habit. She had lots of free time on her hands and so she channeled it into her newfound hobby.

After a while, she took it a step further and purchased more books on the topics that interested her, like those on adventure and romance, to keep her company during her long, leisurely days. She did not know where to purchase these books, so she asked her husband. Esme would know where to get them, but she did not ask her because Esme would insist on going to get them herself while Justina stayed behind, safe and secured in the manor.

Justina got up to go to Wenceslas and tell him of her new quest. She thought he might think the idea ludicrous or decide to send a servant in her stead, but she had her mind set on going herself, and she was determined to convince him. It would be easier to talk her way out with him than Esme. She needed a time out; she wanted to be away from the manor and its confining walls, even if for just a day.

She had been behind walls all her life, growing up in her cousin's castle. The only time she was allowed to occasionally leave the castle was at her mother's memorials. Her mother was an aunt to King Matthias, and he paid his respect to her on her memorial days. On those days, they would ride out of town to her mother's hometown, where they would visit her resting place with fresh flowers and fond memories. Justina looked forward to those days during her time at the castle as they provided her with some respite from her restrained life. Although the difference was not much, as they always left with a company of fifty soldiers, and she was never allowed to stray too far from her cousin's watchful eyes. He always had a guard on her trail who showed up whenever she moved too far from the camp. She learned about her cousin's plan of having a guard trail her after she got caught trying to steal away twice. After those encounters, she learned to be more careful and bid her time. Her big break was supposed to come when she got married. It was the reason she decided not to put up too much of a fight and succumb to her cousin's will, but even marriage couldn't provide her with the freedom she so yearned for.

Wenceslas, like her cousin, kept her locked up behind his manor walls with servants and handmaids. He hardly ever left the estate and turned down invitations to soirees and balls. He said he didn't see the point in them, so she never even got to host one. The only time anyone left the manor was to get supplies, and that was a job strictly restricted to the maidservants and stewards. He would not hear of it if she requested to go buy the supplies herself, get milk from the cows or even hunt. This was her one chance to be away and alone by herself, to decide her boundaries and limits, to be free and visit the places she wanted without having to look over her shoulder or ignore the nagging feeling she was being watched. This was her one shot, and she was going to make it count.

When she got to the door of the study, she fixed up her dress and plastered a huge smile on her face before she knocked lightly on the door. When she hears nothing again, she knocks a second time. Wenceslas answered on the second knock. He probably did not hear the first. She pushed the door back slightly and entered with her dress trailing beautifully behind her. Wenceslas did not look up; he probably thought it was one servant who came to deliver a light snack or run an errand. If that were the case, they already knew not to disturb him, so they simply did their business and left as quietly as possible. She stood for a minute, watching him pore over the books before him with ardent attention. After a long minute with no sign, he was going to look up, so she let out an exaggerated cough. It worked. It caught his attention, and he looked up.

"My love," he said, putting down the magnifying glass he had been using to peruse the book before him. Justina had gotten used to hearing him address her that way after having heard it consistently for a year. He sat up straight and indicated for her to take the empty seat directly in front of him. She waltzed graciously over to the seat and lowered onto it.

Wenceslas's eyes twinkled, and she suspected it was proba- bly because he thought she had come to discuss books with him. If that was the case, she would oblige him by asking some questions before she got to the real reason for her visit. She wanted him in a pleasant mood when she made her insanely unconventional request.

"What books are you studying, my lord?" she asked.

"Ah!" he said with a smile. "They are books on philosophy. Quite captivating, I tell you. It makes one wonder about the essence of life and the reason for our existence."

"Hmm!" Justina replied, but she might have as well said "please tell me more," because that was what he interpreted her reply to mean.

"I know… it has that same effect on me. I have been pondering the words of Aristotle and Plato. I find they are quite related in their principles and the rendition of their concepts and ideas, although there is a bit of controversy as regards their backgrounds. Something about the theft of knowledge, but I was just about to look further on that when you came in… would you care to join me, my love?"

Justina's smile lingered as she tried to think of a quick and easy way to get herself out of that spot without hurting his feelings or making him concerned. She couldn't lie about having a headache or a stomachache because if she did, there was no way in the world he would let her ride out to purchase a book.

"I would love that, my lord, but I have a request to make."

"Of course, my love, go right ahead. What do you desire?"

"Books," she replied.

"Why, I'm impressed. I've got quite a number here. You can have access to as many as you want. I could make some recommendations if you like—"

"I have a few in mind, but I do not think that such books exist in your vast collection."

His eyes bulged in their sockets like she had uttered an abusive word at him, and he stuttered to give a reply. "I... I... I believed I had acquired quite a collection, but clearly, that is not true. So, tell me, my love, these books you talk about, what genre do they belong in?"

Justina cleared her throat and said, "Music, arts, languages..."

"I see," he replied. "I believe I have some books on the latter, but I do not think that I own a single book on music. Thank you for bringing this to my notice, my love. I shall send the steward out at once to get some of those books for me to satisfy your request. And I would like to read them myself when you are done."

"I am very grateful, my lord, but I had a different solution in mind," Justina said.

"Of course, of course, my love. Go right ahead and let me hear it."

"I would like to ride out to town and purchase these books myself." She waited.

Wenceslas was silent for a long time, staring straight ahead. She was just about to call out his name or tap him when he blinked and said softly, "but you do not know how to get to town, my love. And once you get there, how do you propose to find the bookstore? I doubt it's that easy to find."

She leaned towards him, gathering all her womanly allure. "I have you, my lord. That is why I have come here." She knew Wenceslas would not be too eager to leave the manor and go back to that long, twisty, tiring road. She was counting on him to say he couldn't go with her and then she would offer to go alone if he would just tell her how to get to town and find the bookstore.

Wenceslas let out an embarrassed smile. "I am honored, my love. It makes me happy you would think of me like that, which is why it saddens me to say I have never been into town alone, and I do not know how to get there, much more, finding the bookstore. The steward gets the books for me."

"Perhaps I could ask him for directions myself?" she asked. "I couldn't let you do that, my love, but it wouldn't make much difference as he is away right now. He left to purchase some meat and loaf from the town and he should be back about a week from now."

"A week?" Justina's face fell. Her carefully crafted plan had been reduced to nothing in a split second. Why didn't she think about this earlier? If she did, then she could have come to Wenceslas sooner, and then maybe, just maybe, she would have been riding her way into town by now with the steward. Wenceslas noticed his bride's countenance had fallen and moved his chair closer to hers. "I'm sorry, my love. I think I understand what it feels like to not be able to satisfy the yearning for knowledge. I have been there lots of times before, so I promise you this, when the steward gets back, we shall both ride out into town with him and purchase as many books as you would like."

He took her chin and tilted her head up so she could look directly into his eyes and see that he meant every word. She smiled up at him, letting herself get dragged into the warm embrace he offered. He had missed the point completely, thinking she was downcast because of the inability to douse her thirst for knowledge. As much as she would not mind having some new books on arts, music, and language, what she yearned for above all was some time alone. She wanted an opportunity to take control of her life, even if just for a few hours. She could sneak out but that might end up smearing Wenceslas' image with the guards and maids and he has been nothing but nice to her, she couldn't do that. Plus, she believed he was kind enough to let her. She could pretend she was as free as could be and that she had control over her life. She was free to make decisions, dress how she wanted, act however she wanted, and eat the things she was craving when she craved them without having to be a societal puppet passed down from one man to another. She was grateful that Wenceslas was the one she got stuck with and she would not mind being with him for however long as long as she had time to explore life just once.

Wenceslas implored her to sit with him for a little longer, a look of worry on his face about her and he did not want to leave her all by herself when she was looking so sad and downcast. He looked pale and tired too, but all he seemed to care about at the moment was her. He rang a tiny bell, and a servant came running.

"May I get a cup of ale for myself and my wife, please?" Wenceslas requested. He was still as polite as always. When the servants nodded and bowed to leave, he said thank you. The servant came back a while later with the tray of ale and two cups, poured out a cup for each person before bowing again to leave, and Wenceslas said thank you again to the maidservant.

The ale turned out to be of much help. By the time they were done drinking, Justina was in a better mood. She left his office feeling more optimistic that she would ride her way into town in a week. It didn't matter that Wenceslas would be with her. He would be too engrossed in his books to bother her; she couldn't wait, and she counted down to the day with glee.

The steward returned from his trip in a week, just as Wenceslas had predicted, and there was no one happier in the entire manor than Justina. True to his word, Wenceslas requested the steward take them into town the day after because he wanted to give the steward a day to get some rest. The preparations were made, and finally, it was time to travel to town. Justina woke up earlier than everyone else in the Pongrac manor and hurried over to Wenceslas's room to wake him up. Her screams woke the rest of the house, and they hurried to their chamber. When they got there, they found Lord Wenceslas lying peacefully in bed, not breathing.

He had died in his sleep.

CHAPTER TEN

Dark clouds loomed over the Pongrac manor as the entire household mourned the death of their master and husband, Lord Wenceslas Pongrac. It disheartened Justina for many reasons than the obvious. Although her marriage with Wenceslas had been far from a fairytale love experience, he was a good man and kind at heart. It saddened her to see him pass away like that. He was not a perfect husband, but she was warming up to him as a companion. The memories of their time together sitting under the dark sky, discussing subjects he was so passionate about, or the times in his study when she went to borrow books and he would light up with joy that she was beginning to like something that enticed him, came flooding back to her and the tears rolled down freely on her cheeks. She would miss him; she was certain of that. It was ironic that she realized how much difference his presence made in the house now it was gone. She had believed that since he was always cooped up in his study that they shared no connection at all and had little a relationship, but now, all she could think about were the times they were together and the shared laughter over a cup of ale.

"My lady," Esme said, her voice a light whisper under the solemn atmosphere of the Pongrac house.

Justina, lost in thought, did not hear Esme come in or call her name twice as she stood at the door. She was enveloped in her grief, quietly mourning the death of her friend and husband. Esme watched her stare out longingly at the window as tears ran slowly down Lady Justina's face. She made no move to stop them or wipe them off, leaving them to pour out as they would. Esme began to tear up herself but wiped them off quickly with the backs of her hands as they dropped, sniffing back the rest that threatened to come out. She strode towards lady Justina as if to defy the tears and tapped her lightly on the shoulder.

Justina turned slowly towards her, and Esme could see the pain and weakness lurking behind those bright, teary eyes.

"I'm sorry, Esme."

Looking aghast, Esme stooped down to be on the same level as her lady. She placed a hand on her shoulder and soothed her gently. "No, my lady, don't say that. Do not blame yourself for his death. It must have simply been his time."

Justina stared at her maidservant with lost eyes for a minute, trying to reassure herself she could believe Esme's words. After a while, she nodded and lifted her palm to wipe the tears off her face, but more soon flowed.

"The physician is here," Esme said quietly. "I wanted to let you know."

"Thank you," Justina replied. "Tell him I'll be with him shortly. I only need to freshen up."

Esme nodded and departed to do her lady's bidding. Justina got up to freshen up and arrived at Wenceslas' room just as the physician drew a cloth over his face, confirming him dead. According to his wish, Justina had the steward invite the priest over to the manor so they could conduct a private burial for her late husband. Wenceslas had made preparations for his death and how he wanted to be treated before he passed on. It was as though he knew he had little time left. After the physician's examination, he revealed to Justina her husband had passed away because of a cancerous medical condition. Wenceslas must not have told her because he did not want to give her any cause to worry.

The physician's words broke her heart as she imagined how her husband must have suffered alone all the while in silence. As she pondered on that, another thought occurred too. Perhaps her husband might have kept a distance from her deliberately so he could ease her pain when he died. The thought was an absurd one, but it nagged at the back of her mind until it was all she could think about. It seemed plausible; it made sense.

Her knees grew weak, and she staggered backward. The physician jumped in to catch her before she could hit the wall, and in the blink of an eye, her maidservant was by her side. Esme helped her to a sofa while they waited for the priest to come. Another maidservant rushed over with a cup of water and a wet towel for Lady Justina. Esme insisted her lady downed the cup of water and went upstairs to get some rest, but Justina refused, insisting she would wait until the priest arrived. In response, Esme stationed herself beside her mistress, refusing to leave her side for a minute.

The priest arrived after a long wait. By the time he got to the manor, the stewards had dug the grave and every other necessary preparation had been made. All dressed in black, friends and family of the late lord Wenceslas gathered at the gravesite where the priest performed the burial rites and laid the deceased to rest. The kitchen servants had prepared ale and honey cakes for the guests. There were lords from neighboring towns and people that claimed to know him and were his friends when they were much younger. While they clustered together in small groups to reminisce about the life of lord Wenceslas and express their deep condolences to his widowed bride, she excused herself and retired to her chamber.

Justina did not come out for several days. Esme stopped by to coerce her out of her room, but she wouldn't budge. She would go upstairs to Lady Justina's room every morning with breakfast and at noon with lunch and dinner in the evening, but Justina barely ate more than a few spoonfuls, and that was on Esme's watch. She kept to herself and mourned her husband in her own way.

When she showed up outside her room after a week, the servants were pleasantly surprised to see her and expressed their sincere gladness. The kitchen maid offered to make her one of her favorite dishes, roasted potatoes, and the other offered to help her out with whatever she wanted. She was grateful and expressed her gratitude to them, but she declined their offers as politely as she could. She wanted to spend some time in Wenceslas's study. Regardless, the kitchen maid insisted on making her a snack and she obliged her.

The study was clean and arranged. The window had been opened to let in some air and the dust had been cleaned off the furniture. Justina's heart warmed at the thoughtful gesture of the servants. She was grateful to whoever took the time to do that for her. When she asked about it later, she found out each one of them had indeed gone to the study to clean it up, and her heart swelled with pride and gladness. She moved around the study, trailing her finger along the length of his desk and shelves, filled with various memoranda he had liked to collect. She took a seat across from where he usually sat and her memories brought back images of him sitting across from her, with his eyes lit up with excitement. Tears welled up in her eyes again and she wiped them off with her palm. She stood and made to leave the study; she couldn't bear to be there just yet.

She took one last look around and realized how much of a difference his absence made in the room. As she made to leave, her eyes were drawn to a piece of paper on the table, held down by a dried-out quill and inkwell. She felt drawn to it; perhaps he had scribbled his thoughts again. She gravitated towards it and slowly lifted the inkwell lid to take out the paper. It was a will. A written testament and explanation to her. He had sealed it with a cord and his stamp, and she had to break it to read what the letter contained.

Justina was furious when she read it. True to her suspicions, he'd kept a distance between them because he did not want her to suffer so much, thinking about him when he died. He had agreed with her cousin to get married to her and spend his last days with her as a companion for giving up his inherited family estate in Slovakia. At the end of the letter, he declared his will to pass on the Pongrac manor to Justina as an inheritance for her.

Angry tears rolled down Justina's cheeks as she held the letter. She was furious at her cousin for marrying her off to a dying man in exchange for property and wealth. She knew all along there had to be something in this arrangement that would benefit the king, and now she finally knew what it was. She was angry at Wenceslas for being selfish and thinking about himself only when he decided to get married to her and detach himself from her after marriage. She wanted to take out her anger on him, but after several days of pondering over his situation, she realized she could understand him. He wanted to do something for himself, seeing that he had very few days left. She understood what it felt like to not have control over what was happening and she empathized with him, but more than just that, she took a hint from him and decided she was going to do what was best for her, and experience life as she wanted even if just for a short while. Unlike her late husband, she wasn't ill, but she also did not know how much time she had left, so she decided she was going to live before she died. She went and sat down on the side of the river so that she could clear her mind. Her first time going down the creek was because of this event. It changed into a mellow duck-egg blue that exuded an air of calm and tranquility, much like the gentle stroke of a painter's brush. It labored and crept its way past all of the barriers, including the boulders in the river, and made its way to the other side. Small messengers poured over the riverbed's pebbles as twigs danced and twisted on the whispering floor below. The sound was reminiscent of the murmuration made by a flock of starlings.

She wanted to be free, at least taste what freedom was like. She wadded her hands in the water and stared into it.

In the distance, the mountains stood silently, a somber presence of soaring majesty. Snow brooches topped their high peaks, which were ringgit in angel-white garlands. It appeared to be stitched in platinum as it carried its pile of ice crystals. It emitted a distant thrumming sound, similar to the steady thump of a drum roll. It was a breathtaking sight.

Her attention was suddenly attracted back to the turning pages of the book. She took a look at how clear the water was. Wild pea pods began to cover the riverside and surround it. Although the pods' exteriors were dark, within they contained peas that were dainty, delicious, and brilliant in appearance. She gave one a try, and it turned out to be very tasty. Food that has been encased in the satanic cloak has never had the right flavor! As a result, she drank all that she needed to while stooping down and moving her hand through the water. It was enough to slake her thirst. She positioned herself in contrast to a rock, closed her eyes, and tried to simulate the feeling of the sun warming her. She was pondering the beauty of the natural world when she became aware of the exquisite aroma wafting toward her from the nearby forest.

At least it was peaceful. There was nobody to tell her what to do or decide her life for her. She wasn't angry any longer but only felt a wave of peace and calm washing through her. If there was one thing she would choose, it would be to take charge of her life.

Justina did not care about the mansion or wealth or king- doms and glory like her cousin did. What she had always been concerned about and desired earnestly was the freedom to live life to its fullest. She wanted to be able to carve out a path and dictate her fate as much as she could.

And she decided to do just that; she decided to live!

CHAPTER ELEVEN

"My lady," the carriage rider said, "we will arrive at Brasov soon. Better get your things together and be ready to get off."

He gave a loud laugh and sized her up and down with his eyes again. He had been looking at her since she got on the carriage but paid him no attention. As long as she wasn't giving him attention, he would not strike up a conversation or attempt to do anything stupid. However, the carriage rider would not be easily deterred this time. Perhaps it was because he knew she was going to get off soon and this was his last chance with her. She had forced herself into a long sleep throughout the entire ride, pretending to still be asleep even after she woke up. The carriage was comfortable, and the ride had been a pleasant one, but the carriage rider was terrible company, and she was doing her best to avoid him.

"What's a sophisticated, beautiful young woman like you doing in Brasov eh?" he asked.

Justina held her breath at the stench that emitted from his mouth as he spoke. He looked like a sailor. His teeth were broken, browned, and decaying and she tried her best not to look at his face. He had a long scar that ran across his left eye to the bridge of his nose. She wondered what kind of injury he must have had that would leave such a gruesome scar on his face. His hair was tied into an unruly bun with several strands sticking out at the nape of his neck. Justina pretended to be sick, so she did not have to answer his question and unintentionally struck up a conversation with him. She just needed him to get her to Brasov and after that, she would find her way on her own.

Sophisticated? When she got to Brasov, that would be the first thing she would discard from the list of words that identified her. If she hoped to keep her sojourn her secret, she could not afford to let anyone find out about who she was. She was going to live a quiet, fulfilled, fun life away from her cousin.

As she stared out the carriage window at the vast stretch of green lands before her, she thought back to the past few days in the manor before she left, and a smile played on her lips. After she left Wenceslas's study, she stomped back to her room, fuming with anger. She spent the next couple of days after that trying to decide what she was going to do next. Then it occurred to her that if Matthias had married her off to Wenceslas, he probably knew about his health condition. The thought that her cousin took advantage of an ailing man repulsed and infuriated her. If he knew, then he intended to have her inherit this other mansion, and surely, she had inherited it. Wenceslas named her in his inheritance as the owner of the Pongrac manor. Things seemed to go according to her cousin's plan. The latter part would be to have her return to the castle after her husband's demise. What would happen after that is what she was not sure of, and that was exactly what she was trying to understand. There were a few ways things could play out. He could claim ownership of the Pongrac manor by bringing her back under his guardianship and claiming his place as her guardian. Then he would try to seek another suitable suitor, profitable to him, of course, that he could marry her off to again. None of those scenarios was an option for her. She could not bear to go back to King Matthias and become a pawn in his hands again, so she devised her third option, which was to flee the Pongrac manor as soon as she could, before her cousin came calling for her.

Justina arrived at that decision in a flash, and just as soon, she got up to set plans in motion for her move. Esme came into the room a few minutes later to get her ready for her nighttime routine before she went to bed and was surprised to find Lady Justina stuffing her bags with essentials for travel. She looked stunned as she observed the room and knew instantly what her mistress was trying to do. Justina looked up from her mission. Esme was staring at her with a pale face and wide eyes.

Slowly, she put down the things that she was holding in her hand; a book and folded corset and rose to her full height, raising her chin high as she prepared to defend herself against Esme's obvious reaction and judgment. She had known the maidservant long enough to tell what her reaction would be to a situation like this, but she would not let her stop her. She had decided and not even her beloved friend and maidservant was going to talk her out of it. The women stared at each other for a while, and then Esme broke the silence by putting down the tray of spice and ointment she was carrying on a stool beside Lady Justina's bed.

"What can I help you with, my lady?"

Justina heaved a deep sigh of relief and pulled her maidser- vant into a hug, kissing her on both cheeks as grateful tears trickled down her face. "Thank you! Thank you so much, Esme. You're a good friend. I am truly grateful to have you."

Esme nodded and was going to bow, but Justina stopped her. They worked silently, side by side, packing up only the essential things Justina would need. When they were almost done, Justina asked Esme why she did not try to stop her.

"Don't you want to know where I'm going, Esme?"

"It's better I do not know, my lady. That way, I cannot say anything to anybody when I am asked."

Justina grabbed Esme's hands in hers and looked her in the eyes. "I trust you. I know you would tell no one."

"Yes, my lady, but I was talking about the king. The moment he finds out you are no longer here, he will bring me in for questioning. I cannot reveal what I do not know, so it is better I do not know."

"Oh! Esme," Justina said. "Run away with me, or go somewhere else, somewhere far where the king will not find you."

"That would make me guilty, my lady. Don't worry about me. I can take care of myself. I will assure the king that I knew nothing about your intentions to travel and stay back here with the rest of the servants, awaiting your return. But, if I leave and try to escape, the king will find me and when he does, he will show no mercy. He would not believe me if I said I do not know where you are, because my actions would betray my words. So, go, my lady. I will wait for you to return."

Esme had a sad smile on her face, but Justina respected her words, seeing the reason in her explanation. When they were done, Justina dismissed Esme and requested she send another maid upstairs to her when she was done. Esme tried to find out what her lady needed so she could attend to them herself, but Justina insisted she wanted someone else to do it. Esme bowed and left the room, and shortly after, one of the house servants came up to Justina's room to be of service. Justina did not need her, but she cooked up silly errands for the maid to run.

"I would like to have a glass of chamomile ale; would you be so kind as to get me some?"

The maid returned with the ale a few minutes later, and Justina came up with more unnecessary errands. She re- quested to have the windows opened and fresh firewood added to the fireplace. When the last of the errand was done, she thanked the maidservant and dismissed her. Her mission had been to make sure that when the king came snooping around for her and asked questions, the last person to be seen with her was not Esme. She wanted the king to believe she had sent Esme away on purpose so she could secretly leave the manor later that night without her maidservant finding out.

Now she was only a few miles away from her destination, in a carriage with a rowdy rider, looking out at the beautiful green scenery, she hoped Esme was okay and that the king believed what she wanted him to believe.

She opened her eyes when she heard people making a ruckus. She hadn't heard another person's voice aside from her unruly companion for days, so when she heard people talking, it seemed a bit off. She squinted in the bright light. People moved about as her gaze steadied, and at once, she realized where she was. Her face lit up as she took in her surroundings. There was a busy marketplace with people displaying and haggling their wares. Looming in the distance ahead was the town's uncompleted cathedral, it was close to completion now. The sun's rays reflected on the bell as it rang.

"Aye! I see you're awake!" the carriage rider said as soon as he saw her eyes open. "I bet I do not have to tell you we're here already, my lady."

"Thank you!" Justina replied. It was the first word she had said to him in days. The only other time she had spoken to him was before she boarded the carriage to begin the ride to Brasov. The carriage rolled to a stop in an allotted space for a security check before they entered the town's gate.

"Before we part, may I ask what a fine young lady is doing, traveling alone? My conscience will not let me rest until I know you are safe." The man asked her, and Justina sighed. It was suspicious to travel alone, but she couldn't imagine taking anyone else with her through these uncertain stages.

"Thank you so much. My husband lives within the town's gates. I am on my way to meet him."

"Well, then… I bid you farewell." The man muttered to her as the guard at the gate requested to know what business the carriage rider wanted to conduct in Brasov. He nodded to the back. Justina drew the curtain aside as the guard leaned backward to peep, hiding her face with a hand fan. The guard took one look at her, examined her outfit, and bowed his head in greeting. "My lady."

He nodded towards the other guards to open the gate and tapped on the carriage for the rider to move on. As they rode past, the soldier nodded towards the backseat at Justina. She nodded, as she still had the hand fan to her face. The carriage came to a stop as soon as it got into town. The coach master jumped off and came around the back to help her get her load off the carriage. When he was done, he did a dramatic bow and extended a hand to help her down from the carriage. Justina hesitated before taking his hand.

"Thank you!" she said, letting go of his hand as soon as her foot touched the ground. He gave another low bow before he got back on the carriage and rode off into town. Earlier on, he had asked if he could recommend an inn for her to spend the night at and offered to give her a ride to the inn with no extra charges. Justina declined his offer without giving it a thought or waiting for him to finish his sentence. When he was gone, she gathered her bag close to her while she took a minute to decide where she was going to go from there.

The realization that she had finally done what she wanted slowly dawned on her, and she broke out with a huge grin. She would have lifted her hands and danced around, but that would be a bad idea. Standing by the side of the road in a hooded dress with bags around her drew attention. She didn't want to add more eyes to the ones already on her. She took in the length of the city before her, observing as far as her eyes could see. She was overjoyed, thrilled beyond words that she got to decide what she wanted to do, where she wanted to stay, whom she wanted to meet, and what she wanted to eat with no interference whatsoever from guards, her cousin, maids, or anyone.

"Ah!" she said, closing her eyes as she drew in a deep breath, it wasn't as calm and clean as the one back home but she could get used to it.

The sun was beginning to set behind the clouds. Darkness would soon try to claim the city. She needed to find a place for the night. Picking up her things with both hands, she trudged onwards in the same direction she had seen the coachman ride past. She just kept going straight ahead, she would come across a tavern where she could spend the night.

A short distance into the town, a delicious, savory smell floated upon the wind towards her, filling her nostrils and causing her stomach to rumble. It had been a couple of days since she had had a good meal. For most of her journey, she had fed on dried fruits and bread she'd packed for the road, not because she did not have any money, but because she was pretending to sleep for the better part of the journey. The smell of fresh oven-baked bread and soup filled the surrounding air, reminding her of just how hungry she was. Unable to think of anything but satisfy her hunger, she suspended her search to trace the origin of the restaurant responsible for the sweet smell. She found the inn after a short walk of letting her senses guide her until she saw the signpost hanging over the door with the name "Transylvania Delicacy" written boldly. She got in and carefully looked around.

"Good evening, my lady. Welcome to Transylvania Cuisine! Please take a seat anywhere. I'll be with you shortly." The proprietor, who looked clean and proper, and was pleasant to look at, spread his hands out ahead of him across the length of the restaurant.

Justina sat by the booth closest to the door. She was not here for a leisurely dinner. She had only planned to make a quick stop, satisfy her hunger, and be on her way back into town in search of an abode for the night. The proprietor took a while before coming to ask her for her order. He was chatty, like the carriage driver who'd brought her into town, but then, neater.

"I'm sorry, my lady, I had to finish up with some urgent chores back there. My other helper resigned, you see; she's going to be married and needs to move away with the young lad. My wife is out of town on a visit, so it's just me holding down the fort. Would you like me to cook up something?"

He had an apron tied around his waist, a clean towel hanging across from his shoulder, and he positioned his body like he was putting out his ear to hear her. She was going to ask about the food options they had available, but he beat her to it.

"May I suggest you order the night's special, my lady?" "Okay, sir," she replied, "and what would that be?"

"Oh! Freshly baked bread, our signature bread with a side of olives and some chicken dipped in sweet sauce to go with it. It is my recipe," he said, "my wife makes the soups, but trust me when I say you are going to enjoy this meal."

Justina nodded, and he excused himself at once. He came back later with a jug of fresh beer and a mug on a tray, set it down in front of her, and said with a bow, "On the house, my lady. A token of apology for the delayed service."

She smiled. "Thank you, sir. How generous of you." She made to cup herself some beer, but he stopped her and insisted on pouring it out for her as part of the inn's service. Her meal came a few minutes after that, and true to the proprietor's words, she enjoyed every crumb of the bread, and the chicken dipped in sweet sauce. She tried to defend her appetite by saying she hadn't had a meal in so long, so she was only abating her hunger. The inn's proprietor came back with the bill and was pleased to see that she had cleared up her plate.

"Aha! I told you, you would enjoy the meal. As a house treat, I can whip you up some bread and honey for the road."

"I appreciate that, sir, but I'm not traveling," Justina said.

"But the bags…" The proprietor's eyes fixed on the traveling bags Justina had dragged into the inn with her. Her eyes followed the direction of the proprietor's gaze and she smiled. "I just came into town, sir. It's the other way around. I

arrived in town this evening."

"Oh! I see. Then you would need a place to stay for the night, would you?"

"Definitely. It is my first time in town. I was on my way to find an inn or bed where I could stay the night and breakfast before I try to settle in, but I got swayed over here by the sweet smell of your bread baking."

The proprietor laughed and Justina suspected it might not have been the first time someone had said something similar to him. He read out her bill.

Justina reached for her bag, searching in it for her purse so she could pay the bills, and raised her head in alarm.

The proprietor of the inn had been watching her carefully and could find out the situation before she even said anything else.

Justina's face paled and she turned ghostly white. Her money was gone. All of it! She tried to replay her day in her head, searching back in her memory for where or how she could have dropped her purse. Or was it stolen? By the coach master? Or the beggar that gave her directions? Or the kids that she gave alms. Her head was spinning with so many scenarios.

Had it been someone else, they might have wept or fainted. But Justina braced herself and informed the proprietor that she was penniless and couldn't pay for the meal.

He knew what could have happened to her. It was obvious. The traveling bags and curious eyes were of someone who was visiting the city for the first time. He did not ask for further explanation. Instead, he gave her a room for the night.

"Permit me, my lady, but I have an empty room upstairs where you could stay for the night. I could lease it to you at a discounted fee."

Justina stopped at the door and turned back towards him. "Why do you call me 'my lady'? You do not even know me."

The proprietor laughed. "I've seen enough noblewomen to be able to smell them from a mile away. And besides, the way you're dressed and the way you carry yourself with so much grace bespeaks nobility. Of course, you could be a fake, but your dignified demeanor and the calm way with which you speak are not those of a fake."

"Perhaps I am a good actress," she replied deftly. "Perhaps you are, but are you, my lady?"

Justina sighed and relaxed the tension in her shoulders, putting the bags down. "Why would you offer me a place to stay for the night? I do not have any money like I just told you earlier"

"I'm not offering. It's business, you have to pay for it, like I mentioned I am in dire need of a waitress."

There had to be more, and he needed to come clean. She did not say anything, instead, she arched her brows at him and pursed her lips tightly together, arms folded across her chest.

The proprietor shivered and muttered "women" under his breath before he gave her a reply. "I could tell you are not from around here, and you're a noblewoman. If you walked around town looking gorgeously dressed like that, you'll be attracting attention to yourself. All kinds of attention, and it is too dangerous out there at night for you to be walking alone.

"Unless, of course, you want to end up at the Princes's palace and something tells me you do not want that."

Justina observed the proprietor with hooded eyes, he seemed sincere enough and he had not been gawking at her like the other men she noticed when she came into town. He did not seem to be that much older than her late husband, but he gave off a fatherly aura. She wanted to believe his intentions were sincere. He did seem to always speak his mind, so she figured he might have let it slip if he wanted something more from her. She dropped her gaze and extended her hand out for a handshake.

"Thank you, sir, for your kind offer. I'd take the room, it's not like I have options anyway"

"Right this way, my lady."

"And…" she added, "I would appreciate it if you did not address me that way."

"So, what then should I call you?"

"By my name. My name is…" She hesitated, but the proprietor reassured her that it was fine and she didn't have to say it if she didn't want to.

She raised her chin, squared her jaw, and said, "Justina! My name is Justina."

"What a fine name," the proprietor said, "My name is Nicolae, and I own Transylvania Cuisine as you already know. Me and my wife, actually, and she will be back by noon tomorrow."

The proprietor kept talking as they made their way upstairs towards the room he wanted to lease her, but Justina had stopped listening. Telling him her name made her feel like she was finally defying her cousin's hold on her, and it made her feel so good. A warm, fuzzy feeling washed over her, and she was basking in that feeling.

All that was going on in her head was finally, at last, she was free from King Matthias.

CHAPTER TWELVE

BACK IN HUNGARY, KING MATTHIAS'S CASTLE

"Any word from Justina?" The king strutted into the courtroom, his royal regalia trailing behind him.

He was scheduled to hold the weekly meeting with the royal court in a few minutes. Normally, he preferred to be girded in his warrior's uniform rather than wear the royal robe.

"None yet, Your Majesty," the messenger replied.

After the king found out about the death of his cousin's husband, he sent his condolences through his messenger, and so, he was expecting to get a reply from her or, at the very least, an acknowledgment.

"Interesting," the king said. "How long has it been since I sent the message to her?"

"About three weeks, my lord."

"And yet she refuses to reply. I do not presume she is still mourning him. Do you think she is?"

The messenger stuttered, wondering what to say in reply to the king's question. It was the first time the king had asked his opinion on anything. They soon got to the giant door leading to the courtroom, and he was spared from having to answer as the doors opened to reveal the king's court already seated, awaiting his arrival.

"Gentlemen!" The king greeted as he stepped in. All thoughts of his cousin and her "seemingly" malicious act of not replying to him were forgotten

The meeting session lasted the whole morning into the earliest part of noon. As soon as the court dispersed, the royal servants brought in the king's midday meal. The messenger had been waiting outside as the king had not granted him permission to do anything else. He had to be within reach if he was needed, and as if on cue, a message came for the king and he rushed in to deliver it to him.

"Your Majesty," he greeted with a bow, standing far off as he waited to be granted permission to speak.

"Speak!" the king said.

"A letter arrived for you, Your Majesty." "From Justina?"

"I'm afraid not, my liege." "Then who is it from?"

"It bears the stamp of the Saxons," he said with a bow.

The king dropped his cutlery, wiped his mouth with a napkin, and beckoned the messenger forwards.

As the king read the letter, his eyes dimmed with rage and his knuckles tightened around the scroll.

"Send for Lord Sebastian at once!" he thundered.

The messenger, ragged, and lean, squeaked a reply and disappeared. The king's commander returned with extraordinary speed. He saluted and moved closer to inquire what the king's wishes might be. The king handed him the letter without a word, and his face went red with rage as he read it, too.

"What do you want me to do, my lord?" Sebastian asked. "Bring that traitor to me at once," the king said, clenching his fist. "And send someone out to Transylvania and find out how Lady Justina is doing."

"As you wish, Your Majesty." Sebastian bowed and left. "Bloody traitor!" the king roared. The messenger bowed low and retreated, wondering who had betrayed the king and put him in such a foul mood. He feared for the person. King Matthias was not one to be toyed with.

~ ∞ ~

BACK AT THE PONGRAC MANSION

An emissary arrived at the gates of the late Lord Wenceslas's manor, demanding to see the widowed wife on orders of the king. The servants opened the gate to let him in and sent for Esme as they felt she was the better person amongst them all to give answers.

"You are not Lady Justina," the emissary said as Esme arrived. "No, my lord," she replied, head bowed.

"Would she not see me? I have to speak with her directly as the king demands it—"

Esme had to come clean with the truth. Her head might end up on a pike if she disobeyed the king's orders or lied to him. She had known this day would come and had been anxiously waiting for it. They received a message from the king a day after Lady Justina went missing, but she did not dare open it for fear of the king's wrath. The message was in Lady Justina's room, tucked safely away in her dressing drawer. Esme planned to present the king with the letter as proof that Lady Justina had been missing from the manor and had not received his letter.

"I'm sorry, my lord, but Lady Justina is not present at the moment."

"I see." He rubbed his eyebrows like he was worried. "And may I ask where she has gone?"

"We do not know,"

"We?"

"Lady Justina left the manor a few weeks ago. We have been looking for her, hoping to find her soon, which is why we did not inform the king about it. We did not want to bother the king with such news until we were certain that she—"

"You think the fact that the king's cousin is missing is trivial? How dare you think to handle it yourselves," the emissary said, interrupting her.

"I apologize, my lord. If you permit, I shall ride back to Hungary with you and present myself before the king."

"What do you hope to achieve with that?"

"She is my mistress, and I must serve her and protect her to the best of my ability. I intend to apologize for my shortcomings and take responsibility for whatever the king decides to do. I also hope she returns soon, and I want to do whatever I can to ensure that."

"Very well," the emissary said. "We leave at first light."

"Yes, my lord!"

True to his words, at the very first light of dawn, he was packed and ready to ride back to Hungary. Esme tagged along, praying under her breath as they went the king would be merciful and spare her life because she knew something that the others did not. Lady Justina was not coming back. She was gone for good.

CHAPTER THIRTEEN

Justina settled in quickly to her new life in Brasov, blending in with the natives like she had lived there all her life. Nicolae's wife came back the next day just like her husband had said, and she was the sweetest, most hardworking woman Justina had ever seen. She welcomed her with open arms, acting like a mother to her. She helped Justina settle in with ease. The first point of call for Justina was to get new dresses sewn for her. She wanted to keep her down and enjoy a simple, quiet life so that she would not get caught by her cousin. She locked up her expensive silk dresses in a box and went to the town's seamstress with Nicolae's wife. The seamstress took her measurement and in a week, Justina had two new beautifully tailored dresses.

"Wow! You look good in anything. Even rags would look glamorous on you," the seamstress said to her after she tried on the dress at the shop.

Justina blushed and thanked her but the seamstress was not done yet. She offered Justina a job with her. "With that body, and your pretty face, men, and women would flock to my shop wanting to have their dresses made," she said, but Justina declined.

If she accepted the job with the seamstress, she would attract attention to herself, and that was the exact opposite of what she wanted. After picking up her dresses, Justina took a stroll around town, taking the beautiful scenery and everything else the town offered. The town's yet-to-be-completed cathedral loomed high in the distance. She noticed people flocking in and out of the church and wondered if something was happening in there that she didn't know about, but she did not dare to ask anyone about it. She made the sign of the cross at the gate and turned to leave.

On her way back, she noticed a huge building with bright torches around it. Out of curiosity, she entered the building and discovered that it was a play center. She curiously looked around and wondered what kind of plays happened here, she couldn't wait to witness one herself. She had to; she wanted to experience everything that the town offered. The music, nature, the people, and their smiles. Just the warmth that it exuded.

She left the play center with an excited grin on her face. The next agenda on her list was to find a new room to live in, as she could not live with the innkeepers for long. She did not want to intrude and besides, she felt like she had had enough of living with people. She would not be getting the full experience of her freedom if she came down here to live with Nicolae and his wife. She walked around town all morning, determined to find a vacancy for a room in any house before she returned to the inn, but her efforts proved fruitless. Tired and hungry, she suspended her search. She would pick it up some other time, but for the moment, she needed water and some food.

"Hey Justina, you're back," Nicolae said when she walked in but he took one look at her and frowned. "What is it? You look sad!"

Justina chuckled. "I'm just tired and hungry. I took a walk around town today. I wanted to explore it for myself."

"Ah! I see. Why did you not ask for a carriage?"

Justina downed the cup of water he extended to her and asked sarcastically, "Do you have one?"

He blinked. "Where would I get the money to offer such luxury? Do you mock me?"

"No, I do not, Nicolae. I'm grateful to you and your wife, but I'm trying to keep my head down, remember? And riding in a carriage around town does not exactly help with that cause."

"I see. I see," Nicolae replied, "but next time, do not just wander off on your own. How far did you go?"

"Past the uncompleted cathedral to the play center and then, after that, I went in search of a room to live. That was when my futile journey began. I walked across half the town."

Nicolae exclaimed from behind the counter, where he had gone to fetch her some bread and beer. He set the meal down before her and indicated for her to eat.

"Thank you!" Justina said and moaned delightfully when she took the first bite. "Oh! It's so soft and delicious."

Nicolae grinned. "You must be hungry." "Famished," Justina replied, and they both laughed. "Now, about the room to live," Nicolae began.

Justina looked up from her meal, letting the bread dangle in her hand as her face turned bright pink with embarrassment. Nicolae grinned and placed a hand on her free one resting on the table.

"It's okay! I understand. There's no need to look so guilty or embarrassed."

Justina swallowed back her meal and smiled in gratitude. "There are quite many free rooms in some houses back in town. It depends on what you are looking for and how you are dressed. None of these aristocrats would lease their room to a commoner and you look like one dressed like that. I'm sure it must have been those houses that you visited and got turned away."

"Oh!" Justina said, unable to form any more words in response.

"It does not seem fair, but that is the state of things. The upper class socializes and the lower class forms its own circles. But I think I just might help you get a room suitable for a woman of your upbringing, but humble enough to not raise questions."

"This means a lot to me. I do not think that I could ever thank you enough or repay you," Justina said.

"Well, I can think of one way you can."

Her ears perked up, and she sat up straight.

"You could come work here for us. The pay is not much compared to what you are used to, but it should be enough to help you out with some basic needs. Oh, and there are some bonuses too. On some days, they are quite reasonable."

Justina sputtered some of her food as she laughed and quickly placed a hand over her mouth. She grabbed a napkin and wiped it down on her face and hand, then cleaned the surface of the table. Nicolae watched her quietly, patiently waiting for her response. Meanwhile, she was thinking about how unbelievable he was to grant her a favor in place of asking her for a favor. She was glad to find out that there were more people like Esme in the world. It made her feel warm. Her eyes dropped as she thought about Esme; she missed her terribly and it killed her to not know how her maidservant was doing. She thought about writing her a letter but thought better of it. Writing Esme a letter would attest to the fact that Esme knew where she was and she did not want to put her maidservant in trouble with the king; and it would raise brows if they find out Esme can write, it's still a secret that Justina has been giving her lessons while back at her cousin's palace. Besides, if the king ever found out about the letter, then finding her would be easy.

"Justina? Are you okay? You look like your mind was somewhere else."

Justina blinked and refocused her attention on him. She couldn't tell him she was thinking about her maidservant. Although She knew Nicolae had suspected and wasn't sure if he had successfully guessed that she was an upper-class woman. For all she knew, it was still mere speculation, and he had no fact to prove it. He also did not know who she was or where she came from, he imagined her to be from one of the neighboring villages around Brasov, and she did not change his mindset.

"I'm just overwhelmed, Nicolae. I'm surprised and I do not know what to reply to you. You should ask for something as repayment, yet you offer me a job. It's unusual. Thank you, I accept it with gladness. Now, about that tip…" she began, and they both laughed.

~ ∞ ~

Justina woke up the next morning to loud noises from the inn. The house was subdivided into two, with their living quarters placed just above the inn. She woke with a start, rubbing her sleepy eyes as she wondered what might be happening down there to cause such a ruckus. She got up to wash her face and noticed that it was still dark outside, it would take a while before the sun approached fully. She let out a groan and climbed back into bed, determined to drown out the noise. She placed a pillow over her head, but it did little to help. After a while of troubled, noisy sleep, she woke to see that the dark clouds were clearing to reveal clear, blue skies. Slowly, she dragged herself out of bed, washed up, and went downstairs to help the Nicolaes with the breakfast.

The scene she encountered stunned her into silence. The inn was packed full of customers clamoring to have their orders taken and attended to. Nicolae's wife held the fort in the kitchen while Nicolae ran around between tables trying to attend to the customers' needs. While a customer stood to leave after having had their fill, another one opened the door and claimed the empty spot. Now, she understood the reason for the ruckus. But it was barely dawn. How were they all so hungry already, and where did they come from?

"Justina, you're awake," Nicolae called when he saw her standing still on the stairs, observing the chaos.

She smiled, squared her chin, and went to where the meals were cooked. "Good morning, Angela," she said, greeting Nicolae's wife.

Angela replied with a kiss on her cheek, after which she asked her to go into the inn and take orders. Justina straightened and marched out into the inn. The clamoring died down as soon as she walked in. Suddenly, everyone wanted to be served by her, and they will wait their turn until she was ready to take their order. Nicolae, who had been frantically moving around the inn, trying to get their orders and deliver on time, now had so much free time on his hands. He went around requesting to take orders, but they turned him down, insisting on waiting for Justina to take their order, so instead, he filled the mugs with beer and went behind the counter to help Angela with the cooking.

The ruckus died down just before noon and Justina finally got some time to sit and breathe. Nicolae appeared with a cup of fresh ale courtesy of Angela.

"Thank you," she said and gulped the drink down eagerly. She raised the cup towards Angela in the kitchen. "Did you sprinkle magic on this? It tastes divine. No wonder you pack a crowd in here so early."

"It's my grandmother's recipe. I'll be happy to share it with you."

"I would love that." Justina wanted to say more but decided against it. She did not cook; she didn't know how. She had attempted to learn back in Pongrac manor, but the kitchen staff was in such reverence of her they could not believe she was asking. They refused, insisting that they did not want to face her late husband's wrath if he found out that something had happened to her while they were trying to play in the kitchen. That was her chance, but even that was taken away from her.

"Is it usually this way?" she asked.

"Every day, seven days a week," Nicolae replied. "It wasn't always this way. It started when they opened a trade route through the city. Since then, travelers going to other towns for businesses stop by the inn for some early breakfast. Since we are the only ones open at that time, the crowd is massive." Justina nodded, but he was not done. "It's not bad, though.

After the rush hour, we get a break just like this, before the next one comes."

Her eyes widened. "The next one?"

"Yes, but don't look so frightened. It's nothing like what you just did. In the evening, our customers drank and wouldn't require perfection from you."

"Oh, so the next round of the rush hour will be in the evening?"

"Yes, that's when the play center opens, and every other entertainment unit in town, so people come in here for an evening meal or just light refreshment. Every other thing in between is just regular customers stopping by now and then. It's nothing much, it's like one or two customers, and we can handle that individually."

He handed her some coins and, she looked at him, wonder- ing why he was giving her that. "Why are you paying me so soon? I only just started."

"This is not your payment; these are the bonuses from this morning."

"What?" she said, eyes wide. "This much? All of it?" "Yeah," he said with a smile, "the customers were feeling generous today." He winked and Justina laughed with him. Angela came over to them with a tray of food in her hand.

"Here, eat some food and go upstairs when you are done."

"Upstairs?" Justina asked, not sure she heard what Angela

said.

"Yes, for a nap, go and sleep. You have done well. Nicolae and I will hold the place down while you rest. When you awake, you can come and help."

"You both are amazing people. Thank you, but I don't want to nap. I want to get a room of my own to live in, so I think I will just do that."

"You need to rest," Angela said forcefully, "so you can be ready for the evening. You look so fragile. I'm shocked you managed this morning."

Angela was a strong, robust woman, so Justina understood why she would think of her as fragile. Angela has been trying to stuff her with meals since she came back and found her asleep in their guest room. She worried Justina was not eating enough or sleeping enough because Justina was not adding as much weight as she wanted her to.

"I appreciate your concern, Angela, but I am okay. Thank you."

Angela shrugged and returned to the kitchen. It was a simple gesture that said, "I did my best!"

"I hope I have not offended her," said Justina.

Nicolae laughed. "Don't worry about it. Angela can be a little intense, trying to mother everyone that allows her to. She'll be fine."

"She is a wonderful woman. How do I make it up to her?" "You could finish the meal she made for you. An empty plate says thank you better than your words would. Is lovely.

Justina's throat bulged as she swallowed. Angela had made a big plate for her and she was certain she could not finish the meal.

Nicolae noticed Justina's dilemma and reassured her. "Don't pressure yourself. Don't worry about it, you do not have to finish the meal. She knows you appreciate it. I was only kidding."

Her countenance brightened and he stirred the conversation towards something else. "About the room, don't worry about it. I will make some inquiries and let you know about any vacant rooms by evening. You can go upstairs and get some rest. Angela is right; you need to be well-rested before evening. I have friends in town who can help with finding you a room in any nice house, so don't worry about it."

Justina was so overcome with gratitude that she got up and hugged him. She sat down to eat and ended up clearing out her plate; the food was too good. She went back to the kitchen to drop her plate and gave Angela a warm hug, too. She was so happy that at that moment, she forgot about everything else beyond Brasov.

CHAPTER FOURTEEN

TRANSYLVANIA KING MATTHIAS'S CASTLE

A royal guard entered the courtroom to announce to the king that the emissary sent out to Lady Justina had returned. He arrived in the courtroom shortly after, Esme on his heels. The king dismissed the court, leaving him alone with the emissary and Esme.

"Your Majesty!" the emissary greeted.

"Where is Justina?" the king asked before the emissary could get another word out. The emissary opened and closed his mouth as his hands trembled and he looked for a way to say what he wanted to. King Mathias suspected it wasn't good news.

"She's not here, and her maidservant is here. What happened to her? Is she sick?"

The emissary swallowed, lost for words now. He was standing before the king and he couldn't provide answers. He felt so stupid and incompetent.

"Forgive me, Your Majesty," Esme said, throwing herself forward on the king's feet, heads bowed and trembling with fear as she spoke.

"Lady Justina left the manor —"

"Left?" he asked, rising to his feet and unintentionally throwing her off. Esme rolled to the side but picked herself up quickly and returned to a kneeling position with her head bowed and her hands folded on each other.

"What do you mean she left?" the king asked, his voice threatening and menacing.

Tears started pouring out of Esme's eyes like she did not control them. She looked scared but also looked like she had expected it like she knew the king would be furious and had imagined how that could go, but being in his presence and experiencing it in real life must have overwhelmed her. Sweat beads appeared on her forehead. The whole castle was scared and the only one who had the guts to stand up to the king was Lady Justina, his beloved cousin Esme was kneeling here trying to tell him that that same cousin had disappeared into the wind. Esme looked to be muttering a prayer under her breath.

"Speak, woman. What are you trying to say?" the king demanded.

The emissary bowed his head and apologized profusely for something that was not his fault, something he did not know about.

"After Lord Wenceslas passed away," Esme began, lips quivering, "My lady mourned for him. She stayed locked up in her chambers for days and we were all worried for her. Then suddenly, after a few days, my lady came out of her chambers. She was looking much better, and she informed us she would spend the day in Lord Wenceslas' study…"

The king was running low on patience, but he reined in his anger and listened to her.

"That night, I attended to her and she requested for another maidservant to bring her some late-night ale." Esme paused and choked back a sob. "That was the last time I saw my lady, Your Majesty. By the time we woke up the next morning, she was gone."

"And who is this maidservant that attended to Justina later that night? Where is she?" the king asked.

"At the manor, Your Majesty. She's there with the other servants. We have been trying to find the lady ourselves."

The king scoffed. "And do you think you would have been able to find her? How did that go? Did you find her?"

Esme shook her head profusely. "I regret to say, Your Majesty, that she is yet to return or be found."

"And why are you here? Why did you come?"

"As her maidservant, I feel responsible for her, and I… I feel that I should have done better. I feel responsible for being the one to tell you, Your Majesty. I accept responsibility for my mistress' actions." Esme's words betrayed her actions as she trembled like a leaf in a summer's wind.

The king stood, and Esme's heart stopped. His rising meant that he was going to give a verdict. "Well, feel responsible. I committed her to your care, and you lost her. I would have you flogged…"

Esme's heart beat faster, and she clenched her teeth to keep from begging. "Yes, Your Majesty, I accept your verdict."

The king eyed her; she lay prostrate on the floor, not daring to look up at him. She was scared out of her wits, and yet she would offer to take up the punishment for an errant mistress. There was nothing she could have done even if she had been there when Justina was leaving, the king thought. He knew his cousin well enough to know that, and yet this maidservant was here claiming responsibility. I impressed him. He sat back on the throne.

"But my cousin is fond of you, and I can see why. You may go, return to your duty in the castle, and wait for her. Her old chambers need to be renovated. See to it that it is before she returns. I will find Justina myself."

Esme lay still, unable to believe her ears. She pinched herself to be sure that the king's words were real. When she was sure she was hearing the king, gratitude flooded her, and she expressed it in a thousand words.

The king accepted her gratitude and dismissed her to go, but before she did, he said, "For your sake, pray I find Lady Justina alive. If any harm has come to her, I will send you off to serve her in the otherworld."

Esme gulped as he released her to go. She ran out of the courtroom with gratitude, but the king's last words haunted her, and she prayed desperately. Beyond the king's words, she was genuinely concerned for her mistress. It had not occurred to her that Lady Justina could be harmed or brought to hurt, but now it was the only thing she could think about. Her mind concocted different scenarios in which Lady Justina could be harmed, and she became more frantic with each thought.

"Please be safe, my lady. For my sake, please be safe. I would not be able to forgive myself if anything happened to you," Esme whispered, looking out to the night sky. She made the sign of the cross over her face and went back inside. She had sent the prayer out into heaven as a request, and she hoped God would watch over her mistress.

Back in the courtroom, King Matthias dismissed the emissary and requested for the guards to send for an old ac- quaintance of his called Alexandru. Alexandru returned to the palace with the guard and was ushered into the king's presence.

"Your Majesty," he greeted with a bow. "To what do I owe this audience? It's been a while since you requested my services."

The king tossed him a pouch with gold coins in it. Alexandru caught the bag in the air, opened it to take a look, and grinned from ear to ear.

"Pick up the scent," the king said.

"With pleasure, Your Majesty!" he said with a bow, and walked away from the king's presence.

CHAPTER FIFTEEN

"Justina!" Nicolae called as he entered the inn. He was excited about something; that much was obvious. Justina smiled and raised her hand above the counter. She was bent on the counter in search of a spice Angela needed. Nicolae walked to the kitchen behind the counter, where he dropped his coat and kissed Angela on the cheek before going back out into the inn to help clear out the dishes of a customer that had just left.

"Guess what, Justina, I have excellent news!" His eyes twinkled and Justina wondered what it could be to have been so excited and pumped up.

"I do not think I can put a word to whatever has made you this happy."

"Try it?"

"Okay, let's see… Did you get an invitation to meet with the Prince of Brasov?"

"Huh?" Nicolae said.

Justina shrugged. "I'm sorry, I told you before. That was the only thing I could come up with."

"It's fine. It was a fair try, but… get ready for it…" He took in a deep breath and exhale and signaled for Justina to do the same. She obliged reluctantly, and he said, "I found you a room in the upper part of town where most of the upper class live, and it is close to the playhouse and lively spots to spend time…" in one breath. When he was done, he drew in a long breath and sighed.

Justina staggered backward against a table as she took in all the words that rushed at her from Nicolae's lips. A room. In the upper part of town. Close to the play center. It was all too good to be true. The feeling of happiness set in slowly as the realization of what Nicolae was saying dawned on her. She jumped with excitement on Nicolae with a hug.

"Justina, too tight! Too tight," Nicolae said, and she let go. "I'm sorry, I got carried away. I'm so happy. Thank you,

Nicolae, thank you so much. I am deeply indebted to you and Angela. How did you find the place?"

"I told you I have a friend."

"That's true," Justina said. "I see now why you were so happy."

After the evening rush hour, while they cleaned up the inn and tidied it up for the next rush hour, which was to happen at dawn, Justina filled Angela in on the big news. Angela congratulated her.

"I heard about it," Angela said. "I heard you squealing and jumping around the inn."

Justina blushed but did not defend herself. She had been that excited. "I would like to go check out the room tomorrow if that is okay with you. I will leave after the morning rush and be back before evening."

"Of course, we were just talking about it." Angela said, "Please let us know if you need any help moving in. We will be more than happy to be of help."

According to the plan, the next day, after the morning rush hour, Nicolae escorted Justina to the new room so that she could decide if she liked it and wanted to move in. She loved that the room was big as soon as she set her eyes on it. It was well spaced and had places for her to drop her candles or books if she acquired them, so she made payment for the space. Ideas flooded her head about how she wanted to decorate the place, and she asked Nicolae if he could take her to a place where she could get basic household items. They still had a few hours left before evening, so Nicolae offered to go with her.

She bought a mattress, some curtains, and other basic household items she needed. She did not get any kitchen utensils, as she would not be needing them. Every day after the morning rush hour, during the noon break, Justina would buy a bit more of the housing stuff that she needed from the bonuses earned that day and take it to her room. Finally, the room was done and ready for her to move in. It was a small room with a place to cook, and she created a space to bathe. Justina was minimal on the decoration; the space was furnished but did not look too lavish; it was a bit of each, classy, and comfortable.

Nicolae and Angela leased out a carriage to help her move her bags and clothes on the day that she was moving. They closed the inn after the morning rush hour and accompanied her to the new room. Their presence as she moved in helped to reduce the whispers and stares because almost everyone in town knew Nicolae, so no one bothered too much to find out who Justina was.

Nicolae and Angela helped Justina move all her stuff in, they mostly wanted to see her space and welcome her into it though. When they were done, they shared some cakes and drinks that Angela had packed up for Justina. At first, they refused, insisting that they had plenty more in the inn and did not want to be a bother to her, but Justina insisted and they gave in. The couple departed a few hours before evening and informed Justina not to bother coming to the inn later that evening.

"Get some rest, settle in properly."

"The evening rush… how will you cope?"

"We will manage just fine," Angela answered, pulling her into a hug. Angela smelled like clean soap. "I will see you tomorrow," she said, and Justina nodded in reply.

After Nicolaes and his wife left, Justina looked at her room, and then she went out to sit on the balcony and enjoy the evening breeze. The wind blew lightly in her hair.

"I'm proud of you, Justina. You did it. You are a strong woman," she said to herself and stood to go back in the doors as the evening was getting cooler. A flashing light in the distance caught her attention as she stood. She grabbed a coat and walked out the door. Her legs carried her down the streets in dainty low heels until she arrived in front of the town's square. She had seen the flames from the torches on the street as they led down to the open space right before her balcony and all her fatigue suddenly had melted away.

She stood back and as she took in the space and people, enjoying the feeling of being in that moment with a proud smile on her face. Her stomach fluttered with excitement and she giggled from the adrenaline rush. There were multiple stalls and stands, some filled with fresh food and others with items she had never seen before. The market was still bolstering with life despite the sun had taken its leave.

"Excuse me, my lady," a merchant called, but Justina did not turn to look. It had been a while since anyone addressed her after she adapted to her new life, so she couldn't have imagined she was the one being addressed. The voice came again a second time, closer, with a light tap on her shoulder. Justina turned sharply from the shock and almost hit the attendant, who apologized profusely.

What exactly are you apologizing for? I am the one who almost hit you.

"I presume you are here for the town's trade fair, the most popular part of the Moonlight Festival around these parts."

Justina nodded and the round merchant with curly hair continued, "Then right this way, my lady. I will show you the finest items the kingdom offers." He led the way. There was a queue forming at one stall that smelt incredibly delicious. The merchant caught Justina's gaze before she turned her head and a knowing smile emerged on his face.

"Would you like to try some of our delicacies, my lady?" He asked, and Justina pondered on it for a quick second.

Well, what do I have to lose? She gave him a brisk nod.

The merchant led her right past the line to the front of the stall and made small talk with one attendant. He snagged her two of the roasted pigeons that had been propped on a stick and thoroughly spiced to meet the people's tastes.

"Thank you," she said, and the merchant looked genuinely surprised to have heard her say that to him. Justina tried to pay for the meal, but the merchant had refused vehemently, insisting she instead come have a look around his shop.

"A noblewoman like you purchasing one of my fabrics would mean much more for my business than payment for a roasted bird," he said, and Justina followed him gracefully.

It wasn't until after she had left the streets that she realized how he had recognized her as one of regal blood. It was her outfit that gave her away. She had picked a fancy outfit from the ones that she traveled with into Brasov and paired it with a beautiful white mink coat.

Upon getting to the store, it seemed like more customers were awaiting the friendly merchant.

"I think this color is much better. What do you think, Julia? I would say it's perfect, but Ana-Maria might have a different opinion. I say we wait for her to return from wherever she ran off to."

"Ah! Yes! Ana-Maria, better avoid what happened the last time."

The merchant opened his mouth but a woman who Justina assumed to be his friend came into the store at that moment and the loud calling and cackling that followed drowned out his voice.

"Over here, Ana! You need to come look at this!" The one referred to as Julia said, waving the soft-looking silk fabric back and forth to attract Ana-Maria's attention.

"Shh! You're causing a ruckus, Julia. There are other people here." the other lady said and turned to apologize to the two of them before her. "Sorry about that, sir, ma'am."

The friend whom Julia had been waving to, the one that Justina now identified to be Ana-Maria, saw her friends and walked across the space to them. She looked to be the most glamorous and sophisticated among the trio.

Justina turned back to the merchant slowly, having satisfied her curiosity about the drama going on before her. She put the ladies out of her mind and thought that would be the last time she would see or hear any of them. The merchant had just opened his mouth to start selling his trade.

"Excuse me, ma'am, I can't help but ask if you are new here," One lady piped and Justina gave her a small smile.

And just like that, she found herself face to face with the three ladies.

"Thank you very much for answering her, ma'am. She can be a bit... nosy," the other lady said. "I'm Elena, and these are my friends —"

"Julia and Ana-Maria," Justina said.

"Wow! How did you know that?" Julia asked, impressed that Justina had guessed their names accurately.

Justina chuckled. "It's not a magic trick, trust me. I heard you both talking when we walked into the shop, and you mentioned names."

"I see," Ana-Maria said, "I think I like you."

The other ladies laughed and one of them said, "You like that mink, that's for sure."

Ana-Maria rolled her eyes. "What can I say? It's nice to meet someone around these parts who understands the gracious, unique art that is fashion."

Elena smiled apologetically. "Forgive me. I apologize on her behalf because I have to say that once she starts, she goes on and on and it is difficult to turn her off."

Justina laughed, and the others joined in, but she soon found out that Elena's words were true. It was not just Ana-Maria, the ladies talked on and on into the night.

"Oh, can we join you as you see the town tonight? You seem responsible, and my father would be so glad I'm in good company."

Justina had lost track of who was who, they all just blended into one and they were talking so fast that she wanted to shove something in their mouths and get them to stop. She nodded, just trying to be polite as she said, "Sure, join me, ladies. I don't mind."

"I'm sorry, Lady Beatrice, you've spent your time dedicated to shopping because of us. I assure you, we're usually not this chatty."

Ana-Maria coughed, but she didn't need to. Justina could already tell that they were always that chatty. She understood Elena was only being proper by apologizing for all of them and trying to preserve their dignity.

"To make it up to you, Lady Beatrice, how about some late- night ale?" Ana-Maria said, and the rest of the ladies consented loudly.

"We know just the right spot," Julia said, and Justina was grateful when they got to the spot and she found out that it was somewhere else other than Nicolae's inn. She wouldn't have been able to handle it if the ladies called her Beatrice in front of the couple. Or worse still, if the couple called her Justina in front of the ladies.

Justina said a quick goodbye to the merchant after a promise to return and view his wares.

After the introduction where she completed the names for Elena, the ladies wanted to know her name, but she couldn't risk telling them. So far, she had observed them to be quite chatty, and not that they were bad people, but they were quick with their words and might spill a secret without even knowing it. Of course, Elena was more conservative than the rest, but it was too early to have favorites among them. The question of her name came suddenly to her, and she didn't want to be rude by saying that she could not disclose it to them; saying that would have raised more suspicions about her, so instead, she said the second name that came to mind—Beatrice, her cousin's second wife. The first name that came to mind was Esme.

She had so much fun with the ladies that night. After getting ale, they took her around town on their carriage to explore other places in the city. By the time Justina returned home, it was late at night and dark clouds already covered the moon. The ladies stopped her a few blocks away from her house as they also lived in that part of town, and she walked the rest of the way home to her new room. As she trudged towards the house, she couldn't help but get the feeling she was being watched. She turned back to check just so that she could ease her suspicion and was alarmed to see a silhouette dart away from sight and hide behind a building. Her pulse picked up, and she walked as quickly as she could into the building, headed straight for her room, and bolted the door behind her. It wasn't until she had freshened up and was now lying securely under her quilt that her pulse slowed down to a steady rhythm. She reminisced about the activities of the night and giggled as noteworthy moments replayed in her head. She had turned heads everywhere she went with the ladies that night, but that was not unusual for her. At the ale spot, Ana-Maria had alerted her to a young man buying a treat from the stall closest to where they stood.

"I think you got yourself an admirer," Ana-Maria said, but Justina dismissed her words, not even when Ana-Maria insisted that the man could not get his eyes off her since the theater and had followed them there in the guise of wanting to get some ale himself.

"I know him; he's a nobleman. A good-looking one at that, so what's holding you back? It wouldn't hurt to get a little fun and get your hay a bit of sunlight." Justina did not understand the meaning of Ana-Maria's last words, but she did not bother to ask her about it or think too much about it. She ignored Ana-Maria, focusing instead on the amazing time she had that night. She had never felt so alive and so free. She rolled on her side and dragged the blanket up to her neck.

Just before she dozed off, three words played in her head. "Long live Beatrice! Long live Justina!"

CHAPTER SIXTEEN

Alexandru stopped by an inn to rest his head for the night. He had been on the move since he left King Matthias's palace that day with an instruction from

the king to 'find the scent.'

Alexandru was the most fearsome private investigator in all of Hungary. He found things that did not want to be found, that was his specialty, but Alexandru was not exactly welcomed by any king into their kingdom because he owed no allegiance to anyone. His allegiance was to the money. He rendered his service to anyone willing and wealthy enough to pay, but once he decided on something, he would not let go until he found what he needed. He was efficient at his job and that earned him the nickname of the Hunting Dog.

It was unclear why the king needed his services. The terms of their business were known only to both of them, but with the happenings at the palace, there were a few speculations. No one knew about Lady Justina, but they had seen the army commander bring back a prisoner, so the word around the castle was that the king was conducting a private investigation about the prisoner before executing his verdict. It was one thing the locals loved about their king, he was a just and fair man despite the many shortcomings he might have. The locals were assured that he treated everyone justly, irrespective of who they were.

Alexandru opened the door to the inn and set off a bell. "Welcome, sir!" the owner said, raising his head above the counter and sitting up straight on what would be the reception desk. He was old and looked tired with gray hair. "How can I be of service to you today?"

"I would like a bed for the night," he said and tossed a gold coin across the countertop.

The man swallowed, and Adam's apple bulged. His eyes grew wide, and he almost fell off his seat. When he regained himself, he jumped down and came around the front to where Alexandru was standing.

"Right this way, sir. Let me show you to one of our finest rooms," the owner said and walked ahead as fast as his short legs could carry him. Alexandru followed, keeping up easily with long, easy strides.

They arrived at the room and the inn owner opened it with a dramatic flair. "Here you are, sir, our finest suite."

Alexandru walked into the room with a bored expression on his face. It was just as he had suspected. There was nothing fine about this room that the owner claimed to be a suite. It was dusty and cramped, with a huge bed that took up most of the space in the room. At least the bed would be compensation for him, as he was quite tall, and it was always a chore to squeeze into smaller-sized beds. If the finest room was less than satisfactory, he did not want to think about what the regular rooms would look like. He had known from experience the state of inns like this which is why he never ended up in the regular room if he could help it.

The owner watched Alexandru's expression and did not look surprised by his expression. It was quite the usual with guests who requested the best suite. They ended up regarding the suit like a filthy piece of rag, which was not exactly far from the truth, but his concern was the money and he had that in his pocket.

"Sir, do you have luggage? Would you like me to help you with it?" This part always came with a tip from grateful guests. "No, thank you," Alexandru said, much to the innkeeper's disappointment. He recovered quickly and tried another

approach.

"How about a meal, sir? We offer some of the finest cuisines and our in-house cook is an expert. I'm talking about age-long family recipes, handed down through the generations —"

Alexandru interrupted him. "How about a tavern? Is there one around here?"

The innkeeper was taken aback by Alexandru's question, wondering what a fine young man like him could want in a pub that early. It was then that he took the time to look at Alexandru. He observed the sturdy boots up to the robes and further above to the less than a regal shirt that clung tightly to his chest and finally to the hat that topped his hair.

Sighing in resignation, the innkeeper mouthed, "Just another crook," and turned to leave the room.

"How about the pub?" he asked loudly, but the innkeeper did not stop. He shouted a reply over his shoulder and muttered to himself back to his station at the reception. His hopes of making more money off this guest had been thrown into the wind. He climbed back to his seat and waited for better luck with the next customer. At least he was lucky to have even gotten a gold coin out of this one.

Alexandru returned to the reception a few minutes later, dressed and ready to hit the tavern. He noticed the innkeeper's apathy and found it quite amusing. He was no stranger to the streets, so he knew what made the innkeeper so unfriendly suddenly. As he walked out of the inn, he stopped by the innkeeper and tossed him two bronze coins as a tip. The innkeeper's face lit up, and he was once again eager to guarantee the utmost customer satisfaction for their guest. Alexandru had a different use for the pub than the innkeeper assumed. He needed it for business; it was part of his trade. Shady information people did not want to see the light of day found its way around in the darkness of a pub. If he was going to get any leads about his current mission, he was certain he would find them at the pub.

The interior of the tavern was dimly lit and filled with the stench of wine and drunken men. Alexandru made his way to the bar counter and ordered a cup of rum. While he sat there waiting, he perused the pub, looking for who might be most susceptible to his charm.

He found a drunken man at a table at the far end of the room, telling tall tales to the others who cared to listen about outrageous feats he claimed to have performed. Some of his listeners scoffed and guffawed, but they listened anyway. Alexandru observed him for a while, pretending to nurse the jug of rum in his hand.

When he noticed that the drunken man was alone, he requested for another jug of rum to be delivered to him. The drunken man looked up when the rum was placed before him and followed the direction of the waiter's hand to Alexandru.

Alexandru bided his time, and sure enough, the drunken man arrived at the counter with a cloud of foul stench that filled the surrounding air. The smell was so suffocating that Alexandru had to put some distance between them without being concerned about whether they stood the risk of having their conversation heard by others. He was convinced the drunken man had not bathed in weeks and was oozing an accumulated stench of dried beer and body heat. Despite that, he ordered another mug of rum to be served to his smelly companion, and the drunken man chugged it down noisily. Alexandru requested yet another mug. He needed his companion to be drunk enough to spill and not remember what he said by the next morning.

After four mugs of rum for his companion, while he held onto the initial mug he ordered, Alexandru got the information he needed. He left the pub that night tired to the bones and with a nauseating feeling in the pit of his stomach because of having sat close to such a foul-smelling individual, but he was pleased.

He left the inn the next morning at first light, with another destination in mind. He had been headed in the wrong direction all the while, and his undesirable, late-night drinking buddy showed him the right way to go. He had picked up on a new scent.

CHAPTER SEVENTEEN

The gates leading to the dungeon creaked as they opened. The hollow space surrounding the dungeons amplified the noise as it echoed off the walls. For a

place so quiet, loud noise as this was sure to send chills down the spine of whoever was imprisoned beneath. Vlad Tepes laughed at himself for being so shocked when the noise came. He was certain that was exactly the point King Matthias had in mind when he'd built the dungeons. They were like-minded people; tough, brave, and unforgiving, but fair and just, which was why he was not so afraid for his life. He would quiver with fear and try to find a way out of imprisonment if he did what the king was accusing him of doing. He was not stupid. He would not dare betray King Matthias. They were far too alike for him to act recklessly. One could even say that the king had Vlad Tepes's respect and loyalty, not just because he swooped in with his army to save the latter when the Ottomans were trying to take over his region, but because he had heard tales and experienced firsthand the legend that was the great King Matthias.

He had nothing to fear; he did nothing, so why should he be afraid? Which was why he laughed at himself for being so jumpy when the gates above opened. Footsteps thumped down the stairs and he could already guess he was going to have a visitor. It wasn't time for meals yet. They gave the prisoners two meals daily, but he suspected

King Matthias wanted to fatten him up before the slaughter if he indeed found out Vlad tried to betray him, so Vlad got three meals with protein, which he enjoyed wholeheartedly. However, he has not received that preferential treatment in a while. The reason was simple, Vlad Tepes had been in a foul mood the last time his meal was brought to him and the ignorant guard had been foolish enough to taunt him. What followed happened in a flash, with a quick sprint, Vlad Dracula swung his legs forward, sweeping the guard off his feet. Immediately, he jumped him, raining punches on the guard's face with hands still bound.

Other guards arrived later to rescue their colleague, but not before Vlad had given him a bloody beating. The restraint on Vlad Tepes was doubled and he was left in isolation until now. A soldier marched up to the gate of his cell and unlocked it without saying a word to him. Vlad Tepes sat up in his bed, surprised and wondering what was going on. The soldier saluted and moved to stand by the side at the entrance of the cell. That was when Vlad Tepes understood what was happening.

King Matthias was behind the soldier, dressed in his military regalia as he liked to when he was not officiating a court meeting with his officials. Those were the only days when the king liked to don his royal regalia. Every other day, aside from that, he dressed in his military outfit. The king entered Vlad Tepes's cell and looked around it as if it was his first time being there. He observed the environment and placed his hand against the walls to test their strength.

"It is quite sturdy, Your Majesty," Vlad Tepes said, attracting the king's attention to him.

The king sat on a stool another soldier had brought in for him, facing Vlad Tepes on the bed. "How have you been? I heard of your…"

The king let the words linger in the air, but Vlad Tepes knew the king was going to speak of his brutality towards the guard. But since the king did not finish his statement, Vlad Tepes saw no reason to tread in that direction. It would be wise of him to not provoke the king if he wants to be alive long enough to prove his innocence.

So instead, he gave a courteous reply: "I am well catered to, Your Majesty," Vlad responded. "I believe I have you to thank for the hospitable treatment."

The king scoffed. "Enjoy it because soon, I shall find out who wrote that letter and for what purpose. And when I do, you better hope for your sake that I would owe you an apology and not revenge, because if it is the latter..." he paused and stood, leaving his words to dangle in the air.

Vlad Tepes knew the king's words would haunt him if he left like that, so he made a quick statement. "How soon until you find out the truth?"

"Eager to end your misery, are you?"

"Yes, Your Majesty, but not in the way you intend. I hope I can dine with you by the end of the week and return to Transylvania after that. It's been twelve years since I have been cooped up here."

The king turned his back on Vlad and exited the cell without another word. The dungeon gates snapped shut again with a loud bang and soon it was back to the usual silence. Vlad Tepes closed his eyes and listened to the silence around him as he patiently waited for the end of this torture.

~ ∞ ~

Meanwhile, as King Matthias returned to the surface above the dungeon, he had a message waiting for him. Someone had arrived with a message strictly for the king and had been waiting for him. A royal guard approached the king as he ascended out of the dungeon and informed him of the unexpected visitor.

"What business does he want with me?" the king asked. "He said he had a message from Alexandru, Your Majesty."

The king dismissed his guards and went into the courtroom to meet with the supposed visitor. He was a short, sturdy man, the owner of the inn Alexandru had slept in. He had a written message for the king and extended it towards him, hands stretched out and head bowed as the king came in.

"A message for you, my liege."

The king eyed the man suspiciously, but he did not pay too much attention to him. Alexandru had a knack for using the unruliest set of persons for his businesses. The king took the scroll from him and waved his hand for him to stand straight from his bow. The message in the scroll was short and simple.

I have found the scent!

The king's face filled with a broad smile, and he thanked the messenger, dismissing him. The innkeeper accepted the king's gratitude but stood rooted to the spot. King Matthias looked up, raising an eyebrow.

"Ah!" He nodded towards a royal guard, who tossed a small pouch with bronze coins in it to the messenger. The messenger got on both knees as he struggled to reach the pouch before it dropped to the floor. He picked it up, tucked it safely into his breast coat, and thanked the king profusely as he made his way out. Halfway through the door, the king's voice stopped him.

"If you ever pull such an attitude with me again and stay back after I dismiss you, I will have you kept in my dungeons as a royal guest."

The innkeeper swallowed hard at the king's words and scrambled out of sight

When he was gone, the king folded up the scroll and tossed it into the tray. He asked a guard to send a message to his travel party, asking them to get ready, as he would make a trip within the hour.

He had found the answer to his question, and it was time for him to deliver the consequences to the culprit. Ideas came to life in his mind and he entertained the best of them. He had waited so long; he would not waste any more time. His guards were ready when he walked down the stairs. They all mounted their horses after the king and rode out with him into the unknown. No one asked where the king was going, they followed obediently behind, but they could tell that the king meant to settle scores.

CHAPTER EIGHTEEN

"Justina, are you okay?" Angela asked. Justina nodded as she placed a hand over her mouth to stifle the growing yawn.

Angela clapped loudly. "There! That's it. That's what I'm asking about. You have been rather slow this morning and you've been yawning through the day."

Justina sat up straighter and blinked several times to get the sleep out of her eyes, but it was a futile mission. The truth was, she was tired. In between juggling her day and night lives and trying to keep both from clashing, she had very little time to get rested. Her new friends, Julia, Elena, and Ana-Maria, whom she fondly referred to as "the trio," were a fun-packed riot and they made it a mission of theirs to make sure their new friend "Beatrice" had the most adventurous time ever in Brasov. Coupled with everything else was the fact Justina could not shrug off the feeling of being watched. Several times after that night, she had felt like she was being followed and had glimpsed a silhouette before it disappeared. About a week ago, she had gone outside the inn at night to dispose of trash to be burned later and had caught someone scurrying off as she came out the door, but she couldn't tell Angela and Nicolae about all that. She didn't want them to worry.

So, instead, she yawned and said, "I'm sorry, Angela. I'm just tired."

"I understand," Angela said. "This job puts a bit of a strain on you, and not just physically." She leaned closer to Justina and whispered, "I swear sometimes I just want to yell right back at the customer and tell them where to shove it when they come in here demanding to be attended to immediately." Justina bubbled over with laughter. Angela was such a prim and polite woman that it felt strange in a good way to hear her almost cuss. Part of the undesirable side of spending so much time moving about the city on a fun spree was that she got to discover the good, pleasant, and ugly sides of the city. And she had been around a lot of rowdy people and heard them cuss to know it was not exactly a pleasant trait. But, with Angela,

it sounded innocent rather than offensive.

The bell above the inn's door rang as the door opened, and both ladies turned to see who it was. A young man with a firm, strong build stepped into the inn, wrapped in an air of mystery. He was dressed completely in black, with a hat over his head to conceal his face. Although his face was not seen, the rest of him that could be seen when he took off his coat was appealing and attractive. Angela cleared her throat as he took his seat at a booth close to the one where Justina and Angela sat. She nudged Justina to get up and take his order while she went to the kitchen to get ready to cook.

Justina stood skeptically, watching the customer as she went to his seat and told him all they offered at the inn. She felt like there was something about him she couldn't quite place.

Perhaps she had seen him before. She gasped as another thought occurred to her. What if he was someone she had seen before, but not in Brasov? She had met about a thousand men in her cousin's castle and all their faces blended into one, but she could feel her guts telling her if she had met someone before.

He was a mysterious-looking man, with jet black hair and an athletic body. He looked rough and weary like most travelers did, but

Justina could bet that underneath all that travel dirt and stress, he was a handsome man.

He seemed molded from a different caste, as he had a handsome appearance that was unusual for most people. He radiated energy and artistry, lacquered and enamel coated by the sun. His high cheekbones appeared to have been sculpted by a master artisan. In reality, they possessed sharp features, giving the impression that they had been carefully created and honed to perfection. They hypnotized anybody who came under his unwavering gaze, along with the fact that his eyes were as brilliant and alluring as the North Star.

They shone with joy and sparkled like blue pearls set in snow. They were radiant.

She went over to his table to get his order, and he flashed her a handsome smile as though he recognized her, but she did not know him. He was polite as he gave his order, and not once did he take his eyes off her as she continued with her usual work routine. She stole glares at him occasionally and caught him staring back each time their eyes met.

Justina did not know this stranger from anywhere, but she knew one thing; she was attracted to him. With just one look, he made her insides turn to jelly.

She had expected him to take his hat off, but he did not. He scanned through the menu and pointed at an item he would like to try.

"Excellent choice," Justina said, trying to get him to talk. "Would you like anything else?" He shook his head in response, and she went to the counter to relay his order to Angela. While she waited, she kept her eyes fixed on the handsome stranger, trying to jog her memory to recall where she might have seen him or known him in the past.

"He's quite the eye catcher, right?" Angela said, breathing down Justina's neck as she handed her the food. Justina jumped from the shock. She had been so focused on the mysterious customer that she didn't hear Angela ring the bell to alert her that her order was ready. She didn't even hear her move close enough to her to whisper down her back.

"I feel like I know him," Justina said and picked up the tray.

She dropped the meal in front of the customer along with a tankard of ale and excused herself to go sit at the counter with Angela. The customer dug into the meal, still with his hat on, and Justina tried her best to get her mind off him and not make a big deal out of it. But, while it seemed like he was focused on the meal before him, she couldn't shake off the feeling she was being watched. She looked back just in time to see him bend his back towards his meal.

What if this guy is one of your cousin's minions? You know he would try to find you, right? The thought crossed Justina's mind in a flash, filling her with a dread that her newly established life was about to hit an untimely death, but even as she stared at the mysterious man munching down his meal, she didn't feel threatened. Instead, she felt drawn and attracted to him. Of course, her mind told her she was crazy. They didn't look harmful until you were in the back of a carriage,

riding out to Hungary. She waved her hand to dismiss the thought, reassuring herself that she did a good job of covering her tracks and it would not be easy for anyone to find her. She tried over and over again to convince herself she was safe and that her cousin had n't found her out. Even if she was, she would not return to Hungary. She would do whatever she could to preserve this newfound freedom of hers. With that, her pulse slowed to a steady rate and became more at peace, but the doubt had already been sown. She couldn't help wondering what if her cousin had caught up to her, and this customer, with a mysterious air around him, wasn't helping her hold on to her convictions.

The customer got up when he was done, strode to the door to pick up his coat, and exited through the front door into the street. Justina ran after him to remind him he had not paid for his meal, but when she got outside the inn, he was nowhere to be found. He had blended in with the crowd and she didn't know his face. She returned to the inn and headed straight for his table to clear out his plate and was surprised to see he had left the payment under his plate, along with a huge tip for her under the beer mug.

She wondered about the reason for his behavior, but could not come up with any tangible explanation. She dropped the plates in the sink behind the counter and handed over the money to Angela.

"Looks like someone else has been trapped under your charm," Angela said.

"What do you mean?"

"That is quite a generous tip."

Justina groaned. "Yeah, I know, and it's killing me. I'm trying to understand why he would do that—"

"What do you mean it's killing you? What else do you need to understand about a tip?"

"Was I the only one in here? Did you see him? He was a gruff, mysterious, good-looking man."

"I would have to agree with the last words, the rest... not so much. How do you know he is gruff when you've never even heard him speak?"

"You just said it. I mean, I give the best service and not a word from him. Not even a thank you, or a yes, or no?"

Angela dragged out a long sigh and looked sympathetically at Justina. She asked, in the kindest, sweetest tone, "Honey, is there something else bothering you? You know you can tell me, right?"

Justina was touched and shocked. For a minute, she was tempted to speak. Perhaps Angela was referring to the fact that she was concerned her cousin had found her. But Angela's next words had her stopping the words from spewing out of her mouth and wondering about something else entirely.

"He is quite the man, and it is understandable if you are attracted to him. You are a grown woman and these feelings are natural. It shouldn't get you all riled up."

Justina heaved a sigh of relief, glad she had not just spilled her secrets over to someone who had something else in mind. Her feelings of being attracted to that strange customer were the last thing on her mind and the least of all her troubles, but now that Angela had brought it up, it filled her thoughts, and she couldn't shake it off. She kept seeing his firm, strong build with every other customer that came in later that day, placing their faces over the image of his body that she had in her mind to determine which one would be the best fit for him. She found none. She couldn't decide on what face would suit that body, so she ended up with none as a fit.

That night, as she lay in her bed, she realized she did not get the feeling of being followed or watched. She had walked back home alone after work, and not once did she feel unsafe or that she was being followed. She laughed at herself for entertaining ridiculous thoughts like her cousin finding out where she was and trying to drag her back. She was safe, enjoying her quiet, normal life in a city where no one knew her or was bothered about her. It was just another regular day for her, except for the unexpected intrusion of a mysterious customer that has refused to leave her head. He was still with her even as she laid down, and she went to bed carrying him in her head.

~ ∞ ~

Justina's days in Brasov continued with just the right amount of pomp. She was in charge of her affairs and schedules so she could determine how much was too much for her and what she wanted or did not want to do. It was as blissful as she had imagined; she was living an ordinary life in a town where no one knew her. There was one minor issue, though, and that was the attraction she felt to the mysterious man who now frequently visited the inn. She had got over her hunch that he was probably one of King Matthias's spies when she saw him repeatedly after the first visit and with each visitation from him to the inn, her attraction to him grew.

Angela noticed and would tease her about it, but she would shrug it off and act like it was all nothing. What she couldn't shrug off, however, was the thought that perhaps he might be attracted to her, too. Although her friends, the trio, thought he might be attracted to her and she should just go for it, she was waiting for something to happen. Something like him making the first move or outrightly telling her he was attracted. Frankly, Justina knew her attraction to him was not emotional. It was more like a physical, irresistible urge. She wouldn't dare admit this to anyone else, but she thought of him like a yummy snack she wanted to devour.

During his last few visits, he had given her reason to think he might be attracted to her in the same way, but it was nothing forward or concrete. His eyes would linger on her when she went to serve his table, on her chest rather than on her face, and when she met his eyes, the look in them would send fiery sensations throughout her body. His eyes burned with ferocious intensity, and it made her wonder what he would be like if they ever got under the sheets. Embarrassed by the direction of her thoughts, her face burned and she placed her palms over them.

"Why do you look so pink?" Nicolae asked innocently as he passed by her on his way to dispose of some trash outside the inn.

"I think I might know just why," Angela quipped and winked at Justina, causing her to blush even deeper.

"Lady secrets, huh?" Nicolae said to both of them. "I better stay out of this one."

The bell over the door rang, and the door opened to reveal the object of Justina's imagination. He looked a lot better today than in the previous times. His clothes were more colorful. His shirt was a deep shade of orange and it complemented his skin. It was tight fitting and she could trace out the outline of his biceps through his shirt. He seemed to be aware of his effect on her because he came up closer to her and flashed her a smile before taking a seat at the booth where she was seated. She got up to fetch a menu for him and his hands grazed her thighs as she passed. She couldn't tell if it was intentional as he had his back turned to her when she looked up at him, but she could tell what she felt at his touch.

"Get a grip of yourself, Justina," she mouthed as she got the menu and handed it over to him.

It was still summer, but the last day of it, so the sun burned bright in the sky and the weather was relatively warm. Justina returned with his order to find that a few of his buttons were undone and his chest was exposed.

"Here's your order, sir!"

"Thank you."

It was the first time he had ever spoken to her or anyone else at the inn since he began his regular visitation. His voice was rich and strong, with a nice baritone ring to it. Justina nodded to acknowledge his thanks and he flashed her yet another of his charming smiles. He finished his meal and lingered a bit longer before he requested the bill and as usual, he left a generous tip for the waitress. Nicolae came back into the inn just as the customer was leaving and said: "I haven't seen him here before."

"Oh! He's a regular," Angela replied. "And I bet ten gold coins that we will be seeing him around some more."

Good thing that Angela did not put her money down on the bet as she would have lost a fortune. Justina's mysterious stranger did not show up at the inn again for a long time.

~ ∞ ~

Summer had finally ended and winter came in with a strong force. The cold wind blew with violent aggression, coating everything in sight with frosty white air. The inn had been working overtime since the beginning of winter to serve cold customers with warm meals and beer to combat the cold, and Justina was getting a real feel of the not-so-pleasant part of being an average woman, but she girds her loins and handled the difficulties like it was nothing.

Justina was glad to see the day end, the inn had closed for the night and everyone else had gone home, leaving Justina alone to lock up. She had offered to, seeing how exhausted Nicolae and Angela were. They refused at first, claiming that she also needed to rest, but Justina insisted on account it would help clear her mind. She was cleaning up and getting ready to lock up when the bell rang.

"We're closed," she said, without looking to see who it was. She was just as tired and wanted to be done with the cleaning as soon as she could.

"I was kind of counting on that," the customer said.

She looked up from the table she was wiping out and saw a familiar face staring back with unmasked desire in his eyes. It was the same mysterious man that had been coming by for a while. His gaze roamed her body, leaving no doubt what his intentions were. Justina almost cried out with relief when she saw him. He had not stopped by the inn in a while, and she was wondering where he was. They stood staring at each other, each one sending a heated message to the other about what they were feeling without words.

His eyes trailed the length of her body down to the place beneath her stomach and back up again. She gulped back air, suddenly feeling so hot right in the middle of winter. Her insides spilled over with a thousand unnamed sensations, and she felt herself gravitate towards him, but just as she drew closer, she noticed that the man was soaked to his feet. When she asked, he told her it was raining outside. She wondered why he had come in the rain but did not voice out her thoughts.

She decided she was going to fix him a cup of beer and send him on his way. If he came to get a meal, she was sorry, but she couldn't help him.

She offered to get him a beer and went back to the kitchen to fix him a cup. On her way back, she tripped over the broom she had been using. The cup went flying, dumping all that brown liquid on the person who had made it.

Justina was mortified and stood up, red-faced, apologizing profusely. She ran for the kitchen and returned with a napkin to clean up some of the beer off his skin. She dabbed at his wet shirt, which now clung to his skin like a second layer, and as she brushed him hastily, she accidentally popped a button and her warm, soft hands came in contact with his cold, tough skin. Subconsciously, she ran her hand over the rest of the skin, tracing a line down to his belly. She caught herself and let go immediately, coughing loudly to cover up her embarrassment. She looked up at him to apologize, and the desire in his eyes swallowed her whole. He dragged her back just as she was about to put some space between them.

"I have wanted to do this since the first day I saw you," he said. "Just say the word and I will stop and walk away." With that, he pulled her against his chest and claimed her lips in a hot, passionate kiss, savoring the taste and feel of her lips with his tongue. He tasted her and relished her as he kissed her, letting his tongue explore her mouth. When he let go, she was panting hard for breath and her eyes were darkened with desire.

"Now's your chance to stop me," he said, "or I will not be able to let go."

When Justina said nothing but stare at him like he was a figment of her imagination, he said, "I assume you want me, too."

Justina clung to him when he pulled her in again for another kiss. She yelped when his hands went under her skirt and made their way up toward her buttocks. His hands trailed a heated line from her thighs up to her behind, filling her with a heady rush. She gave in to the thirst and wrapped both her legs around his waist, grateful he could carry her weight. His hands traveled up her skin, coming to rest on the fullness of her breasts. He fondled and squeezed her, teasing her nipples with two fingers until she felt she could not take it anymore, but he was not done yet. He had more in mind for her, an accumulated outpour of weeks on end of sexual frustration.

He lay her down on the table she had been cleaning so that all of her was within reach and in full view. Still hanging both of her legs on his hips, he bent after her and deftly undid the strings of her corset, then moved to the buttons of her blouse. Her blouse opened easily and her breasts stood out at him, well rounded and aroused, eagerly awaiting his attention. He bent his head over her and took one of her breasts in his mouth while his fingers squeezed and caressed the other nipple. Subconsciously, Justina arched her body forwards toward him, wanting to get as much of him on her as she could. He looked into her eyes and she grabbed his hair with both hands, bringing it back down to her. Letting out a mischievous grin, he took in her other breast.

He staked his claim over her body with hot, wet kisses. He planted kisses on her neck, around her breasts, down to her stomach, and her belly button and, using a free hand, pulled her skirt so it slid down to her ankles while the other hand held both hands above her head. He went down on her, taking her into his mouth. Justina stiffened, but the pleasure soon overcame her and she moaned passionately, inching closer to him. He ravaged her with his lips and tongue like a starving man. Justina did not know she was screaming until he placed a hand over her mouth. When he got up, she felt sore and raw, but more alive than she had ever been. She felt slightly disappointed when his head came up, but he nodded upwards, gesturing to the people up there.

The last thing she remembered was grabbing her coat off the hanger and going out into the rain with the handsome stranger. As soon as they both got into her room, she yanked his shirt off him and lost herself in the feel of his warm, hard chest. She gave in to the pressing urge to feel him and ran her tongue over his skin. With a sharp intake of breath, he pinned her to the door, raising her to wrap her legs around his hips. Justina felt his arousal against the pit of her stomach and ran her tongue over her lips. As they ravaged each other's mouths, drinking in the essence of the other, she slipped her hands into his pants and held his testicles in her hand. She massaged them softly, sending him over the edge with ecstasy, as he had done with her nipples earlier at the inn.

He let out a deep, throaty groan, and she knew she was hitting the right chord, so she brushed her hand lightly over his shaft before shifting her hands to take the other testicles in her palm.

He trailed a hand down the length of her legs to the warm opening between her legs while his other hand supported her weight. He opened her up with his thumb and slipped two fingers inside her. Justina gasped when she felt his finger penetrate her, letting out a guttural moan as waves upon waves of tantalizing sensations washed over her. He slipped another finger in, sending her over the edge.

She clawed at him, begging him to stop and continue at the same time. Her body melted against him as a sweet sensation washed over her. She felt so light, like she was floating on the waves of passion. His hands were so strong and skilled, and they inched upwards inside of her until his finger found her most sensitive spot. He stimulated it with his fingertips, and she shattered under his influence. Everything else faded into the dark, and at that moment, it was just her overwhelmed by a sensual wave of passion. He slipped his fingers out slowly. He placed both hands on her buttocks, lifting her slightly as he entered her with a quick, deep thrust. Justina moaned, relishing the bittersweet feeling. Instinctively, she tightened against him, enjoying the feel of his shaft inside her. She could feel him close to her stomach and a mischievous grin played on her face as she relished the fact that he was big and strong. She adjusted her hip to accommodate him better. He pulled out and penetrated her slowly, deliberately, watching her eyes roll back in her head as he teased her. He set a steady tempo, thrusting into her slowly as he began, but taking up the rhythm with each thrust. He went hard and fast, losing himself in the tight, warm feel of her vagina and the sultry tone of her moans. He rode her fearlessly, passionately, and she moved with him, matching him stroke for stroke. He took up the tempo with each thrust, transporting them in bliss beyond words. They climaxed in a burst of ecstasy.

She clung tightly to him after they were done, pleading with him to let her bask in the union of their naked lower bodies together for a while longer. He responded by kissing her on her breasts. As she curled up in bed with him later that night, straddling his thighs with hers, she felt sore, raw, aching, and throbbing with a rising hunger for him. She was ready to go again, and she felt like she would be throughout the night. She now understood why her cousin's wife made such loud noises at night.

She had never felt so alive.

CHAPTER NINETEEN

The previous night was like a fairytale dream to Justina; it was simply too good to be true, as most things have been of late. There was also the fact she had never

acted that boldly before and could not believe that she had been that spontaneous and brazen with a man she barely knew. It simply could not have happened. She might have imagined it all in her head, but the feeling between her legs begged to differ. A hand cupped her breast, and a tingling sensation ran down her spine. She was not thinking up things. It was real. It had happened.

She purred and wiggled her body slightly in bed, with her eyes still closed; if it was a dream, she didn't want to ruin it by waking up. She had not planned to have a sexual escapade when she fled the Pongrac manor to Brasov. But now she had experienced what she did last night, she saw no reason she shouldn't enjoy it. Although she felt a sense of shyness, nobody knew about it, so it was still good.

Ana-Maria's words from the night when they went out came back to her. "…It wouldn't hurt to get a little fun and get your hay a bit of sunlight…"

She sighed in reaction to what her spontaneous lover was doing to her body. In her head, she agreed with Ana-Maria. She was going to get some sunlight for her hay. She had no reason to be afraid, she was her own woman and she would get the best experience out of her freedom because she knew her cousin was bound to look for her. Before he caught up to her, she would make sure she did what she wanted, even in satisfying her physical desires.

She gasped when her companion's hand slid down her stomach to rest on the edge of her thigh. Her stomach grew tight with anticipation. Instead, his hands dangled and moved back and forth across the tangle of hair between her thighs.

She opened her eyes, and he said, "Good morning, gorgeous."

She sat up, but he pushed her back down, straddling her, and leaned down to kiss the space between her thighs. "I just can't get enough of you."

Justina's nipples hardened in response, sticking out to taunt him. Justina grabbed the sheets tightly with both hands as he teased her with his tongue. Her better senses took hold of her, and she decided to at least find out the name of her paramour.

"Who are you?"

"Someone irresistibly drawn to your charm," he joked, then added smugly, "My name is Daniel. You can call me that when I drive you crazy."

He did not ask for her name, and she did not bother to tell him. She tested his name in her mouth, but it turned into a sensual moan when his finger invaded her. She had barely sighed through the pleasure of his first finger pumping in and out before he slipped in a second, then another. She could no longer hold it in. Her arousal dripped all over his fingers and onto the sheets, dampening them with her thirst. While his fingers went to work in the sensitive opening between her legs, his tongue trailed a line of heat from her stomach to her cleavage. She squirmed under the weight of the pleasure and called out his name in a throaty whisper. His appendage grazed her thigh as he moved back and forth on her, tasting her with his tongue. He moved up to her and devoured her lips with intense hunger, biting and sucking with a fierce passion. She wrapped her legs tightly around him, forcing his hips down closer. He caressed her most sensitive spot, and she exploded under him, shaking violently. Looking pleased with himself, he came to rest both hands against her backside. He buried his face in between her breasts, blowing hot air on her skin. He drank in her smell, her taste, her feel and his eyes rolled like it intoxicated him.

He got down to a kneeling position and pulled her up to sit on his lap while he entered her slowly. With his hands holding firmly to her backside, fondling and squeezing, he entered her with a quick, deep thrust so that she would bounce off him with each thrust, giving him twice the pleasure. They ascended drunkenly with pure exhilaration, but their sensual bliss was cut short when Justina's door flew open.

Mortified and irritated, Justina screamed and grabbed a cloth to cover her bare chest, then looked over her shoulder. She disentangled herself from Daniel as King Matthias stepped into her room, sizing it up. A sturdily built man followed him and some of his royal guards. Walking straight towards her, he grabbed her by the hair and slapped her across the face. Seething with fury, Justina let the cloth over her chest fall and raised her chin in defiance. She rose to her full length, completely naked. "Will you also have your men look upon my nakedness?"

The king waved his hand, and they all dispatched, including the unknown man.

"To what do I owe this visit, my lord?" she said with a mock bow as she picked up her discarded linen chemise and pulled it over her head.

"I hate to spoil your fun, and it seemed like you were having quite the escapade, but I think you've had your fill. It's time to go back." He looked furious and embarrassed and would probably have done more than just slapped her, but there were other people in the room.

It would not do Justina any good to defy the king now. She found the subtler means to irritate him and display her obstinacy. "I would have offered you a seat, but I was not expecting a guest, so forgive my manners."

The king waved off her excuse and nodded at Daniel to get lost. Daniel picked up his clothes and pulled on a hose to cover his legs. He bent to kiss Justina on the lips, but was dragged by the neck by King Matthias.

"Playtime is over," he said. "That is the last you will see of him." He added in a dangerously low tone, "If you do not want to mourn him."

He let go of Daniel and the latter left the room as honorably as he could. Justina did not, however, miss the look he gave her on his way out. She was certain she would see him again if her cousin did not bundle her back to Hungary first.

She did not plan on giving in so easily. She had become rather fond of her new life in Brasov, and she was none too eager to go back to the confinement and dictatorship of her king back in Hungary.

"Did you fancy yourself a peasant just because you dress like one now and even live like one?"

She did not reply. He was trying to goad her, and until she could think of a way out of this scenario, she was better off not getting angry.

"You're royalty, Justina; it's in your blood. You can do better than that commoner who was strangling you when I came in." "And I assume you have someone else in mind, don't you?"

"I do, and he is the perfect match for you. A powerful ruler."

"The last time you had a perfect match for me, how did that turn out?"

"Wenceslas was nothing like this man, and you will not speak to me like that again."

"I would rather not speak to you again at all."

His eyes constricted and Justina knew she had hit him where it hurt. King Matthias might be a lot of things, but he cared for his cousin. Any other would have done her serious harm at this point.

"He is really what you need; a strong and powerful man. He is hosting a dinner party at Bran Castle on Saturday. I will see you there, Justina. I will give you some time to say your goodbyes and get yourself in order. A carriage will be here for you on Saturday, don't play tricks with me," King Matthias said.

At the door, before taking his leave with his men, he turned and said, "Get rid of that filth that you are wearing. It is beneath you." With that said, he left and slammed the door behind him.

Justina cried her eyes out after he left, screaming and wailing with pain on the floor. King Matthias had brought an end to her freedom. She was not eager to end things soon or start bending to her cousin's whim, so she stuck it out at Brasov for a while.

The rest of the day was a drag for Justina. She could not put a name to how she was feeling. Her emotions were in turmoil, alternating between furious, sad, angry, wanting to take revenge, and feeling helpless. After hours, she pulled herself together and made the most of what little time she had left. Now that her cousin had found out where she was hiding, she could only hope to be given a bit of leisure time here. Whatever time she had left would be regarded as a gift. All she could do was delay, but she could not get the king to change his mind. In the end, she would have to give in. Not even her stubborn, fiery self could be a match.

"Get up, Justina. It's not over yet. You're not riding out already, so pick yourself up and make the most of what you have."

She dragged herself in for a bath, all the while speaking to herself to boost her morale. She was far from being her usual self, but she held her head up and made her way to the inn with a smile plastered on her face.

"About time, huh? Honey, she's here. Look who showed up," Nicolae said when she walked in.

Angela stuck her head out through the opening that con- nected the kitchen to the counter. She was ready to give Justina a proper talking-to, but one look at Justina's face and the couple's anger melted away into compassion. They were both beside her in an instant, asking to know what had happened to her. Justina tried to shrug them off, telling them she was fine and it wasn't important.

"What do you mean, not important? Your face looks puffy, like one of those doughs I use for pastries."

Nicolae gave his wife a look. Angela did not get it, or maybe she did, but decided against his advice. She had always been one for tough love and seeing Justina look downtrodden, she wanted to squeeze out the information from her and very well be on her way to getting things fixed. She was going to give whoever was responsible for the look on Justina's face an earful. An earful from her was enough to make anyone dread what she would do. But, in this case, not even Angela could help.

She would end up getting hurt if she tried to interfere, so Justina kept her mouth shut. She didn't want to hurt this kind of family who had been nothing but good to her since she came into town. She would have told a lie, but then she would feel guilty about it and they would sniff her out in an instant. "I love you both so much, and I truly cannot thank you enough for what you have done for me."

"Did you hear that, honey?" Nicolae said, his tone laced with hurt and pain, "That means she will not tell us anything. She's thanking us instead. That's the end of the conversation. She's done talking."

After trying effortlessly to find out what was going on, to no avail, the couple finally let her be. Justina drew in a deep breath, placed a smile on her face, and went about attending to the customers at the inn with a sunny, bright expression. Nicolae stared at her with his mouth wide open as she attended to her business at the inn. Angela shrugged and turned back to her cooking. Justina worked herself to the bones that day, amidst pleading and coercing from her employers to get some rest.

The inn closed early that day, much for her sake. The couple closed the inn just after sunset, which was unusual. The inn stayed active until twilight most days. Justina suspected they might force her to go home. As she walked back to her home, she made plans to go to the play center and meet with the girls later that night. The play center was their rendezvous point. Justina was trying as much as she could to be detached from them, so she did not let them know where she lived. They couldn't even exchange letters.

She hastened towards the room, excitement building within her as she made plans of how she was going to spend the night. She thought about what dress to wear and what places she wanted to visit with the girls. She had seen about everywhere that there was to see in Brasov. There was no way she would spend that much time with Elena, Ana-Maria, and Julia, the town's party trio, without spending every minute on an adventure. They knew about every nasty place there was in Brasov, spending lavishly to have a good time. It was all they did with their time; they did not have to work for money. They were wealthy aristocrats with tons of gold from their parents and admirers to spend. They might have their struggles, but Justina did not get close enough to find out what they were. It was all flings and momentary pleasure when she was with them and that was what she needed at the moment. She wanted to indulge and get a headrush from having so much fun, wanted to live in the moment and forget about whatever new plan, new man, or new agenda her cousin had in mind for her.

She was so obsessed with her thoughts that she did not notice the person hiding in the shadows when she got to her door. She put the key in the lock, and just as she turned the knob to get in, strong hands grabbed her and pushed her into her room. Panic filled her as she tried to think of a way to get free from her attacker. She couldn't believe it. Would her cousin stoop so low as to have her kidnapped and brought back? What happened to the time he promised her so she could put her things in order before she left? Matthias was truly unbelievable.

Her attacker turned her against the door as soon as they both got in so she couldn't see his face. She knew for sure that it was a man because no lady could own such strong hands, not even Angela, with all the hard work that she did. She struggled to get free from his grasp, but he held her hands above her head and pinned them there. All the while, he said nothing to her, instead, he hissed at her when she wouldn't stop struggling.

She wanted to get a look at her attacker's face, but her animosity soon melted away as his finger drew a straight line from her spine down to between her buttocks, it was a familiar touch. She stiffened. She willed herself to be calm and try to think of a way to outsmart her sudden attacker. As she relaxed her nerves to clear her thoughts, she subconsciously caught a whiff of her attacker's scent. It was a familiar scent, one she had smelt so often on her skin, her clothes, and her bedspread. She had solved the mystery of who her surprise guest was, but she did not give it away. This was a fantasy that she had nursed for a long time, so she planned to go with the flow for as long as she could manage. Still, with her hands held above her head, the other hand massaged the space between her thighs with his palms, twirling the hair around it with his fingers while he breathed hot, raspy breath on her skin. He dragged his hands up, trailing all five fingers upwards under her dress to fondle her breasts, squeezing and pinching; he was doing it all just like Daniel. Against her will, she felt herself relax, shooting her body towards him, hungry for more. When he felt she was relaxed and had stopped struggling, he let her hands go but said in a deep, throaty voice. "Stay!"

She wanted to say his name, but he placed a hand over her lips. "Shh!"

She tried to look back at him, but he wouldn't let her. It was probably his intention. They both knew that she had identified who her secret lover was, but he did not want her to break the spell by affirming it. She loved it. The thrill of anonymity fueled the burning passion. It was exactly what she needed, what she had been planning to get with the ladies later that night: a wild, heady rush. But this was better. This was being delivered with the right level of expertise, mystery, and flame. She embraced it, letting the passion take over. She relished the hunger, the pleasure, soaking in every bit of sensuality without apology. She didn't have to do anything; her mystery partner did all the work. She pleasured him by soaking in and reacting to every touch and stimulation.

He did not bother to undress her. With skilled expertise, his hands slipped back down. He groaned and entered her with one quick move. She gasped and threw her head back at the sensation.

* * *

The pent-up annoyance and frustration of the day melted away, and she felt so relaxed and peaceful. She knew all along it was Daniel, but she confirmed it when she saw his face later. She wanted to ask why he had been so secretive and anonymous, but decided against it. It wouldn't do her much good to find out; instead, she enjoyed it and kept the memories preserved in her head. She did not know who he was, he revealed nothing about himself, and she did not ask, just as much as she did not tell him who she was and he didn't ask.

It was just as she wanted: a wild, adventurous fling! And Daniel brought the heat every time.

CHAPTER TWENTY

HUNGARY, 1475 THREE DAYS BEFORE KING MATTHIAS SHOWED UP IN BRASOV

"Your Majesty," a royal guard greeted, bowing low as he stood before the king.

King Matthias was standing out on the balcony, waiting to have a meeting with his army commandant, Sebastian. He had sent Sebastian out on a mission during the week, and he was waiting to get feedback from him. He wanted the exchange between them to be as discreet as possible; hence he chose the rooftop of the castle. It was one of his favorite places aside from the courtroom, also known as the throne room, where he held his meetings with court officials. He spent a lot of time in the courtroom, but with the rooftop, he could enjoy the evening breeze along with the view of the kingdom. He did that exact thing when the royal guard walked in.

"Send him up," King Matthias said. He didn't need to be told who it was. He could already guess who would request to see him.

"Your Majesty," Sebastian greeted with a bow, his long blond beard even had stains of mud just like the rest of his clothes. The king smiled at him and signaled for him to move closer.

He dismissed the royal guard with a wave of his hand and they were soon alone.

"Feeling a little sentimental, eh, my king?" Sebastian teased. The king patted him on the back. "I can't deny my humanity.

So, what did you find out?"

"A false letter. It's a fake."

King Matthias was quiet for a while, staring out into the space beneath the rooftop. Sebastian stood by patiently, taking in the view of tiny villages and houses spread across the kingdom. Beyond the habitual settlement was a large stretch of vast green lands, where some of the local people owned farms and grew their crops.

"I suppose it's time to let him go, then."

"Who would have tried to set him up?" Sebastian asked. "That part is obvious. It would be the ones who sent the

letter, the Saxons. What I'm trying to understand is the intention behind their actions."

"I see. The throne, perhaps?"

"Yes, there's that, but I think beyond that, there is an underlying motive. I cannot help but feel this was indirectly intended for me and woe unto whoever was stupid enough to try to fool me. I will find them… not just for me, for him, too."

"Tepes?"

"Yes, Dracula. If I know anything at all about him, it would be that he is not so forgiving. I am certain even at this moment, his mind is awash with a thousand different ways to repay the perpetrators of this foul trickery."

"Perhaps the intention was to cause a rift between you both. An alliance between the two kingdoms would create a force that is formidable and fearsome."

King Matthias's face lit up with understanding, and a mischievous grin spread on his lips. "It all makes sense now," he said and laughed a mirthless laugh.

"How about a surprise, then? If the intention was to cause a rift between us, then I have just the perfect reply to that. An alliance, and the most formidable one at that."

The king laughed maniacally, and Sebastian watched, wondering what exactly he planned to do this time.

After the king met with Sebastian, he requested that their prisoner, Vlad Tepes, be released and given a chamber to freshen up.

* * *

Vlad Tepes was taking a troubled nap in his cell when the dungeon gates opened, the hinges creaking, protesting the weight of the gates. He sat up, mentally preparing himself as he did not want to be shocked like he was the previous time. He was calm and relaxed when the door to his cell opened and a guard bowed and stepped to the side. Vlad grinned when he noticed that. None of the guards had even bowed to him since he was imprisoned or acknowledged him as a Prince, so why would this one act differently? He waited for King Matthias to stroll through the door and fill up his tiny cell space with his brooding presence, but he got a knight coming to announce his release.

"My lord, His Majesty has requested you be released and escorted to a chamber he has prepared for you."

"Released?" Vlad Tepes mused. "Then does that mean the king has proven my innocence? Ah! Then, if so, he must know who handles my unplanned vacation in the king's dungeon." A mischievous grin turned up the corners of his lips. "I would love to see them and extend my most heartfelt regards. Thanks to them, I have had lots of time to think, and oh, the thoughts that have brimmed in my head." He cackled loudly, giving everyone a jump at his loud voice.

The knight stretched his hand ahead of him, leading the way out of the dungeon. Vlad Tepes followed as graciously as he could. They escorted him to a chamber where the king had ordered for a bath to be made ready for him along with female servants to attend to his needs. Dracula grinned when he saw the arrangement. He knew what the king had in mind with the maids, and he did not object. He had been feeling rather restless and finally hopeless with all those long years in the dungeon, sitting around with nothing to do. Letting the maidens attend to him would be just what he needed to ease himself.

The guards bowed and excused themselves, leaving him alone with the ladies. Vlad Tepes moved towards the ladies shyly and cautiously; it's been so long since he has touched a woman and he wondered if he'd still know how to do it right. He had nothing to worry about because the moment his skin came into contact with them, everything fell perfectly in place. The guards stood outside the chambers with straight faces, despite the loud noises and ruckus going on behind the doors. The maidens walked out later with rumpled dresses and untidy hair. One of them had an unruly glow on her face, while the other bowed her head and disappeared quickly from sight. Later that day, news spread around the castle of Vlad Tepes' ferocious, manly prowess. The king invited Dracula for a meal, and he was escorted to the courtroom where the king dined with the same guards who were keeping watch over his chamber.

"Your Majesty," Vlad Tepes said, looking almost like a different man now that he was properly washed, in clean clothes, and with his hair cut.

"Prince Dracula, congratulations on your release. Please, sit. Dine with me?"

"It doesn't feel so much like a release with those guards." He gestured towards them. "Following me around and watching my every move."

"They are simply there to act as guides. You have never been to my castle before, and it can be quite intimidating. They know their way around, and they will help you move around with ease."

"Ah! I'm honored. I take it that the king has found the answers he seeks," Vlad Tepes said, picking up a drumstick and biting into it.

"Yes, certainly." The king replied as he also picked a piece of chicken to savor. "I trust the maidens treated you well?"

Vlad sighed heartily, leaning back against his seat in a relaxed pose. "An excellent gift, Your Majesty. They took good care of me; one was so shy and the other wild and exciting. It helped to ease off those years of celibacy in your dungeons."

The king laughed, and Dracula joined in, too.

"Pray tell, Your Majesty, did you find out who sent you that gift on my behalf?"

The king knew he was talking about the letter. "I did, and I have a counter strike prepared for them."

Vlad Tepes sat up in his seat.

"An alliance," the king said, "and the most formidable of them."

Dracula paused, his eyes narrowing as he sought to un- derstand what the king was trying to say. Did he hear him correctly? An alliance? With him? He was already in alliance with the king and if it meant paying back the people that put him in prison, he would very well agree to an alliance with even the emperor himself. He held no grudge against the king, it wasn't his fault he spent all those years locked up.

"But we already have an alliance, Your Majesty."

"After I found out the source of the letter, it troubled me to know that someone out there would try to make a fool of me. I intended to reciprocate their actions, but first, I needed to understand their motive."

"And what was the motive?"

"To cause a rift between us. As you said, we are alike in so many ways. The first strike of vengeance will be to let them understand their plans failed woefully. All things being equal, I would have executed you on account of treason, but you are a smart man and the whole situation helped me sniff out the scheme. So, here's my offer. A marriage with my beautiful cousin, the fairest Justina, and yourself, uniting both lands and kingdom in an unbreakable bond."

A wide grin spread across Vlad Tepes' face. The king was apologizing. It was the only explanation he could come up with for such a beneficial alliance. Of course, the king would benefit too, but it was too sudden.

He did not voice his thoughts. The king never apologized to anyone. Vlad was lucky to be out of the dungeon, sitting across from him, dining and laughing.

"I heard Lady Justina was married."

"He died about a year ago."

"My deepest condolences."

The king waved his hand. "She no longer mourns him. Now, what do you say?"

Vlad Tepes was ecstatic; he had seen the king's cousin before, and she was a beauty. He was instantly charmed by her gorgeousness and to think the king would offer her in marriage to him was too good of an opportunity to pass off. There was that, and then an alliance with the king. There was only one answer.

"I agree, Your Majesty. I accept this alliance between us. When do I get to meet with Lady Justina?"

"That is up to you to decide."

"I will throw a party in castle bran to commemorate my return. Thanks to the news spread around by your men, my people believe that I have been away in battle with you and we did mighty deeds, so, when I return, they will honor me with a feast."

"Send an invitation, and she will be at the party."

Vlad Tepes nodded, but there was something else still eating him up and he couldn't just let it go. "Who was it?" he asked. "Who wrote the letter, Your Majesty?"

The king passed him the scroll. Vlad Tepes perused it and was surprised at how well and how carefully his writing was mimicked.

"An expert did this. The semblance is truly mistakable. How did you find out?"

"Sebastian! I had him tour the cities, ask many people, threaten a lot too, and eventually, the truth was revealed."

Dracula's knuckles tightened against the scroll. "Please, Your Majesty, who did this?"

"Old friends with old grudges."

"The Saxons?"

The king nodded.

"I should have known."

"I understand what is in your heart, and trust me, I will help you get revenge. Not just for you, for myself too, for thinking someone can easily fool me."

"I do not want to hear about it, Your Majesty. I do not want to be told how they suffered before they died. I want them to suffer at my hands. I want to inflict the measure of pain they had me go through in double quantity. I want to hear their screams and see the anguished pain

158

in their eyes. I want them to look at my face as they restitute for their sins, so please, Your Majesty, let me have my revenge."

The king looked at him with a proud look in his eyes. "You are one impressive man, Dracula. I like it." He took a loud sip of wine, placed the goblet down, and looked Dracula in the eye. "When I said I would help you get revenge, I meant together. You will get to torment those charlatans to your heart's content."

The king raised his glass, and Dracula reciprocated at the other end of the table. When they were done, the king had a chariot prepared for him to ride back to Transylvania without delay. Vlad Tepes rode back to his kingdom that night, determined to put his life back on track and make up for all the lost time. His starting point would be to track down the ones who made him lose much time.

One thing was sure, when he found them, death would be the highest form of mercy.

CHAPTER TWENTY ONE

CASTLE BRAN, DRACULA'S CHAMBERS TRANSYLVANIA

Vlad Tepes stood with his goblet, staring outside the courtroom and reminiscing about his unplanned and unpleasant vacation to King Matthias' dungeon.

He slammed the goblet hard against the far end of the wall. The goblet clattered to the ground with a resounding bang echoing throughout the courtroom. One of the castle maids rushed in frantically to clean up the mess, jumping at every little sound.

He had almost finished conquering these ghosts, the ones that felt it was safer to run from you than to you. Yet he couldn't run. He tried. Each time, he spiraled.

Vlad Tepes was as gruesome as he was handsome, and he was very handsome. He caught the eyes of almost every lady in town, and tales of his sexual prowess made him even more popular and appealing. He was not one to forgive an enemy and came up with creative ways to pay them back inch for inch. But he was a just ruler and hated injustice as much as he despised his enemies. Cruel, mean, and detached as he seemed, he was a good ruler, one who prioritized the needs of his subjects and would protect them even if it cost the last drop of his blood. The town has seen him go out to battle and ensured their protection countless times, and that has earned him their respect.

Vlad Tepes paced about his courtroom, causing the already frightened maid to panic even more. He grunted and slammed his hand on the table with a loud bang. The maid yelped in fear; she had had her back turned to him and did not know the cause of the noise. With lightning speed, she finished up her cleaning and hurried out of his presence. Vlad's mind was occupied; he was seething with rage and anxiously waiting for a way to get his revenge and get the anger out of his system that he took very little notice of his environment and was even less of a cleaning maid.

Since he had left King Matthias's castle, he had been having trouble sleeping and had been restless and jumpy at every creaking sound because of the prolonged time of being locked away in the dungeon. He had female servants attend to him to ease him, but often he would suddenly jerk awake at night and cannot go back to sleep.

In his absence, lots of duties had piled up for him to attend to and he was lucky to still have a kingdom when he returned because King Matthias had had someone take charge while he was away. The king had trusted his words despite the doubts that he had and had given him a chance to prove his innocence. It was solely because of that act of mercy that he was still alive. He had his previous standing and relationship with the king to thank for that; otherwise, he would probably have been executed in an instant and done away with. He folded his fingers in a fist, and his knuckles whitened as he squeezed tighter and tighter. He needed to thank his enemies for almost getting him assassinated. They had made a mistake by not thinking their plans through, and because of that, they were going to pay dearly! He needed to get peace and move on, and the only way he could do that was after he had satisfied his need for justice. He was a just ruler, and that meant he would always get justice, even for himself. And making them pay for what they did to him would be justice.

The courtroom door opened and a young man with a tough, muscular build walked in. He was dressed in a military outfit, with shiny buttons lining the middle and sticking out for all eyes to see, a sign that he was a part of the Prince's military force and a high-ranking official at that. He looked travel- weary, but it was hard to tell at first glance.

The Prince's face lit up. He had been waiting for him. It was the information he had been waiting for since he had left Hungary. The information would lead him to the last stage of his horrible nightmare that had lasted for too long and give him the needed peace and justice that he sought. It was the start of his payback.

"Sir Augustus," he said as the knight walked in.

"My lord," Sir Augustus said, kneeling, his head bent.

"Ah! Come on, tell me quickly what my ears are itching to hear."

Sir Augustus rose and said with a knowing smile on his face, "We found them, Your Highness."

Vlad Tepes clapped once in a loud manner. "Tell the stable to get my horse ready, and we ride out within the hour. Inform the commander to get me a troop ready and meet me out front.

I want them all captured. Let no one escape, understood?"

Sir Augustus saluted. "Yes, Your Highness. I'll get to it straight away."

Sir Augustus was Vlad Tepes's friend and had been by his side as a right-hand man. He, more than anyone else, understood Vlad's pain, and he wanted those scoundrels to be captured as much as Vlad Tepes did.

The troop assembled in front of the castle, armed and ready to march. They had received Vlad's order and acted with urgency as soon as they got the command. If Vlad wanted to ride out with them, then it must be a pressing issue. Their lord came out of the castle door within the minute, elegantly dressed in his military regalia. He strode towards the horse waiting for him with confidence, determined strides. A stable attendant was waiting for him and went down on his knees to help Vlad mount his horse. Vlad Tepes mounted, pulled the reins, and, with a loud noise, urged the horse forward. The others journeying with him moved out after him. Sir Augustus mounted and caught up to him, riding at his side.

Vlad Tepes traveled for several days and nights with his troop, stopping to rest for only a few hours during the day before they resumed their journey. Sir Augustus led them through a discreet path, trying to keep their scents off their targets.

After traveling all day under the scorching heat of the sun, with little food and wild fruits to eat, the soldiers were getting quite exhausted, and Vlad Tepes noticed. He was tired, too, but his mental strength kept him. But he needed his troop to be alert and in the best physical condition when he ravaged his enemies and reduced them to ruins.

"Let's stop here for the night. The sun is almost down. We will get some rest, get refreshed, and continue by morning. Have some soldiers scout the bush for edible fruits like berries and persimmon so that the soldiers can have some food in their belly."

"Yes, Your Highness!" Sir Augustus reiterated Vlad's orders. Vlad's horse trotted to a stop, and the others with him did the same. Soon enough, they had made a fire and roasted some of the wild rabbits that were caught in the forest, along with some wild berries to go along. The soldiers ate their fill and sat around the fire, making gaudy jokes and comments. It was the first time since they left the kingdom and set out on their journey that they were this rested and had such good food to eat.

While the troops refreshed their bodies, Vlad Tepes strate- gized with Sir Augustus on how to take out their enemies.

"How much longer before we arrive?"

"About a full day's ride, Your Highness," Sir Augustus responded. "We are already late. The Saxons heard about your release and escaped to the distant mountains to hide. We have to be vigilant as we draw closer. I would suggest we leave the horses and every other thing behind. From here on, we go on foot and be as discreet as possible."

Vlad Tepes stared into thin space, lost in thoughts. He nodded after he had processed Sir Augustus' words, agreeing with him. "And the Ottomans?"

"They used them. They broke off their alliance with the Saxons after they got them to do their dirty deed by framing you. The Saxons are helpless, which is why they tried to escape and run far away."

"Why do you sound like you feel pity for them?" Vlad Tepes asked. "You make them sound like pathetic victims."

Looking flushed and agitated by Vlad's words, sir Augustus denied it vehemently. "No, Your Highness. Not at all."

Vlad Tepes twirled his mustache and said with a wicked smile, "They should have gone farther."

His words, and his expression, chilled Sir Augustus to the bone. After a short pause, Vlad said, "Inform the men we leave at first light. If we have to go on foot for the rest of the journey, then we might as well start early. I do not want the Saxons to get even the faintest hint of our coming… I want to catch them at their happiest, unguarded hour and strip them of joy, laughter, and everything like they did to me."

He had a distant look in his eyes as he spoke. When he was done, a cruel grin split his face and developed into a loud, mirthless laugh.

CHAPTER TWENTY TWO

SAXON HABITATION, TRANSYLVANIA ALPS, CARPATHIAN MOUNTAINS

The weather grew freezing as they arrived in the mountains. It was freezing, and that it was winter did not help at all. The temperature dropped around the mountains.

The Saxons built their tents just around the foot of the mountain. Only an insane person would decide to travel that far in winter, and Vlad Tepes was just the right amount of crazy. Rage drove him further than anyone could have imagined, further than the Saxons dared to believe anyone would venture. Having made a hideout in the mountains, the Saxons had adapted slowly through the summer into winter. The Ottomans betrayed their trust longer than Sir Augustus knew, and they had to escape faster than he realized.

The surrounding hills made good spots for a stakeout, and Vlad Tepes' men surrounded the perimeters of the Saxons' new habitation, camouflaging themselves with the environment to make a good cover. Vlad Tepes observed the Saxons, mobbing back and forth across dwellings, clad heavily in thick. They built tiny fires to keep warm and sat around them to keep the smoke as minimal and seen as possible. The setting was just as he wanted it, unguarded and unsuspecting. It was a regular day in their lives. The Saxons were about twenty men or more based on his prediction, and he assumed the others were not as lucky. A bitter smirk split his face. The missing numbers amongst the Saxons were probably the handwork of the Ottoman sultan. He was a cruel, dubious man whose words are not even worth a pinch of salt. He played dirty, pulling tricks, and betraying whoever just to get what he wanted. Only a desperate fool would dare try to ally with him. Vlad did not know what category the Saxons fell into to have made a pact with him; neither did he care, but he did know what they would be now he had found them. Dead!

He signaled for the soldiers to advance slowly and spread out, covering every escape route. Slowly and stealthily, they moved forward toward the Saxons' camp, taking cover in the hills, bushes, and piles of snow. The Saxons suspected nothing, heard nothing, until, with shouts, Vlad Tepes' army charged into their camp, ambushing them from all sides.

They were trapped, with nowhere to run. Vlad Tepes' army trapped them in the middle, closing in on them and forcing them to close in on themselves. The Saxons formed a circle in the middle, standing back to back, with their backs to each other. At their leader's signal, they unsheathed their swords, arms stretched in front of them, ready to swing if anyone dared come closer. The Saxons were mercenaries, so they knew to stay armed at all times, with their swords at their sides, as they were often attacked without warning like this. Having surrounded them, Vlad Tepes' soldiers stood ready and alert, arms were drawn and ready to strike on their Count's command. Vlad Tepes had informed them he wanted all prisoners alive, which was why they did not attack immediately. Observing that the soldiers merely cornered them and did not attack, the Saxons guessed they were probably wanted alive and tried to threaten the attackers by swinging their swords at them. The soldiers parried and blocked but did not attack. All this time, Vlad Tepes had not appeared. He was covered by the shield of his soldiers so his face would not be seen. He wanted to enter and relish the looks on the faces of his enemies when they saw him.

Rhythmically, the soldiers parted and made way for him to advance toward the Saxons. He moved forward with his head down, dressed in a long robe with a hood that covered his face. The Saxons looked with curiosity as he advanced. When he got to the front, he made a dramatic gesture of removing the hood and revealing his face with an ominous smile. Whimpers and gasps rippled through the crowd of Saxons, replacing the confused, curious stare that were on their faces with a petrified look.

One of the Saxons drew a dagger out of his waist girdle and tried to slit his own throat to avoid being captured. Dracula caught his movement from the side of his eye and reacted quickly, drawing out a dagger hidden in his glove and aiming it straight at the mercenary's hand. The dagger hit the target, sticking to the flesh.

The mercenary groaned in agony, and the dagger fell out of his hand, spiraling downwards. The others dropped their weapons and tried to escape, but Vlad Tepes gave an order with a nod that they were to be captured and bound immediately.

Yet some others tried to be brave and not go down without a fight. In a swift, clean move, Vlad Tepes and his soldiers took them on, separating their limbs from their bodies with a sharp swipe of the sword. They clattered to the ground, groaning as the snow swallowed their blood. Vlad Tepes' soldiers captured them still, wrapping up their wounds. Vlad Tepes ordered that his soldiers search the surrounding area and capture any other Saxons. The soldiers did a clean sweep and returned to the camp to confirm that all the Saxons had been accounted for and captured.

Pleased with himself, but only slightly, Vlad Tepes ordered that they ride back to Transylvania. The prisoners were tied to horses and dragged back to Castle Bran, through the treacherous rocky roads, cold weather, and every other hazard on the way, but Vlad Tepes kept them alive until they got back to Transylvania. He ordered medical treatment for any of them that was ailing, losing blood, or infected from the wounds and nursed them back to health.

As they rode back into town, he sent a message to King Matthias informing him he had apprehended the perpetrators of the crime for which he was falsely accused and also telling him of the plans that he had to mete out punishment on them. The king read his letter with a proud grin on his face and promised to visit Transylvania soon. The people cheered for Vlad Tepes as he returned, thinking that their Count had gone out to fight a war and returned victoriously with war prisoners. They came out to the streets to cheer for their monarch while they dumped dirt, abuse, and insults on the prisoners. They hurled stones at them, booing them.

When they arrived at the castle, Vlad Tepes ordered them to be imprisoned in the dungeons and requested that the royal kitchen make a palatable meal for their dungeon guests. His actions left no doubts as to his intentions; it was the fattening of the ram before the slaughter.

That night, Vlad Tepes held a feast, inviting everyone that cared to attend for a sumptuous buffet. His prisoners got an invitation too and were special guests at the feast. He humiliated them, asking them to dance naked and hold pageantry for the entertainment of everyone present. The most demoralizing thing for a swordsman would have him humiliated and unable to defend their honor, and Vlad Tepes did just that to his prisoners. He made them embarrassed with shame, seethe with anger, boils with bitterness, and incapacitated them able to do anything about it. The older Saxons that were weak and sickly were all killed. The young ones were put out and beaten mercilessly. Some were even used as temporal slaves. They were stripped naked and jeered and snared at.

None of them were allowed any item, so they would not use it as a weapon against Vlad's men. They knew they were all going to die, Vlad was just using them to boost the honor his people gave him.

One of the Saxons who was fed up tried to defend himself and tried to escape. He pulled out a sword from one guard like a madman. Though his leg was in chains, he was able to defend himself for a while.

"Yes. I've got you now. Who's gonna die now?" He said, while holding the sword forward with two hands. He smiled as all the guards gathered around him and pulled their weapons. "Drop that weapon. And then we'll let you off easy," one of

the fierce guards said.

The rest of the Saxons cheered their brother happily for his courage.

"Oh. I know you're never going to let me off easy. You are never going to spare my life. And I will not go down without a fight." The cheers increased, and with that, he made the first move and charged forward. All three guards charged back to kill him.

One could tell he was a very skilled swordsman with the way he blocked their strikes. He was probably one of their warriors.

The smaller guard struck his sword at the Saxon with all his might. He missed and immediately the Saxon pulled his sword in and out of his stomach. Blood spurted out of his mouth.

He killed two guards and got a smote from the back at once. Although he didn't die just yet, Vlad ordered them to stop. He was going to be a scapegoat for the rest of them who thought they could be heroes.

Vlad ordered that the Saxon should be tied to a horse and dragged to his death. It was so gruesome that when they stopped, his head had been detached from his neck.

Arms and legs bound in chains, he had them wrestle for the people's entertainment. They looked like idiots as they fought and the people laughed and jeered at them. After stripping them naked, he dangled their clothes in front of them and they struggled to grab hold of it and cover their bodies. The more they tried to reach for the clothes, the farther he became, so they kept struggling. If they got tired and tried to give up, a soldier struck them with a whip made of sharp spikes, and they soon hopped about to catch the errant piece of clothing. The people laughed at them and made bets on who would get their clothes first or who was the biggest idiot, or who had the finest body. They spat their beers on them or booed them if one of them got weak and tired.

Vlad Tepes kept up the charade through the night, and by the next morning, he had one of the Saxons impaled on a pole. The rest of them, he had sent back to the dungeons to resume their clown show again the next evening. The people soon looked forward to the evening entertainment brought to them by the Count's prisoners. He spiced up the competition by sparing the life of whoever grabbed onto their clothing. Of course, it wasn't a complete pardon. He only spared their lives until the next day, when they had to compete again.

The new clause and promise of pardon made them even more eager to grab onto the clothing, and they competed with seriousness. However, no matter how much fun they gave the people, by the next morning, one of them would be impaled again. The knowledge of impending death and feeling of helplessness, knowing that they could do nothing to stop it and that Vlad Tepes planned to impale them all but was just having his fun with them, messing with their minds. They begged and pleaded for mercy as death stared them in the face in the most gruesome way before it came for them.

Every morning while Vlad Tepes impaled one of them, he made them all come out and forced them to watch as one of their comrades was impaled on the pole. The anguished cries of the dying men haunted them throughout the day until the next morning, and so terror filled the minds of those still alive and they slowly lost their minds. Their numbers diminished as Vlad Tepes impaled one person per day until they were all wiped out. There was no order in which he chose them. He just pointed at whoever he felt like and had them impaled. He left them hanging on the pole after they were all dead, gracing his castle walls with the acrid mark of vengeance. He wanted to remind the kingdoms that he was no less brutal than he has always been, and he was never to be toyed with ever again.

Every day he spent in the king's dungeon had been filled with the fear of death, as he was at the King's mercy and feared that every day might be his. He had exuded calm and fearlessness, but all the while, his mind was in turmoil and he had held onto the hope he could take revenge when and if he left the dungeons alive. That hope kept him going and gave him strength, and now it was finally fulfilled. He saw that same dread, that same fear replicated in the eyes of every one of the Saxons before they died, and it gave him relief from his agony.

The news of Vlad Tepes' actions traveled far across the kingdoms, sending dread and terror into his enemies and giving him the nickname of "Vlad the Impaler." The people feared him, and tales of his acts kept his enemies at bay. When King Matthias heard about Vlad Tepes' actions and the reputation they earned him, he felt proud of the Count. Of their own accord, kingdoms came to be reconciled with Vlad

Tepes and tried to build an alliance with him. He became powerful and wealthy, feared across all kingdoms in a few months.

King Matthias saw then that an alliance with Vlad Tepes would be more profitable than he thought and stirred up his cousin to be married to Vlad.

King Matthias was not one to be on the losing side. He pictured the benefits of having Vlad Tepes as his ally, and he knew just the right person for the job. It was for his gain, well, of course, for his kingdom too.

CHAPTER TWENTY THREE

King Matthias was never one to bluff, so Justina had learned to take his words seriously. Sometimes she felt like even if he wasn't king, his words would still hold integrity. He was a man of his word and did not give light promises. The few times she had gotten him to swear an oath, she had held him by his words, and he respected those words even though it cost him.

It was based on this that she believed when he said he would send a carriage for her to take her to Castle Bran for the meeting with the prospective suitor. It was also the reason she was being careful with her escapades with Daniel; her cousin was not bluffing when he said he would kill him if he was proved to be a distraction.

Following his last visit to Brasov, she had spent most of her nights with Daniel. His desire for her was insatiable and infectious, and it was never boring with him, plus he had a unique method that ensured he never left his seeds in her, so there was no way she could get pregnant; it was fun without consequence. He was full of energy and mischief and tricks to get her burning with excitement and sexual thirst. They spent most of their time in her room, exploring and satisfying their lustful desires. Usually, Daniel stayed until the first light of dawn or sometimes disappeared in the night after their nightly escapades, but today he was with her till daybreak, passing the morning with terrific sex.

It was Saturday, and just like her cousin promised, a carriage had arrived and was waiting to carry her to Castle Bran. The carriage driver had come up to her room to knock and inform her of his presence. She had informed him she would be with him shortly. Still, it was taking much longer to get dressed, with Daniel taking off every piece of clothing that she put on to fill her up with enough love to last the duration of her absence. She would be gone for about two days if she left Castle Bran immediately after the celebrations were over, but there was no way of telling, especially if her cousin was going to be attending the party.

She was almost done now. She had kept her clothes on and was now sitting in front of the dresser with some cosmetics laid out. She was a remarkable woman even without makeup and fancy dresses, but she was determined to put up quite a show at Castle Bran for her cousin's benefit so he could leave her alone for a while. She was dressed in a gorgeous sea-green dress that complemented her eyes and creamy skin. She applied some, then put on a bright red cosmetic to make her lips look full and juicy. On her way out, Daniel pulled her into a long, passionate kiss that left her feeling breathless and took some of the lipstick with him.

Throughout the ride to Transylvania, her lips throbbed with a dull ache, and she loved it. It brought a mischievous smile to her face, which she wore to Castle Bran. Engrossed in her guilty pleasure, she couldn't have imagined the surprise that awaited her in Transylvania.

CHAPTER TWENTY FOUR

CASTLE BRAN, DRACULA'S HOME TRANSYLVANIA

Vlad Dracula threw one hell of an impressive ball at the castle. Justina could not believe her eyes when she walked in. The hall was tall with beautiful torches lit all over, the interior architecture surpassed the outside, and the outside was super impressive already. There were paintings around and sculpted animals on pillars, the castle was packed full of impressive men and women, and she was glad she had taken the effort to look pretty. She had never seen such a jolly crowd before, except in Brasov, at the play center. If this man knew how to live freely, then he was something different. The royal attendant at the door took her coat and asked for her name. His face brightened when she said, "Justina." He fawned over her at once.

"My lady," he said with a low bow. "Right this way." He led her into the hall and another guard came up to them immediately.

The previous guard must have signaled him. He didn't ask for her name like the previous one. Instead, he led her through the crowd to a private party on the rooftop. She spotted her cousin surrounded by a couple of dashing, valiant men, some of whom she recognized as his knights and others she hadn't seen before. She tried to guess which of the unfamiliar faces seated with her cousin was going to be her newly betrothed. She wasn't very impressed by any and was glad about it. She would stay through the night and be on her way once the night was over.

"Finally, Justina," King Matthias said.

Conversations around the king trickled to a stop, and soon, knights were clamoring for a chance to be chivalrous and noble by offering up their seats for her. She did not very much like this part. It placed her on the spot and made her the center of attention. She did not appreciate it and did not know how to react to it.

"Thank you, kind sirs," she said and took an empty seat away from her cousin. The night sky was lovely, dotted with bright, twinkly stars. She lost herself in space, gazing at the beauty of the night sky while around her, the men talked about their glorious war feats. After a short while, she was bored and got up to go for a stroll or join the party in the main hall. Halfway through, she bumped into someone. She staggered backward but was caught just in time by strong, steady hands.

"Are you okay, my lady?" a rich, baritone voice asked. The arms steadied her on her feet and escorted her away from the rooftop. She was swooning and she would have loved to attribute it solely to the fact that she almost fell, but she also knew that this intoxicating, manly aura and woody scent that her savior was giving off contributed to her dizziness more than anything else.

"Have a seat. I will get you some water."

He returned shortly with a cup of water, and she drained it. Her gaze steadied, and she could see his face. He was handsome in a daunting, daring way. His shoulders were squared and broad, and she had felt how strong they were when she bumped against him. He smiled at her when she kept staring, flashing the most brilliant set of white teeth. He took her hand in his, raised it to his lips, and kissed her knuckles. There was an explosion. Her sensory neurons malfunctioned, releasing a myriad of sensations through her. For a man as masculine and tough as he was, he had such slender, long fingers. She took note of them when he brought her hand to his mouth.

"I hope you'll be fine. I have some business to attend to. Take care."

When he left, her cheeks burned hot at the thought of what those long, slender fingers could do and where she wanted to feel them on her body. She gasped and drew in a long, deep breath. Daniel had filled her head with so much passion that she was now imagining things with a stranger's hand.

Get yourself together, Justina.

She stood, adjusted her dress, and gracefully made her way back into the hall. She was supposed to be a prim and proper woman, modest and pure, not one to entertain such randy thoughts. But all that had changed since meeting Daniel. He made her feel so alive, so aware of her body, and opened her mind up to unimaginable pleasure. She was still supposed to be seen as the proper, modest woman she had always been, even though now, she was aware of her body and her needs, and she embraced them. Meanwhile, as her savior walked away, she was thinking about how astoundingly gorgeous he was with his dark sleek hair, tall frame, and bulging muscles. Her cousin was in the hall when she got back. He waved her over and she went without delay. The sooner she did what he wanted, the sooner she could leave. He was talking to someone who had his back turned on her, so she did not see his face until she got to her cousin.

"This is the man that you are to be engaged to," her cousin said. "Vlad Tepes."

The stranger turned to face her, and she almost passed out from the shock. It was him! The man from earlier on, the one that she bumped into, the one that caught her, the one that made her stomach flutter and her heart skip a beat, the one that she wanted to feel his fingers, it was him – Vlad Tepes. She looked like a fierce angel as she walked up to him smiling and revealing her perfect glistening teeth.

Her skin glowed under the light. Her hair was well packed up with adornments. Her smile made Vlad's heart throb as she got closer to him with her slick curves behind that dress. He could swear that she would look good in anything.

Especially in his bed with him.

Justina couldn't believe what was happening. She fanned her face with her hand.

"My lady," Vlad Tepes said with a charming smile and took her hands in his, bringing them up to his lips for a kiss. Her pulse raced when his lips touched her skin, and she just stared at him, completely smitten and at a loss for words.

"This was the business I told you about. It appears it might be destiny. Would you walk with me?"

Justina nodded and placed her hand on his arm. He led her outside to the garden and asked if he could get her anything. She found her voice and replied that she was okay.

They sat side by side, sparks flying, and stared at the night sky. Vlad started a conversation, and she spent long hours talking and laughing with him. He was impressed she was so knowledgeable, and she explained it was mostly things that she read from her late husband's books.

"It is a great pleasure to make your acquaintance, my lady," he said, with his warm brown eyes fixed on her.

Tucking some strands of hair behind her ear, Justina smiled. "You are not bad, either. It is rather enjoyable talking to you."

"Oh, tell me. What do you think about this castle?"

"You pulled quite an impressive party. I'll say I'm impressed." "You flatter me." He laughed. His strong set of white teeth glittered. The man she barely knew mesmerized Justina. Her thoughts went off Daniel. This man's beauty is one to behold.

She liked his hands and physical features as they showed how manly he was.

"You flatter me the most."

"I wouldn't want to get on the wrong side of a beauty like you. It's not common to find someone as arrogant as you are." Justina laughed. She could admit he swept her off her feet. Vlad Tepes was easy to talk to, he listened to her, and so she talked about what her life was like with her cousin in the palace before she got married and a little of her life now in Brasov; on and on into the night while he looked at her with a dreamy, longing look in his eyes. The sparks were mutual.

She was not the only one smitten.

The party was winding down and a group of ladies came out to the garden, where she was enjoying a cozy time with Vlad Tepes.

"There he is," one of them said, and they all fluttered over. They spoke to him and fawned over him, touching his chest as they spoke, making no attempt to hide their intentions. Their actions were suggestive and Justina grew annoyed watching them. Vlad Tepes did nothing to encourage them. Despite that, she felt jealous that many women wanted him. It made her anxious, and she tried to dismiss the feeling by telling herself that she had her fling and he was allowed to have as many flings as he wanted. It made her feel better to think of them as flings, and she fancied herself to be the one who would hold his heart. Although she had every right to be jealous, seeing as she was engaged to him. Her unstable thoughts wearied her, and she excused herself.

She rose and turned without looking back. The longer she was there, the angrier she would become.

Vlad Tepes caught up to her. "My lady, are you leaving so soon?"

She forced a smile. "It's getting late and…" she yawned, "I must get some rest. I feel so tired, and I think I might come down with a headache."

He grabbed her hands. "I can't let you go… not unless I know." When she said nothing, he prompts, "Will I see you again, my lady? Will you honor an invitation from me?"

She stared at him for a long time, looking into his eyes with a longing gaze, and nodded in reply.

"I will feel much better, my lady, to hear you say it."

"Yes, I will."

His face broke out into a smile. "I will send an invitation, my lady, soon. I can't wait to see you again. Until then, I shall treasure the time we had together today." He kissed her hand and helped her get into the carriage.

Justina kept sighing on the journey back to Brasov. He was not just good-looking, and strong, but he had a way with words, too. His deep baritone voice stayed in her head until she got to Brasov. Throughout the long, tiresome journey, her mind kept replaying their encounter together, and her stomach tightened with anticipation at the thought of seeing him again soon. He made her giddy and excited. She couldn't help but imagine what it would be like with him. She wanted to find out, but then that would mean leaving Brasov and she was not keen to leave just yet.

Daniel was waiting for her in her room, none of the candles lit; he must have been dropping by ever since she was gone. He grabbed her as soon as she entered the room, telling her how much he had missed her and how badly he wanted her. Justina had forgotten just how sweet he was and how he made her feel things she couldn't describe in words. He soon refreshed her memory.

She had not gotten over two words out when his mouth devoured hers while his hands roamed her clothing. He seduced her through her clothing and carried her like she weighed nothing to her dresser, sweeping out the cosmetics that lay on it with a swipe of his hand. He explored her with his tongue, running his tongue along her body with a steaming hot breath. Spreading her legs with his hands, his tongue explored the hidden treasure between her legs, sending wave after wave of pleasure through her.

Justina exploded with a low groan, and her body shook violently. When she opened her eyes, it was no longer Daniel but her current admirer, Vlad Tepes. She grabbed Daniel's head, seeing Vlad Tepes on his face, and drew him closer to the sweetness between her legs that was pulsing with moist heat. He ravaged her with his tongue, and she groaned with pleasure. She was getting heady from the sensations pulsing through her and tightened her legs around him, drowning in an ocean of lustful pleasure. Throughout the night, they made love, but while Daniel was here in her room, in her head, there was someone else.

By the break of dawn, she was alone, curled up in sheets with dull aching, and sweet memories.

CHAPTER TWENTY FIVE

The royal guards knew not to disturb the king after he had retired to his chamber for the night unless it was a pressing issue. A message had arrived for the king, requesting to be directed to him personally and no one else. After a short consensus and fear, a guard headed for the king's chamber. As the guard drew closer to the king's chamber, he heard strange sounds, sounds that he was quite familiar with, and made an about-face, going back to inform the others and the late-night visitor that the king would not be disturbed. They allowed the messenger to stay in clean quarters for the night, so he could deliver his message to the king in the morning.

Queen Beatrice of Naples, the king's third wife was a rather haughty woman who created a rift between the king and his subjects. The king eventually grew tired of her, and rumor had it their marriage was one of convenience and political gain rather than anything else just like most royal marriages. So, after their first year of marriage, the couple grew apart. The queen spent most of her days away from the castle, going on trips around the lands and visiting kingdoms, while the king stayed back to attend to state matters. Although alone, the king found his way to relieve his physical desires and needs. He was a powerful monarch after all, and the fantasy of most females in the kingdom, he could have his pick of whoever he wanted, and he did. An unsentimental person, the king never grew attached to any of his late-night companions.

It was a great luxury to have the king invite any of his previous lovers back to his bed. They were all well-compensated, but none of them ever saw the insides of his chambers again. None that is, except one. A woman named Barbara Edelpock. She was not known, nor was she born to any noble family. She was the daughter of a citizen of Stein in lower Austria. No one knew her family lineage or her name, at least not the name that she was commonly called. It was the most ironic twist of fate that the king would be involved with someone so simple, so ordinary, and pure at heart while he was the direct opposite of all that. It was funny still, that she was hidden in plain sight.

About thirty minutes before the message arrived for the king, the guard headed for the king's chamber to inform him, the king had secretly escorted his clandestine lover into his chambers. He locked his chambers and retired to his bed, where he watched her after asking her to dance for him. She started slowly, timidly working up the courage as she danced. He watched her, picking grapes from a tray set on a small stool beside his bedside, registering every move and twirl of her body. After a short while, he asked her to get rid of her clothing and dance naked.

"No! Slowly," he said in a raspy voice.

She relaxed a bit, drawing in a breath, and continued her dance, slowly and seductively getting rid of her clothing until she was down to her shift.

"Wait!" The king slipped her hands down to her waist. "Just a minute." He soaked in her image, salivating at her creamy, smooth skin. She waited for him, standing in a pose.

"You are so refreshingly gorgeous and beautiful. I can't get enough of you," said King Matthias. It was a shocking admission from the king, and it caused his lover to tremble.

"The top one first," he said, and she slowly and gradually took off her chemise. She held onto the straps with both hands and bounced them up and down so that it looked like her boobs were bouncing with them. The king stared attentively, captured by her charm. She let the clothing go, revealing a set of perfectly rounded breasts with hard pink nipples, aroused with desire. She resumed her amorous dance, running her hands from her stomach to her breast, up to her neck, and back again. She teased him by sliding her hands down to her waist, into her undergarment, and letting him imagine what her hands were doing there. She kept up the dancing and the teasing for a while, squatting down low and spreading her legs wide apart. She slid down to the floor slowly from her squat position with her back against the floor and raised both legs, then spread them wide apart before placing them against the ground in an arch. She raised her upper body halfway through, supporting her weight with one hand while the other hand went over her undergarment. She trailed a straight line from the middle of her feminine mold, lingering just at the tip of the opening of the skin down there before running the rest of the line upwards to her belly button. The adrenaline had kicked in now and the passion filled her with boldness, carrying her to make daring, taunting moves.

"I am your king, and you would dare to tease me so?" the king said, captivated by her charm and paying close attention to her performance so that he did not miss even a second.

She laughed and got up to her feet, walking majestically towards him on the bed. She climbed on top of him, straddling him with her feet, then pushed him back lightly with her fingers against the bed frame. The king leaned back, playing along with her as she wasn't strong enough to throw him back against his will.

She slipped her hands under his night robe and stroked him softly, running her hands back and forth against his chest. Then she leaned in closer to his ear, ran her tongue over it, and said in a stimulating, low whisper, "You can have the last piece, my lord."

She reached for his hand and placed them on both sides of her hips against her undergarment to leave no doubt what she meant. The king got her message clear and reacted with stimulation of his own.

"I can't seem to understand how you are so bold and so modest," he said when she giggled like a kid at his touch. He pushed her back against the foot of the bed, strapping her under him with his hands on both sides of her head to support his weight.

"Let's see how high those long legs can stretch now, eh?" he said, responding to her teasing him by stretching her legs high and wide when she was dancing. Without waiting for a reply, he raised her legs to his shoulders and hung them there, spreading her legs apart to leave her open and defenseless against him.

"Ah! Such beauty," he said, referring to the skin that opened up before him like a budding flower, pulsing with blood and desire. Her undergarment was a thin, transparent piece of clothing that did very little to cover up the mold of flesh that it was designed for so the king could get a good view even before taking them off. It was like a tease, a sneak peek before the main attraction showed up.

She felt self-conscious as the king studied her every outline with his eyes, devouring her with an intense look that sparked a burning heat in the place between her legs. She tried to turn her body, so that she wasn't so open and bare before him, but he turned her back around, trapping her hands over her head.

"Allow me a good view please, would you?"

Her eyes softened at the fact that he was asking, and she unconsciously relaxed, taking pleasure because she provided a good sight for the king's eyes. She had obsessed over him from afar but did nothing about it, not until the last time that she returned to Hungary and he had made a move on her. She had resisted, trying against her own needs to fight his charm. She thought perhaps he was drunk, and she couldn't bear the thought of being a drunken, momentary fling. Her resolve did not hold for long; however, her strength faltered, and her body betrayed her when his hands touched her. He was just as she had imagined in her head, in the many fantasies that she had about him, and she couldn't find the strength to resist anymore, so she gave in. That night was magical. It was a memorable one, and she decided she was going to cherish it for as long as she lived, even if it was just for that night. She let herself go that night, soaking up all the love and pleasure that he had to give, squirming under his touch, reacting to the feel of his body, opening up eagerly for him to enter. She wanted to reach the heights of passion and she did, so that when morning came, and he looked at her like a stranger, she had no regrets; she had the memories from the previous night to keep her warm.

In life, things do not always go as planned, and in this case, it wasn't such a bad thing. She had a planned arrangement in her head. In the natural order of things, he was never to look at her again. Never to want her or invite her into his bed, and she was fine with that. She had built herself and prepared her mind for just that scenario so that the pain doesn't hurt so badly when it happens.

Fate was determined to shock her. He came for her the next night, and she shared his bed again. And then the night after that. And the night after. And now, she was here again, trapped under him in his bed, taking in the feel and smell of him while he ravaged her with his eyes.

This was a far cry from the plan in her head and she couldn't help but dread the intensity of the pain that she would feel once this ended. And it would; everything does. She was prolonging the inevitable, and yet she had no intention of cutting it short. She wanted to ride the waves for as long as they would last.

Who knows, fate might have another surprise in store for her, and it did!

She was cut off from her nostalgia by an overwhelming erotic sensation. She felt wetness on her skin, drenching her undergarment and making it stick to her skin like an extra layer. It wasn't her own wetness; it was an external heat generated by the hungry lips devouring her. His lips sucked on her through her undergarment, creating a suction that filled her vaginal hole with cool air when he released his lips. Her head spun with pleasure, and she secreted her own wetness. He kept up the acts, doing it several times after that, until she was squirming under him and begging to have the undergarment removed so she could feel him against her skin. He slipped his hands in when she thought he was done, letting his fingers grope around her vagina like a man moving around in the dark. She clawed at the bedsheets, curling her toes in pleasure and unwittingly closing her organ around him in a tight squeeze. When he pulled his fingers out, she was overwhelmingly aware of her own body, but not in a self-conscious way. Every nerve, every fiber, every muscle of her tingled with exhilaration and pure desire. She opened her eyes just in time to see him bring his fingers to his lips and taste her, sending another spark of desire through her.

"You taste like grapes…"

"You just ate grapes, my lord,"

"I know, and I can't seem to get enough… so irresistibly, tempting and yummy," he said, with his eyes fixed on the tempting spot between her legs.

He placed both hands on her waist, lifting her easily like she weighed nothing, and turned her around on the bed. He let her undress him, taking her time to reveal the skin underneath with each button that she popped open until he was completely nude. His graceful, lean body stretched out before her, and she admired him reverently. She couldn't believe how beautiful he was, and how toned his muscles were around his skin. She ran her hands lovingly over his flesh, from his shoulders down to his ankles and back up, fondling and caressing his tight backside. He leaned across the bed to pick up some grapes and pop them into his mouth, then stretched himself up to take her nipple into his mouth. He licked and sucked with the grape still in his mouth, savoring the taste of both items as they came together. He bit her lightly as he chewed and continued to suckle on her breast.

"Do you still worry about her?" he asked, making a pop sound as he let go of her nipples.

"Yes, my lord. I do."

"Why?" he asked, popping another grape into his mouth as he took in the other nipple.

"I can't explain it…" she replies. She slides her hand down his body, reaching out to touch his appendage, but he stops her.

Staring her in the eyes, he says, "I want to take it slow tonight. If I feel your warmth around me, I could not hold back."

She stares into his eyes and sees that he is serious. He meant what he just said, and emotions welled up in her throat. She swallowed it back. She couldn't avoid feeling anything. It would only make the pain worse when the time comes.

"Are you worried that she would find out about us?" he asked again, trailing his tongue from her shoulder to her neck. "I'm more worried about how she's doing, and yes. I'm afraid of how she would react if she found out."

"Don't worry, she will not be coming back to the castle." She gasped, "What do you mean, my lord?"

"I have other plans for her, and they are already in motion." "So, you mean to keep this up?" she asked.

"Are you tired of me already?" he asked, fondling both her breasts passionately while his lips tasted and explored hers. Her breathing was rushed and hot when he stopped, she had her legs wrapped around him, and her body arched forward towards him.

"…I suppose not," he said in reply to his question. "Your body is still as responsive as ever. And that is the problem. I can't seem to get enough of you, and for as long as I want you, I intend to take what I want."

His tone was forceful and authoritative, but she did not feel offended, instead, her face filled up with heat and traveled around her body.

"You are such a pure, kind soul. Perhaps that is why I am attracted to you," he said, running his hands lovingly through her skin.

He flips her over, so that she is lying with her back on her bed while he kneels on the bed above her. He pulls her leg up to his waist and drags a pillow from the bed, which he places under her back. She wrapped her leg tightly around his waist as her female part pulsed with excitement and expectation. Placing both hands on the curve of her waist, he pulls her close to him so that she could feel his arousal just at the edge of her lady part.

In a voice made rough from the desire, he said, "My cousin can take care of herself. Stop worrying so much about her. She's fine. You, however, have more pressing matters to attend to…" he said, nodding towards the hard erection between his legs.

"… My dear Esme, or should I say, Barbara Epeldock."

He entered her with a swift move that made her eyes roll behind her head, and she released a deep-throated moan just about the same time as when the guard got closer to the king's chamber. The guard got the message; The king was closed for the day, and all matters would be attended to the next day, and he turned right around without delay.

~ ∞ ~

The next morning, the king was informed about his late- night guest and demanded the person be brought to him.

"I have a message for you, Your Majesty," the visitor said after saluting the king.

"Go on then, speak!"

"He said to tell you that the sparrow still visits the dove. He said you would understand."

The king requested a clean scroll, quill, and ink. He scribbled a note and sealed it with his seal, then handed it over to the visitor.

The letter had only two words in it. Kill him!

CHAPTER TWENTY SIX

Justina was finally getting back her rhythm of life in Brasov, at least until the king ordered her to leave for good. The incident of her cousin showing up unannounced in her room, the invitation to Vlad Tepes' party, the attraction between her and Vlad Tepes, and everything else that happened during that week was all behind her. She had her spirits back up, and she was once again back to enjoying her free, unrestrained life in Brasov.

Nicolae and Angela noticed the change in her and commented on it. Business at the inn was booming, the couple was making remarkable sales, the tips were as generous as ever, and whenever Justina was not at the play center or traveling around town with the girls, she was in her room, cuddling up under the sheets with Daniel.

Life was just perfect, even though she was now engaged, she was determined to enjoy every bit for now and everything was right with the world. What could go wrong?

Justina woke up happy and refreshed, like every other morning. Daniel had slept over the previous night after they had spent the night making love and devouring each other like men starved of food. She lingered in bed longer that morning and they had a quick tango under the sheets before she got up to get dressed for work.

Her countenance was clear and bright throughout the day, and she bounced around with a spring in her step. They never made plans to see each other before now, they just met up whenever and hit things off spontaneously, but that morning had gone so well that Justina suggested they meet up again later in the evening. She wanted to splurge; even though things were running smoothly, she had a feeling that the quiet would not last that long. Daniel was one for doing whatever Justina wanted to do, so he agreed without question.

The day seemed to go on forever, even though it was the same as every other day. Justina kept her ears open for the bell, waiting for hours to go by. By the end of the day, she was more than happy to take off her apron and hit the front door for the road.

When she got to her house, she screamed her lungs out. Daniel was lying there in front, in a pool of his blood. She shrieked and dropped to the ground beside him. She was out of her mind with worry, anger, and fear. It was an accusation, but she knew Daniel was murdered and she suspected she knew who was behind it. Her cousin had warned her to stop seeing him and the fact that he was lying dead outside her door meant he had come to see her, it was enough proof that had riled her cousin.

Daniel was so happy that she just could not get enough of him as much as he did too.

He had reached a point at which he would do anything she told him to. He had always fantasized about getting married to her and taking her farther away to a place King Matthias would never find.

All day he had anticipated spending another night with her, he strode to her house earlier than usual.

He got there and noticed the door was locked. She had not come back from work yet. It was quickly getting cold as night time came. He was going to wait out for her. That was how much he loved her.

He rubbed his hands on his arms for warmth and leaned on the wall. The sound of a chariot closing disturbed him. His heart was filled with fear, as he knew who it was. He had the chance to run, but he didn't. This time, he was going to face King Matthais. Somebody had to stand up to him and tell him the truth.

King Matthias wanted to see his cousin that day. Turns out she was still in that awful place she so much loved. He always wondered how someone with royalty would suddenly want to become a peasant. With the looks of it, she already was.

He set off in his chariot, along with two guards, to meet Justina. Getting there, he found that pitiful smug she called her lover standing outside her door. He was furious, however, taken aback by the young man's sudden courage.

"I see you have refused to listen to my order!" he thundered. "Pardon my stubbornness, your majesty," Daniel replied in the most mocking tone.

King Mattias waved his hand at his guards, signaling for them to arrest him.

"Although there is something I have to say, though." The king ordered them to stop. He wanted to know what this pitiful rat had to say.

Daniel stared at him in so much anger and hate. "Lady Justina is not your puppet! Arrest me now and I will have her in the dungeon if I wanted to!"

The King smirked at his guts and moved closer to him. "You have shared her bed, and now you think you can share her arrogance with me?" He was just going to dump him in the dungeon, but with that disrespect, he crossed the line.

He pulled on his sharp sword, and Daniel stared at him without a flinch. With just one strike as a skilled swordsman, that was all it took, as Daniel died instantly.

He smiled at his corpse, knowing fully well that Daniel was out of the way now. He didn't care how she felt. Daniel was just going to spoil the plans he had. With that, he left with his guards.

What started as a pleasant, calm day turned dark and murky. And the days that followed were even darker. She had grown fond of Daniel and his absence deeply felt like a dagger had gone through her. He was a wild fling, but she had grown fond of him and he was human and did not deserve to die a cruel death.

The months following Daniel's death were tough and lonely. She felt the gap that his absence left on every cold winter night, but she gradually recovered. She hung out more often with the girls, spending her days at the inn and her nights at the play center. Eventually, she moved on.

Vlad Tepes was feeling a bit more relaxed after taking his revenge on his accusers, and he felt it was the perfect time to pursue other pleasant needs and desires. He never stopped thinking about the last time he held a banquet and Lady Justina showed up. She had been on his mind ever since, but more so this last couple of days. He had made her promise she would see him again and honor an invitation from him to come over if he invited her. So, he did just that. He threw a party, smaller and with fewer guests than the last time, and sent out an invitation to Lady Justina.

The invitation arrived in Brasov the next morning. Justina was in bed, weak and sick from consuming too much wine the previous night, a knock sounded on her door. She slurred her reply, but her voice was too weak and too low for the person at the door to hear that the knock came again. She got up and headed for the door grudgingly, dragging her weight behind her.

"A letter from the king, my lady," the messenger said and left as soon as he handed her the scroll.

Vlad Tepes had sent the invitation for his party to the castle in Hungary, thinking that Lady Justina was there. When the king received the invitation, he sent a message to Justina in Brasov through the guards he had secretly stationed to keep watch over her. The content of the letter was simple and straight to the point. He asked her to return to Hungary and be prepared to attend Vlad Tepes' party. As always, he wasn't asking for her consent; he was simply informing her of a decision that he had made and asking her to go along with it. Justina was still too sleepy and tired to give any reaction to the king's message. She read the letter drowsily and dropped the scroll on her dresser before climbing back into bed. By the time she woke up hours later, she was feeling much better, and she remembered the letter. It would have been an otherwise difficult decision to make, but Justina felt like she had had her fun and made the best of the time that she was given, so she had no regrets.

Daniel was dead. She could not stand the thought of any other person who she knew and related with in Brasov being harmed because of her. She particularly had Nicolae and Angela in mind. They had been so good to her, and she owed them a lot. She could not bear to see them come to any harm for her sake. She knew her cousin well. He could get testy when he was not having his way or things weren't going as planned. She did not want to test him. She didn't want to find out what he would do next, so she made a wise decision for herself. She lived her last days in Brasov to the fullest, spending time with Nicolae and Angela when the customer rush hour died down. She read books and poems, attended brunches, and ticked off everything she wanted to do while she had the chance off her list.

When she was ready, she packed up her things and began the journey back to what used to be home. Brasov was home now, and it didn't matter that she would no longer be there. She would always remember it in her heart as home. No matter where she was. It was the place where she had found herself and was free to be Justina without fear or apology. The memories built there and she would always treasure the good times in her heart.

CHAPTER TWENTY SEVEN

KING MATTHIAS CORVINUS' CASTLE HUNGARY

Justina's return to the place where she grew up, her cousin's castle, left her with mixed feelings. She was glad to be back. She had missed the people, more so her maidservant Esme. She had missed the friendliest of the townspeople and the late-night secret soiree they had held.

She drew in a deep breath as the carriage advanced towards the castle. It felt like ages since she was last here and even the fresh, clean air and the smell of mountains brought back nostalgia. Everything she loved about Hungary was around her; the lush green fields, the smell of spices, the sound of laughter on familiar faces, and the easy way of relating with everyone. Here she knew people that loved her for being the king's ward unbiased. She did not need to hide her identity like with Brasov, but all that aside, the major reason that Hungary quickly lost its appeal was looming ahead of her in the distance, tucked behind the cold, concrete walls: the king. If Justina could take all the beautiful features that she loved about Hungary without her cousin in it, she would be much better. He was family, and she hated him for everything he had done.

She arrived at the castle gate quietly without hassle or delay. No one knew she was coming back, not even her cousin who had sent the letter demanding her to return, so there was no loud noise or festive welcome back party and she loved it. It was going just as she had planned. If her cousin knew she was coming back, he would have wanted to make some noise and put up a public display of being a compassionate and wealthy king by holding a feast in her honor. She was certain he would still do that, but at the very least, she had had her way and made her quiet comeback. By the time he threw his feast, she would be mentally ready for it.

The guards at the castle gate stopped her carriage, demand- ing to see who they brought into the castle and what business they had with the king. It was an official protocol. The carriage slowed, and the guard moved around the back. She drew the curtain aside, staring straight ahead so only her profile was showing, but the guard still couldn't determine who she was.

"My lady, please turn your face?" the guard asked.

She was hoping the guard would see her clothing, as she was dressed like a noble lady, and allow her in, just like with Brasov. But this wasn't an entrance at the city gates. This was an entrance to the king's castle, so naturally, the security and scrutiny would be tighter. Revealing herself at the gate would jinx her perfect plan of coming back unannounced. Once the guards verified her identity, the next point of call would be to inform the king of her return. She could ask them not to do that, but it would seem suspicious. Matthias may have them punished for not announcing her return to him.

With a sigh, she turned her face fully towards the guard. At once, his face lit up with recognition, and he jumped back in surprise.

He bowed. "Welcome back, my lady."

"There goes my secret return," she said with a dry laugh. When she got to the palace, Esme was standing outside, waiting for her. She ran towards her and grabbed her in a tight hug as soon as Justina's legs came off the carriage.

"I have been so worried about you, my lady," she said, still holding on to her. "You look well. Have you been well?" Then, dropping her voice down to a whisper, she asked, "Did you have fun?"

Lady Justina chuckled and returned the hug. "I guess my return was not as discreet as I had thought."

Esme had a guilty look on her face, and Justina laughed, waving it off as no big deal.

"I will answer your questions, Esme, but can I get some rest at least? It's been a long journey."

"Of course, my lady," Esme said, helping her with with her bags and leading the way into the castle. "Your chamber is ready. I cleaned it every day while you were away."

"Thank you!" Justina said. It wasn't just for the chamber; it was for everything else. For the thousand and one things that she couldn't recount. All her gratitude was encapsulated in those two words, and Esme knew she meant it from her heart. She smiled at her and received it cheerfully.

Gasps and whispers erupted among the maids and servants when they saw Lady Justina show up and was escorted to her chamber by Esme like she had not been away for over a year. She left the castle when she was to be married to Lord Wenceslas. Thinking about it made her smile. It felt like it was ages ago when that happened. She thought about the study where he buried himself most days, the garden where they had consummated, the front yard where she spent her evenings, and the servants, those wonderful souls. She has not corresponded with them since she left for Brasov. But she was back now, and she decided she would reach out to them. She made a mental note to ask Esme about them later. She must have given them quite a scare when she left the manor without warning.

She eyed Esme walking happily beside her and smiling like she had received an early winter gift and wondered how she had managed the king's wrath in her absence. She had put her in a tough position and she needed to make it up to her. Her head and mind were flooded with deep-seated memories. Memories she had tried to repress all came rushing back now. "Ah!" she breathed. "So many memories. So much to catch up on!"

Esme looked at her with a smile, concurring.

What Justina did not know, however, was that a lot had happened in the castle since she was away, and she was the one that needed to catch up more than anyone else.

She was in for big news!

$\sim \infty \sim$

Things were spiraling quickly out of control. There was no plan for this; there was no way she could have expected it. Esme took a deep breath, drew a hood over her head, and headed for the left wing of the castle to the king's chamber. She had been struggling with whether to honor the king's request to see her. Lady Justina was back in the castle now, so it would not be that easy for her to sneak around and about, warming up the king's bed.

There was also the fact that she felt strangely guilty because she was keeping a secret from Justina all the time she's been in it. She wanted to tell her, but she could not summon the courage. But while she mused on what to do, a tiny part of her mind reminded her he was the king, and she dared not defy him. She got out of bed, pulled on some clothes, and sneaked around, headed for the king's chamber. She had a lot on her mind that night, and she needed to speak with him.

As she approached the king's chamber, the candle burned bright inside; he was probably waiting for her. She paused at the door and took a deep breath, trying to ease her mind. A random thought flashed through her mind, and she shivered. She had imagined the king would show up at the servants' quarters demanding to see her if he waited for another hour and she didn't show up. It wouldn't matter to him to disclose her identity as his mistress, but it would matter to her. She wouldn't be able to face Lady Justina again after that. She was yet to reveal her real name to Lady Justina, and she wanted to be the one to tell the Lady about her affair with the king so she would say it with meekness and apologize. She shook her head.

She knocked and pushed open the door slightly. The king was on the bed, dressed in his night robe, a goblet of wine in his hand. It was obvious he was waiting for someone, for her. The setting in his chamber gave off that much. His robe was slightly open, and she glimpsed his skin and her face turned red.

"Finally, you show up?" the king said, noting the reddish tone of her face, he followed her eyes to his exposed skin and sighed, shaking his head. "You are an unusual one."

She had seen him nude several times before. She had touched him and felt him inside her, so he couldn't understand how she could still be so affected by the sight of his naked body. He took off the robe, exposing the rest of himself and enjoying her demure shyness. Her eyes widened, her face turned a deeper shade of red, and she gulped. He laughed and patted the space beside him.

King Matthias was a powerful man and the fact that Barbara worshiped him with her eyes, hands, and body every time that they were together intoxicated him, at least in her eyes. It appealed to his ego, and that was also why he could not get enough of her. She was so simple, so modest; there was no pretense with her. She wore her emotions on her face, and it was easy to see her reaction.

She climbed beside him, and he drank in her scent. He leaned closer to her, nuzzling her neck while he went to undress her. He flung her garment aside as soon as he ripped it off her skin and buried his face in the curves of her body.

Barbara, which was who she was when she was with the king, closed her eyes and tried to get the words to form in her mouth. She needed to speak now, while she still had control of her senses and before her mind became befuddled with pleasure, and she would not be able to make any other sound except deep, throaty moans. The king preferred to refer to her as Barbara, and she instinctively referred to herself that way when she was with him. That way, she wasn't a maidservant; she was one of the king's subjects, one that warmed his bed at night. Somehow, not thinking about herself as Esme gave her the courage that she needed and loosened her tongue.

"Your Majesty."

The king paused and murmured a response. When she said nothing else, he lifted his head and, seeing her hesitation, urged her to speak.

"Is this about Justina's return? Are you scared?" He was about to go off at her for being interrupted for such a trivial issue as his cousin. He never really cared about Barbara's reservations, but he tried to respect them. But now, if she was going to fear Justina more than him, he needed to remind her who was king and lord over them both.

"It's not about her, my lord," she said quietly before he could let out his rage.

He paused, stared into her eyes, and when he saw she was telling the truth, said, "Speak."

She lifted his head from her lap and climbed out of bed, going down on her knees with her head bowed. The king was perplexed.

Barbara had been contemplating this moment and now she had started it, she couldn't hold it in. She tightened her jaw, determined to pull through with it even if it killed her.

The king sat up and leaned his head against the bed frame. She drew in a deep breath, let it out slowly, and said, "I am with child, my lord."

Her voice was so low it was almost a whisper. He was still, and she felt he might not have heard her. She repeated herself, louder this time so that she was sure that he heard her, but there was still no reaction, just a still silence.

The king got out on the other side of the bed and walked towards her, during which she prayed desperately for her life to be spared. She quickly sat up with a gasp as panic seeped in and her eyes went wide and her hand immediately went over her stomach as if to protect her unborn child, although she knew he wasn't cruel enough to hurt the baby. She pleaded with the king that it wasn't an intentional act on her part. She begged for mercy and promised to go far away to have her child if he would spare her life.

The king took her shoulders and raised her to her feet. She quivered.

His voice was dangerously low. "Are you sure?"

She nodded vehemently, unable to get the words to form. The king observed to be sure she was speaking the truth and not trying to tease him. Then suddenly, he folded her into a tight hug, squeezing her against him. Barbara was confused; this was the last thing she had expected. When he released his grasp, she coughed from being squeezed too tightly by strong hands, but she had never felt so relieved. The king pulled her close again and peppered her face and stomach with kisses.

"Where would you like to go?" he asked, and her counte- nance dropped.

Of course. He wanted her gone. Why was she so quick to be happy? She couldn't blame him; she had offered a minute ago to leave the kingdom and go far away, so why was she feeling so blue at being told to leave? But the king was not done yet. She had merely let her emotions get ahead of her.

"I am going to make you a comfortable estate where you can live and give birth to my child. You cannot keep working here, so tell me where you would like to go, and I will make plans."

She smiled. He was sending her away to care for her and the child. She might not have his love, but regardless, she was glad that at the end of it all, she would have no regrets. She would not spend the rest of her life wondering what could have been. She had dived in, and she was glad she had. She would happily take whatever came next.

"I have to speak to Lady Justina before I leave, my lord," she pleaded.

The king nodded. He lifted her and lay her down on the bed. She giggled happily as he loomed over her and merged with her most sensually. That night, they had bout after bout of intoxicating lovemaking.

When she woke up, he was gone.

$\sim \infty \sim$

Esme knocked on the door lightly and pushed it open. She had spent so much time deliberating on how she was going to tell Lady Justina all that had happened. After several long minutes of pacing without coming up with any quick fix, she braced herself and just deal with it.

Lady Justina was up already when she got to her room. It was a new development for her, one Esme had noticed since the lady had returned from Brasov. Lady Justina used to sleep for a better part of the mornings, but these days, she was wide awake at dawn.

"My lady," Esme called, peering her head through the door. Justina turned in her direction with a smile and waved for her to come in. "I'm not sure if I like this new habit of mine," she said. "Back in Brasov, I had a job, so I had a reason to wake up early, but here... even the birds are still asleep. Can you believe that?" She giggled.

Esme watched her quietly as she talked. Whenever Lady Justina talked about her time in Brasov, she always said it with a certain glow. Her face would light up with brilliance, and her eyes would shine with joy as she recalled fond memories. Esme also knew that once Lady Justina started talking about Brasov, it was usually hard for her to stop. She could go on and on, smiling and recalling one fond memory after another in clear detail. Esme already knew the wonderful couple, Nicolae and Angela, even though she had never met them. And then there were Elena, Ana-Maria, and Julia. And there was Daniel. She said very little about him. Most of the surrounding conversation was that he knew how to ease her stress and help her relax, and in most of her stories, he was always in her room. Esme did not pursue that detail, and Justina elaborated little.

"My lady," Esme began in a quiet, meek tone. Lady Justina stopped talking and looked at her with a puzzled expression. "I'm sorry, my lady, forgive my interruption, but there's something that I must tell you."

Lady Justina's face softened immediately, melting into worry. She looked her in the eye. "What is it, Esme? Are you hurt? Did the king order a punishment on you on my behalf? Tell me, and I will go to him at once." She was already halfway to her feet.

Esme placed a hand on Lady Justina and slowly narrated what had been happening since Lady Justina was away. She told her about her secret affair with the king and how she had been invited by him to warm his bed every other night. Lady Justina looked like she was listening with rapt attention because her eyes were welling up with a feeling Esme pinned as compassion.

"Does he treat you well?" Lady Justina asked. "I know my cousin. He's a gruff, selfish idiot who doesn't care about anyone but himself. So, tell me. Is he any good… Oh, please, I don't want to hear the details about my cousin's escapades. A simple answer will do." They both giggled.

"I know he doesn't care much for me except to appease his sexual hunger, but I have also enjoyed it for as long as it lasted, so…"

Justina understood her maidservant's words without her having to finish. She knew what that could be like if it was good enough for Esme, then she was fine with it. She is suspicious and wondering if all these while Esme was on her side or just on the King's side, but then she remembered all that they have been through even in Wenceslas palace and all suspicion disappears.

She said as much to Esme and her maidservant jumped at her, wrapping her in a warm hug. With the first hurdle out of the way, Esme felt brave enough to break the other more shocking news to Lady Justina. She told her about her pregnancy.

Lady Justina's eyes popped in their sockets and she made a squealing noise to express her happiness. It was a bittersweet feeling of joy and apprehension at the same time. She couldn't trust her cousin to be a good person and Esme was the sweetest person she had ever known. It was strange how the least predictable things always somehow ended up happening. She couldn't fathom how Esme was attracted to her cousin. It was a purely sexual arrangement between them, but she feared Esme might get her heart involved and King

Matthias didn't do well with hearts. His closest relationship with them was to squash them under his boot in battle.

He had had three marriages. They were all based on agreement, like a contract, rather than mutual affection and companionship. And that explained a lot, such as the reason he would try to dictate his cousin's life and have her matched to be married to the next available villain as long as he was rich and powerful, or a scholarly landowner with acres of land.

Justina was glad her maidservant was expecting a child, but she only wished that it was of someone other than the king.

In later years, however, her cousin would be glad he kept the child, as history would record his illegitimate son, John Corvinus, born by Barbara Edelpock, as his only son.

King Matthias never had an heir aside from him.

CHAPTER TWENTY EIGHT

CASTLE BRAN TRANSYLVANIA

Vlad's small gathering had been in session for a little over two hours now. All the guests fit perfectly into the hall and there was enough food and drink going

around with the servants that served. Vlad Tepes moved within the small circles clustered in the feast, exchanging pleasantries and stopping briefly to make small talk before moving on to the next group. All the while, he kept his ears open, listening for a certain name while his eyes tried to stay fixed on the door.

She had given him her word. It did not matter if a million hours went by; somehow, he could trust her to uphold her word. She was Matthias's cousin and integrity ran deep in the family.

A few more hours went by, and his convictions faltered. He was no longer sure as earlier on. Doubts crept in and he started wondering if she got his invitation. There had been no response from her so perhaps she never got his invite. He folded his hand into a fist as he tried to curtail his annoyance. The way he saw it, the only way Lady Justina would not have found out about his party and the invitation was if King Matthias tried to keep it from her. And why would he do that? Not once did it occur to Vlad Tepes that maybe his invitation had simply been ignored by Lady Justina and she decided not to attend the party. He could not find fault with her. He simply would not, in his head, keep the memory of a beautiful, fair and flawless damsel. There could not possibly be a fault with her. He had been staring so hard at the entrance that he lost focus and simply stared, thoughts somewhere else. A graceful movement caught his attention.

Behold, it was Lady Justina, gorgeous in a velvet, red ball gown. Her lips were bright red against her creamy, white skin. She was easily the most captivating woman in the room. Vlad Tepes stared at her in awe, soaking up the beautiful sight. She smiled when their eyes met and began walking towards him. Vlad Tepes smiled back, and they met in the middle.

"I'm glad you could make it," he said. "I was almost worried you would not keep your word."

She blushed. "I'm sorry. I was on my way, and just a few miles away, I had a bit of a wardrobe emergency. I had to go back and change into this. I hope I am not underdressed."

"I bless that wardrobe emergency," Vlad Tepes said, "You look ravishing! May I have this dance?" He offered her his hand.

She placed her hands in his, and he led her out to the dance floor, placing his free hand on the small of her back. The connection between them was clear to everyone in the hall. They looked like the perfect match, but while Vlad Tepes connected to Lady Justina in both physical and emotional ways, Lady Justina restricted her connection to him to the physical. She needed to know more and couldn't trust so easily.

* * *

The proximity sent waves of sparks through her. Her stomach tightened and her heart stopped every time he pulled her close during the dance. He was a good dancer, and he glided smoothly across the floor, taking her with him. By the time the dance ended, everyone in the hall was watching them, and they gave a loud wave of applause when they were done. Just as soon, the music started again, playing another song, and people flooded the dance floor with them.

Justina had her fill of dancing for one night, and Vlad appeared to feel the same as he took her delicate fingers and nodded for her to follow him outside. He slowed down to a walk and dropped his voice. He had been talking loudly when they were in the hall so that she could hear him above the music. The dance made her remember the first time she had danced with Wenceslas, her late husband and it brought a spark to her heart.

"Would you like to go on a walk with me? Let me show you the rest of the castle."

She accepted, and they walked side by side, keeping a slow, steady pace. The sun had disappeared behind the clouds, and as dusk came, a cool breeze accompanied it. The walk around the castle had been an unplanned, spontaneous decision, so they had both rushed out of the hall without their coats. Vlad Tepes drank in her beauty as they strolled, unable to get himself to stop staring at her. He told her stories about the castle that made her giggle and brush her head lightly against his shoulder. They circled the water fountain several times, but neither of them noticed.

"Maybe I should have brought my coat with me," Lady Justina said.

"And why is that, my lady?" "It is getting chilly already."

Vlad Tepes took off his jacket and placed it around her shoulders. His inner was fitted, and it clung to every muscle on his chest; without his jacket, the shirt was all he had on and Justina was given a view of his perfectly sculptured muscles. "Thank you," she said as they sat on a slab by the fountain. The duo continued their conversation into the night, enjoying the evening atmosphere and the beauty of the night sky. Just before midnight, Vlad Tepes' tone became a little more serious, and he informed Lady Justina that he had something that he would like her to know. He confessed his feelings for her while she sat there, trying to get a grip on her emotions. He purred several reactions from her, but none of it was love. She was confused, she felt beautiful, curious, doubtful, and unsure, and she felt compassion and desire, but she couldn't feel the same way Vlad was communicating to her. He said he could not stop thinking about her, and she couldn't stop thinking about him either, but for a different reason.

In the end, Vlad Tepes proposed to her and asked her to be his forever bride. Lady Justina mused at the choice of words. Forever meant a long time, and she was not yet certain what her disposition was. While she took her time to come up with an answer, he explained to her he had asked her out for a walk so that he could propose. It was a spontaneous event as she would like it; he had given it some thought and decided he wanted to be married to her. "My lady," he said. "Look at me."

When she did, he took her hands in his. "This is not about your cousin. I know the king is trying to make a match with us and wants us to be married to form an alliance, but this is not about that, my lady. This is about you and how much I care about you. I want it to be your choice. You decide if you will have me, not your cousin. What do you want, my lady?" Justina's eyes softened. He'd had her attention throughout the night, but he recaptured it now. Her eyes roamed his body when he asked her to look at him, and she tried to focus them on his face, but then he asked her what she wanted, without thinking, the words that came out of her mouth were, "I want you."

She gasped and placed a hand over her mouth, but Vlad Tepes laughed, looking at her lovingly, and she chuckled. After the laughter died down, she agreed to his proposal. She had already made it slip that she wanted him, and he was right when he said it was her decision and she had gone for what she wanted.

This time, she had been given a choice. It made her feel differently about this marriage, and she looked forward to it. She could already tell it was going to be an adventurous ride and the fact her fiancé would dare defy her cousin by saying he would not marry her if she did not want it intoxicated her. Vlad Tepes was thrilled, and lifting his fiancée by the waist, he sealed it with a kiss.

CHAPTER TWENTY NINE

CASTLE BRAN, TRANSYLVANIA VLAD TEPES AND LADY JUSTINA'S WEDDING, 1575

The sun shone brightly over Transylvania on the day of the wedding. Probably the brightest that any of the inhabitants had ever experienced. The whole town glowed together with the sun, radiating brilliant joy and elation. Since the count had announced two weeks ago that he was to be wedded to his heartthrob, Lady Justina Szilagyi of Hungary, and that both families would be bound in the closest, most sacred form of alliance, the entire town has been in a state of non-stop excitement.

Everyone whispered happily about it, making plans to support the count and his to-be bride in whatever way they could. And when the count announced the invitation was open to all, and the celebration was to last for three whole days, the townspeople did him one better and begin their celebration ahead of time. Men and women flooded the castle with gifts, each bringing their contribution, small and big but filled with love and good wishes towards the intended couple. And now, finally, the day arrived.

Castle Bran had transformed. It was quite difficult to tell what it once looked like. The once cold, dark, and brooding fortress was now a warm, colorful field surrounded by flowers. The castle brimmed with life, laughter, and the sweet-smelling aroma of palatable meals. The castle staff worked themselves to the bone, going over and beyond to ensure the wedding was an event to remember yet none seemed weary or complained about the extra work. They did it cheerfully, much to Vlad Tepes' surprise. He was overwhelmed with gratitude at the display of loyalty and love exhibited by his staff and subjects. Before the day, men from the village arrived at the castle, volunteering to contribute their time and help the count out however they could. They had fixed the broken furniture in the castle, patched up the walls, trimmed the hedges, and done whatever menial chore there was to do. The castle servants worked alongside them, happily lending a hand when needed and glad for the help the townsmen were giving. To reciprocate, Vlad Tepes had the castle kitchen prepare a meal for the men so that every evening after the day's work, the townsmen and the castle servants held a mini ball where they ate and danced.

The women were not left out. They offered to decorate and clean every chamber in the castle, every wing, every nook, and cranny.

Angela scurried down the stairs as she struggled with several boxes of presents. The castle was looming with guests and servants running around with one or two in hand.

"That color is odd!" she said to the servant setting the curtains. "Change the bright pink to a cooler tone." She looked closely at it again, scrutinizing the color combination. She turned and waved her hands in dismissal, then continued with her chores.

Never had they ever imagined Lady Justina was this big of royalty and was getting married to a strong man. None of her friends were left out; Elena brought a gift of an embroidered kerchief she had made herself. Nicolae, one of the lovely and sweet recipes he had, was gifted to Lady Justina.

"For the bride-to-be!" the servant announced as he passed the box of presents to a maid standing at the entrance of the chamber.

Esme directed the servants and maids to get everything prepared as Lady Justina would have wanted it to be. She was simple, definitely, but knew how to get you on your toes if you were not careful.

"No, no, no, Lady Esme!" the head servant said as he tried to bring Esme down from the ladder she was climbing. "My lady strictly said there should be no stressful chores for you. You just sit and we'll do our jobs," he added with a smile.

Esme smiled and blushed. "But I can't sit and do nothing, especially when it's Lady Justina's happy day," she told him. "She wouldn't know if I did anything. She's not here yet!"

"I can't let you do that, my lady. Orders have been strictly set that I must follow. I don't want my head on a plate when she finds out."

"Alright," Esme said, throwing her hands in the air in defeat. "So what did she say I am to do, then?"

"Sit and enjoy the scenery of our beloved castle. I can assign you a guard to show you around the city. I bet you will love it." He smiled convincingly. "And you get a special invite again!" "Well, as much as I would love to help with the chores, I wouldn't want to have you losing your head." They both laughed and left the chamber.

Dozens of women stationed themselves in the laundry room, dishing out batches after batches of clean, pleasant-smelling linens for the chambers in the castle, while some of them sewed new sets of curtains, knitted tablecloths, and napkins, and designed them with beautiful embroideries. The maids cleaned out every chamber in the castle, dusted them out, and aired them for the rest of the day. By evening, they rested and joined the men and the servants for the mini feast.

Lady Justina arrived at Castle Bran a week before the wedding, and the whole of Transylvania was agog with excitement. Kids ran out of their homes, dragging their parents along, and crowded the road she was to take to the castle, screaming and cheering for her.

Lady Justina hid behind the curtains of the carriage, unsure of how to react to the people's reception. She had not expected the town to cause a riot on her arrival and make a big deal of a reception. Their warmhearted gesture touched her and slowly gathered the courage to respond appropriately to their exhilaration. It was easy to react, their excitement was contagious, so as soon as she drew back the curtains on the carriage, a wide, cheerful smile filled her face and she reached out happily to them, waving and laughing and thanking them for the warm welcome. Even after she got to the castle and was escorted to the premarital chamber where she would stay and undergo all the premarital beautification rites, she was still smiling and giggly.

All the while, during her one-week stay at the castle, Vlad Tepes was not allowed to see her. He had heard her arrival, accompanied by the loud noise and cheerful uproar, but he merely glimpsed her before she disappeared, snatched away by the women who were to beautify her for the ceremony.

She had captured his heart, just as he was gradually doing hers. Right from when he had first set his eyes on her, Vlad knew there was something different about Justina. It was like a love that was bound to happen, arranged or not, and he vowed to love her more every day.

He glimpsed her while she was talking to one woman. Her purple, gold-encrusted corset gown rested beautifully on her smooth, silk skin.

While he was being held captive by King Matthias, he received his first glimpse of her. When he had first seen her, the moon's ethereal light had just set the stadium ablaze with silver. She had a pretty figure that gradually became more shapely. The saffron undertones in her skin more than anything else blew his mind when he saw her. Her curvilinear waist didn't even come close. She needed to be a noble, the king's cousin, otherwise, he would have kept the notion to himself, and everyone agreed on that.

When she knew Vlad was looking at her, the arch in her eyebrows made very little upward movement. He let out a scream since he was trapped. Her long, sluggish eyelashes that were the color of velvet fluttered once, slowly as if to invite him, and she smiled at him. As he got closer, he noticed her cute little ears that pointed in the opposite direction and her trendy nostrils. He couldn't put his faith in it as she nuzzled him up against her nose and kissed him. It had become a tradition for her people, and he speculated that either her actions or her actions alone showed that she had fallen in love with him. At first light, love sprang between them. As he took her slender arms, which had red, flowery spherical nails, her brilliant, heavenly-white teeth flashed in his direction.

Her hair looked like a beautiful tumble of golden star beams, and the virility in her eyes made his heart go a-thumping. Her quivering lips drooled with all kinds of deliciousness. Oh! He was completely charmed by her sugar syrup–candy lips and her sophisticated demeanor. She spoke to him in a hushed tone that was as enchanting as the singing of any bird. Her fashionable attire still held a scent that was reminiscent of cinnamon and mint that had just been picked from the meadow. It remained in the bedroom long after she had left, even though she was no longer there.

He smiled as the memories replayed in his head as he sat on the royal chair and sipped his wine. He was lucky. Indeed, he was!

Every other day leading up to the wedding had passed by quickly, filled up with activities, but for Vlad Tepes, none of the activities were long enough to keep his mind occupied. The days dragged on slowly, and even more so because his bride was just within reach, but he couldn't see her. Anticipation and excitement welled up inside of him each day as the wedding day drew closer.

Now it was finally here, his joy could not be contained.

An invitation had been sent out to the priest after both parties involved, which of course included King Matthias, had decided on and agreed on the date for the wedding. The priest arrived with his carriage, accompanied by two other priests, shortly before King Matthias arrived with his convoy. The party location soon filled up quickly after that. Kings and Princes of other territories turned up for the occasion, but not the emperor. King Matthias did not bother to send out an invitation to him, and since he was not exactly a close ally of Vlad Tepes, he did not receive an invitation from the groom, either. Lady Justina's guest size was small; she invited her old friends from Brasov, Nicolae and Angela, and the ladies she had befriended. Esme was in attendance, as well as her maidservants. She had pleaded with the king to be allowed to stay until after the wedding.

The castle was packed full, and the guests spilled over to outside the castle gate. Most of the people in the castle were royal dignitaries and their servants. The rest of the town was seated outside the castle gates. The gates were flung open so that everyone could get a glimpse of what was going on in the castle, but guards were stationed at every entrance to ensure order. It was the most beautiful and colorful ceremony, with every castle servant dressed in ceremonial robes. Every king and royal official were dressed in their official attire, looking fabulously regal.

The fountain where Vlad Tepes had proposed to Lady Justina had been decorated with beautiful, sweet-smelling flowers to look like a vibrant, colorful stage. The decorator had formed a huge arch made of flowers right in front of the fountain, while the perimeter was covered in flowers. It was a sight to see. The fountain poured out water in an upward motion that trickled down to form a pool at the feet of the statue and the flowers danced around freely in the pool. The arch, which served as the main attraction of the stage and the altar where the couple would be joined as man and wife, was interwoven with bright candles.

An aisle was created from the entrance of the left wing of the castle, which was the closest doorway to the fountain to the huge arch. The aisle was a drawn out, long, green carpet bordered by tall pillars laced with white blossoms. Before the ceremony started, servants walked in between the crowd with trays of little snacks and drinks.

The start of the ceremony was announced by the sound of the trumpet blowing to announce the arrival of the Count of Transylvania, Voivode of Wallachia, and bridegroom of the day, Vlad Tepes. The people stood at once at the sound of the trumpet as he strode down the aisle, elegantly dressed in a navy-blue three-piece suit. The outer jacket was designed with clean-cut diamond pieces, with a clean circular cut in front just above the belt line, which made the back of the jacket longer. He wore a hat in the same shade as his outfit and looked every bit a dashing, powerful, and happy groom. The people saluted quietly, standing still as he entered. When he got to the foot of the arch where the priest was waiting, he bowed to the people and moved to stand on the right while he waited for the bride.

The sound of the organ came up shortly after Vlad took his place at the arch, ushering in the bride, escorted by the king. The bride was ravishingly radiant in her beautiful, silver- studded wedding dress. The dress shimmered under the sunlight, giving off the impression of it being lit with a million tiny stars. To further create the perfect ambiance, the torches mounted onto the huge arch at the end of the aisle lit with fire just before Lady Justina waltzed slowly down the aisle. A light gasp swept through the crowd and people murmured amongst themselves about how beautiful she looked. Vlad Tepes was filled with awe and pride at the sight of his bride. He watched her with a huge smile on his face, unable to take his eyes off her.

King Matthias let go of her hand a few feet away from the groom, and she walked the rest of the way alone, taking graceful, calculated steps. She had a smile on her face, but she felt conscious and overdressed. The women that helped her get dressed had assured her she looked every bit a princess, and she knew that. She would have just preferred to tone it down a little. But, right now, as she looked at the expression on the surrounding faces, she understood what the women had been trying to create, and from the looks of this, they did hit the mark.

"You look stunning," Vlad Tepes said when she got to the front and stood opposite him.

Seeing her walk down the aisle to meet him, Vlad lost his breath and senses and muttered some words.

"To love and to cherish, till death do us part. According to God's holy ordinance, and thereto I pledge thee my faith," He repeated after the priest, concluding the vows.

"With the grace of God and the power vested in me, I now pronounce you husband and wife," the priest said, giving them the final blessing.

Justina bit her lip, she was finally his. "You may kiss the bride."

Vlad Tepes obeyed that instruction to the letter.

She was beautiful, even right from the time he had set his eyes on her. Justina smiled; the widest Vlad had ever seen her smile before, that only made his heart skip and rendered him weak in the knees.

The rest of the day passed by in festive activities. The people danced, ate, drank, and danced some more, laughing happily. The couple took the first dance, after which several others joined them on the dance floor. The partying and celebrating continued until late into the night for the Transylvanian residents.

King Matthias stayed for the festivities but left later that night after giving the couple his goodwill and blessings. The priest also left to return to the city, but the Transylvanians stayed all night, partying for long, eating, drinking, and making merry.

"I am happy for you, Your Majesty," one guest said to King Matthias.

"Yes," King Matthias replied with a flush and pride in his voice. It was an alliance that benefited him. That had been his aim since he had been on the throne; to form allies for himself and his kingdom with whatever tactic he had to used to get it. He was a smart king; after all, everything had been planned, set, and predicted by him. Vlad Tepes was a very strong ally he already had on his side.

"I wish them the blessings from above," the man said again. The king didn't say a word but nodded to his servants, who took their leave.

King Matthias was so happy for his unborn child.

Esme lived very far away from him until the baby was born. She stayed in a beautiful and well polished house all thanks to her rich lover. Carrying this child for the King was the best thing she had ever done.

Soon, her belly protruded. She somehow felt that this child was going to be a boy. She remembered the superstitions of pregnancy.

"If it's a boy, the mother will look prettier during her pregnancy."

She had heard her fellow maids gossip about other people's pregnancies. Now she'll be the main center of the gossip, she thought.

Her new home was so comfortable, but she was very lonely.

She hoped Lady Justina was doing just fine in her new home. She had made a new friend, though, Christina. Christina had the kindest heart and even though she was busy most of the time, she always visited Esme and bring her fruits. "Staring at the window again?" Christina giggled. "You must miss your home."

"I do, I miss everyone in it. I guess I'm in my new home now. I should probably get used to it," she sighed.

"I would have loved to take you there, but that would be a risk because we don't want to be having the child in the middle of nowhere." They laughed.

"Why? Are you scared of helping me deliver a baby?" She giggled.

"No no, Esme. I'm only scared of the situation." "I can deliver your baby, why not?" She smiled.

They celebrated their Prince and his newlywed Princess in the grandest style.

The second day of the festivity ended with an inauguration ceremony for Vlad Tepes' new bride, Lady Justina Szilagyi, as the Princess of Transylvania. The couple had held the inaugural ceremony in the evening, just as the sun retired behind the clouds. The castle was a beehive of activities during the day to prepare for the last and final part of the two-day, non-stop celebration. The theme for the inaugural ceremony was an all-black event, to create a mysterious ambiance and to achieve that, the decorations in the ballroom had to be taken down and replaced with dark flowers and decors, with candles lighting the room up with their flames.

By evening, the hall was transformed and ready for the ceremony. The bright amber torches hung from the ceiling, strung together by white string, and suspended from the air so that the string looked invisible, creating the illusion of the fire hanging in midair on its own. Everyone that entered the hall was filled with awe and could not contain their expressions. The flames were lit as dusk approached, further beautifying the atmosphere. The guests arrived and took their seats just like they did two days back when their Prince got married.

The sound of the organ playing announced the soon-to-be-inaugurated Princess and she marched forward in a beautiful mermaid-style, black dress. On both hands, she wore black lace, and her hair was pulled back to reveal the beautiful outline of her face. Her lips were bright red, and they stood out like a vibrant contrast against the otherwise dark background. Vlad Tepes was on the stage, just like at the wedding, close to the officiating priest.

It was just like a second wedding, but with an emphasis on the Princess' coronation.

The Prince of Transylvania had chosen to have both events performed separately, so that night, the focus was on the newly crowned Princess. The Princess said the pledge after the officiating priest and vowed allegiance to Transylvania and her residents before everyone gathered there and before her husband. After the coronation rites, she was bestowed with the crown jewel and proclaimed the Princess before everyone. The people cheered and clapped happily.

The rest of the night was spent in celebration, as a cumula- tion of all the events leading up to that evening. The Prince and Princess opened the dance floor with a dance to which everyone cheered. At the end of their dance, other couples took the stage and danced the night away. Trays after trays of meals rolled out of the kitchen, accompanied by drinks and the people helped themselves to they could eat.

While the party continued in full force inside the hall, the Princess asked the kitchen servants to hand out packs of food for the villagers to take back home with them as there was more than enough.

The people received their packages with gratitude and when they found out it was based on the Princess' instructions, their love for her grew and they chanted her praise outside the castle gates.

~ ∞ ~

The festivities had finally ended, and Vlad was granted the chance to finally be able to spend some quality, uninterrupted time with his bride. Every night since they were joined together as man and wife, he had yearned for her, but tiredness or servants or certain festivity had gotten in the way. Now that it was all over, he could not try to hold back the desire anymore. And he was certain he was not alone in his longing, he had seen the look in her eyes every time they were together, and it had sparked an even hotter fire in him. Finally, he could get to explore that fire all he wanted.

"You look…" he began, but he was too stunned to speak, so he moved closer to her, running his hands through her hair to free them from the pins holding them up in a bun. The hair cascaded down her back in glorious waves. He let his hands linger as he admired every inch of her.

She stood still, enthralled by his spell, unable to resist his charm, and she didn't want to. Every fiber of her being pulsed with desire for him, and she subconsciously angled her body closer to him. He pulled her closer to himself, tasting her with his tongue. He ran his tongue over her lips, her neck, and her collarbone. She moaned and arched her head backward so her upper body lay vulnerable and tempting before him. He ran his hands over her body, stripping off her clothes, then lifted her easily and laid her down on the bed, letting his tongue trail every other part of her body. She was soft and yielding, drunk with as much passion as he was. The feel of her skin on his tongue set him over the edge, and he pinned her down under him, raising her legs to rest on his hips. Justina felt his arousal against the pit of her stomach and ran her tongue over her lips.

As they ravaged each other, drinking in the essence of the other person, she slipped her hands into his pants, pulling them off hastily so she could see and feel his naked body. She ran her hands over his organ, caressing it lovingly. When he let out a deep, throaty groan, she knew she was hitting the right chord, so she placed her hands on his shoulders and pulled herself up. With her legs still wrapped around his waist, she bounced up and down on his erection. Her action was a two-way sword as it pierced her with as much hunger as she stimulated in him. She moaned and gasped, brushing her breasts against his chest with every movement. It was both torture and pleasure, and she couldn't take it anymore. She wanted to feel him inside her and wanted him to bury himself deep inside her curves.

He reciprocated by pushing her back onto the bed and raising her legs so she opened against him, filling his nostrils with an erotic scent. He trailed a hand down the length of her legs to the slick opening between, while his other hand supported his weight. He opened her up with his thumb and slipped two fingers inside her. Justina gasped and let out a guttural moan as waves upon waves of tantalizing sensations washed over her. Her brain went blank, and she could only focus on the feel of his fingers. He slipped another finger in, sending her over the edge.

She clawed at him while her toes curled in ecstasy at his back. Her body melted against him as a sweet sensation washed over her. She felt so light like she was floating on the waves of passion. His hands were so strong and skilled, and they inched upwards inside of her until his finger found her spot. He must have known when he touched it because she drew in a sharp breath. He stimulated it with his hands, and she shattered under his influence. Everything else faded into the dark, and at that moment, it was just her overwhelmed by a sensual wave of passion. Her body tingled and ached, and yet she could not get enough. He slipped his fingers out slowly, deliberately, watching her expression as he did. He placed both hands on her buttocks, lifting her slightly as he filled the void that his fingers left with a quick, deep thrust. Justina moaned as he entered her, relishing the bittersweet feeling. Instinctively, she tightened against him, enjoying the feel of him inside her. She could feel him close to her stomach, and a mischievous grin played on her face as she relished the fact that he was big and strong as she had imagined. He set a steady tempo, thrusting her slowly as he began, but taking up the tempo with each. He went hard and fast, losing himself in the tight, warm feel of her and the sultry tone of her moans. He rode her fearlessly, passionately, and she moved with him, matching him stroke for stroke. He took up the tempo with each thrust, transporting both of them in bliss beyond words. They climaxed together, and their bodies exploded in a burst of ecstasy.

She clung tightly to him afterward, not wanting to let go of the rapturous feelings still washing over her, and he wanted it as much as she did; he was thinking the same thing. He wrapped himself around her, spooning her and massaging her backside with his hands, trailing patterns up and down her hips. She purred softly and nestled her head against his chest.

As she curled up in bed with him later that night, straddling his thighs with hers, she felt so many sweet tingling sensations run through her, with a rising hunger for him.

She wanted him. She was ready to go again, and she felt like she would be throughout the rest of the night.

CHAPTER THIRTY

CASTLE BRAN, TRANSYLVANIA A FEW MONTHS AFTER THE MARRIAGE

Life in Transylvania was a lot better than she had imagined, and so was being married to Vlad Tepes.

He was every bit the powerful ruler her cousin had hinted he was, and she suspected that was why he was so interested in her husband. She, however, was captivated for other reasons. Vlad Tepes was as gentle as he was tough and strong, and although they had been married for a few months and shared the same bed every night since, she couldn't get over how attractive and dashing he was, and she certainly couldn't get enough of him. He was great company, and he made his affections for her as clear as day. And she was loving him dearly.

Every day, he would get her flowers and put them by her bedside. Justina loved him and was ready to do anything for him. Vlad was funny; his sense of humor always blew Justina's mind.

"I was right to guess that I would find you here," she said as she opened the door to his private reading room wide.

"Ah... you caught me," Vlad said as he laughed, motioning her in. "And what surprise do I get today?"

Justina walked slowly and steadily towards the table. She was wearing a bright green, see-through gown and her milky thighs showed halfway. Vlad's eyes traveled down her legs and back to her bare neck, then to her face. He wore a gold robe with crystal stones embedded in the neckline and end seams.

The study was big, bigger than King Matthias', and had lots of books. Vlad was a tactical man, but he wasn't ignorant. Justina sat on the edge of the big table, a few meters away from him.

"What have you been up to?" she asked. "Nothing much, my lady."

"Enough to keep me at a distance?"

"Not at all, my lady. I dare not do that, lest my precious head be food for the birds of Transylvania," he said, faking a bow. "You are the most precious, sweetest, purest, and fairest of all maidens. I dare not defy you or keep you at any distance."

Justina laughed, throwing her head back slightly and for- ward to gain her balance. "You are not forgiven yet!" She crossed her legs, exposing the skin of her thighs. "You shall be punished duly for your offense. I shall speak with the council and decide your punishment myself."

Vlad tried to suppress his laugh and bit his lip. His wife was funny, there was never a dull moment with her, and definitely, she was pure of heart; her intentions were real and true.

"And what is it I may know, my lady?"

"I have decided with the council and some say to send you to the chamber of heavenly ecstasy. Do you plead guilty or not?"

Vlad's eyes lit up, and a smile came from the corner of his mouth. "I accept my fate with a grateful heart and open arms." He rose to his feet, walking towards her. "I guess that's how the heavens have dealt with me. My fate," he paused, "lies in their hands and yours."

She sat well on the table and faced him, her eyes looking up at him with desire in her eyes.

He cupped her face in his hands and looked straight into her eyes. "I am yours, my lady. You can punish me the way you want." His hands slid up her gown and into the middle of her legs, feeling her fresh, soft thighs.

It drove him crazy and intoxicated him like fine wine. Her fingertips traced his jawline and settled on his lips. His mouth came crashing into hers and she devoured every one of his kisses in ecstasy. She felt hot on the inside with passion and want. He pulled her closer to him, feeling every part of her body. Her nipples were erect, standing out of her thin gown, and made him go hard with desire.

She slowly directed his hand to her bosom, squeezing it with her hand on his.

"Would you take me to the chamber at which I shall be punished, my lady?" he asked in between the kisses.

"I decide where your punishment shall take place," she whispered in his ear.

A naughty smile appeared on his lips. Placing his hands gently on her waist, he went for her neck, kissing it hungrily. Soft moans escaped her compressed lips; her inner wear was already damp. She put her hand around his neck, throwing her head back.

Slowly lifting her gown, he felt her wetness, making her moan loudly. Sliding two wet fingers into her, he felt her close around them. She was enjoying it and so was he. He would tease her until she became wild with desire, wanting every part of him.

Her rings of pleasure rang through the whole room. She wanted him. She wanted to feel him down there and bring her to new heights.

"What do you want, my lady?" he said into her ear. "I want you," she said amidst the pleasure.

"Tell me how you want me, my love. I shall abide by any of your punishments."

"I want you in… to feel your mightiness in this riptide of pleasure."

He smiled and kissed her. Sliding his fingers inside and out of her, he stopped suddenly, jolting her back to the present.

"What is wrong, my love?" she asked with a puzzled look. "Did I hurt you?" Perhaps he had dug his nails too deep.

"My punishment, my lady. I hope I shall not have my hands cut off from my body?" he asked, running his hand through her hair.

Her husband only intended to tease her. She understood what he wanted to do. "If you do not carry out your punish- ment well, I shall have no choice but to take your fingers away," she replied. She spread her legs on the table. She licked her fingers and slid two into herself. Vlad's eyes went wide with excitement. He closed the little distance left between them and crashed his lips onto hers.

Giving her a view of his shaft, he teased it around her welcoming spot, causing her to go wild in her desire.

"Don't take away these fingers, my lady. It won't let me do the work of serving my punishment well," he replied, smiling naughtily from the corner of his mouth. Gaining full balance and control, he slid in, letting out a guttural moan. He knew how to please her, the right spots to touch, and it made her go crazy every time they did.

He thrust slowly, and she followed his pace, which became heightened as they were both close on the verge of ecstasy. As he shoved in hard, her eyes rolled grabbing him tight and her nails digging deep into his skin; he followed suit, filling her up with his seed.

The days after their three-day wedding ceremony had been spent mostly in the company of the other. She blushed as she remembered those days. The only way to describe them would be magical. After such bouts of pleasure and intense copulation, it was only natural that she would have news for him.

She woke up feeling light-headed and her chest felt like there was stuck in there. Like a meal she had the previous night. She turned to the other side of the bed and didn't feel him there. She opened her eyes and the sun almost blinded her.

"What did I eat last night?" she asked herself as she scratched her head. Immediately, she got off the bed and ran to the bowl resting on the table in the middle of the room and almost vomited her insides out. Her head rang, and she sat on the floor to support herself.

Slowly, she walked back to the bed and sat on the edge. Vlad would be in his chamber reading or sorting some things out and she wouldn't want to disturb him.

"Andrea," she called her maidservant.

"At your service, my lady," she said curtsying.

"Fetch me the court physician." She lay down and covered herself. She didn't understand why she was feeling feverish and nauseous. "And not a word to Vlad." She didn't want her husband to worry if he understood there was something wrong with her. Maybe she had eaten too much and had to relieve her bowels by taking some herbs. She wouldn't want to disturb her husband over something she could handle by herself.

Immediately, the maidservant scurried out of the room, closing the door gently behind her and heading straight for the royal infirmary.

The court physician, Ervin, was busy mixing some herbs for the young patient sitting in front of him. Andrea whispered into his ear and immediately called his younger assistant to continue his task and left the infirmary quickly.

"The court phy—" the servant announced but was cut short by Lady Justina.

"Let him in."

"Your Grace, you called for me," he said as he paid his respects.

"Yes, I did, Ervin. I have been feeling sick these days, although my lord doesn't know about it yet," Lady Justina explained. "I woke up feeling feverish, and I vomited all morning. I have been waking late and feeling sleepy, too."

The court physician sighed. He had worked his whole life as the castle physician. His father had before him, and his son would after he was gone. He was comfortable to be with, with squinting eyes that showed years of seeing a lot of things. He was mostly quiet, not usually talking much, and mostly observing. When Lady Justina saw him for the first time, she must have thought his hair was unusual with the look she gave him, her eyes lingering above his head. It was very long and winter-white. He had crow's feet in the corners of his eyes. He had a fine, defined jawline that suggested he must have been handsome when he was younger, and that must be why everyone liked him and wanted to be around him. His teeth shined like piano keys, and his eyes were a brilliant cerulean blue that had never been seen before.

However, it became difficult to tell his age, and Lady Justina estimated he was probably in his fifties. He may wish to seem a bit aged, as though life and age are getting the better of him. This may be the case when he is speaking. However, he has always maintained a refined and correct appearance, and his experience in the fashion world has not derailed him.

He put his hand on her temple and then on her belly. He took her small, delicate hands and checked something on her palm. Lady Justina watched him as if he was telling her future. His fingers rested on the center of her hand, and he checked her eyeballs. How would he know what was wrong with her by just reading her palm? Well, of course, he knew immediately, but he still wouldn't jump to conclusions. She might be short on enriching herbs and needed to take more to help the flow of blood to the proper places.

"You look pale, Your Grace," he said and picked up his bag. "I shall get back to you soon enough. Don't be afraid. There is nothing alarming wrong with you," His calm voice echoed the confidence and surety of his job. He smiled at her and bowed before leaving the room.

He looked at her again before closing the door and gave her another smile that was almost brighter than the candles. It transformed his face, and the years dropped away.

Lady Justina didn't do or eat much. After checking up on her husband, she spent most of her time with Angela. She was friendly with everyone in the castle, just as she was when she lived in her cousin's castle, and they all liked her.

The physician came back minutes later with a smile plastered all over his face. Justina wondered what made him suddenly beam with joy.

"What is wrong? Did anything happen?"

"Nothing of concern, my lady. I have brought good news you would be pleased to hear." He settled the tray he was holding on the bedside table.

"Tell me what it is." She sat up. "I can't deal with the suspense."

"Please be calm, Your Grace, I will tell you. But first, I want you to use these. They will allow you to eat and prevent throwing up." He handed her a bowl of herbs.

She drank and her face went sour, her brows arched together in disgust, and her lips firmly pressed together.

"I thought you said it wasn't bitter."

He chuckled. "I didn't say if it was bitter or not, my lady."

Lady Justina eyed him and laughed. He wasn't bad after all and not weird either.

"Spare me the suspense. Please, tell me," Justina asked. "My lord is expecting an heir very soon, my lady." He bowed.

Lady Justina couldn't believe her ears. "You mean I am with child?" she asked, and the old man nodded while smiling.

It had taken her a while to come to terms with the new reality, but when she did, she couldn't get over the feeling of unspeakable joy, and she glowed. She never realized she would be that happy over such news.

Vlad Tepes was in his chamber when she found him because she had been moving around the whole castle in search of him. He was rarely in his chamber these past days as he had been preparing to go on a trip, where he was to be crowned as the Voivode of Transylvania. She had been so proud of him when she received the news, and she still was. She lingered at the door when she got to his chambers, watching him quietly for a moment, trying to think of the different ways he might react to the news. He caught sight of her when he turned and called out to her.

"My lady…" he said gently, motioning for her to go to him. "You look so lost in thought. What is the matter?"

She smiled. "Oh, it's nothing," she said, then corrected herself. "It is something. I have something to tell you."

Vlad Tepes tried to keep a calm and composed demeanor as he waited for her to spill what was on her mind. He would have been alarmed, but her expression calmed him down. She looked happy and shy, and it made him curious. Not once did the possibility of the actual news cross his mind.

"I was sick the other day," she began, and his cool demeanor broke off at once. His brows creased with worry, and he was beside her, feeling her temperature and trying to find out if she had a fever or any symptoms.

"Are you okay?" he asked, his tone deeply laced with concern. "Do you need me to call the court physician?"

"Well, I have seen the court physician, and he... he sent me a message for you..." She gave a mischievous grin.

He led her to sit at the edge of the bed and sat close to her, just in case it was news that he couldn't take while standing.

And it indeed turned out to be!

"I'm pregnant!" Lady Justina said, looking into his eyes and waiting for his reaction.

"What?" he gasped. Relief washed over him, coupled with tons of other overwhelming emotions such as joy and pure love. He threw his head back in laughter, and when he was done, he lifted his wife and embraced her in a warm hug, pelting her face with kisses. He was truly overjoyed.

He drew her closer, placed his lips against her ears, and whispered just how much he loved her, then kissed her lips.

Vlad Tepes departed from Transylvania about a month later with his men, leaving her in charge of the affairs of Transylvania as Princess of the kingdom. He told her how much he would miss her and promised to write as often as he could, and made her promise to reciprocate. They set out immediately, and she watched from the balcony as they departed.

* * *

The baby bump grew as each day passed, along with mood swings and funny, weird cravings. She would walk to the garden every day to sniff the flowers and sit among them. One would think she was performing a ritual or an experiment to discover a new fragrance.

Lady Justina was in her room one sunny afternoon when she heard a knock on the door. A petite figure with curly hair in a fine, flowery gown walked into the room, smiling as she came in.

"My lady, are you okay?" Angela asked as she sat on the edge of the bed, worry written all over her face. She had volunteered to stay with her until Justina gave birth. Esme was a mother now and had the duty of taking care of her newborn baby.

"I am fine," Lady Justina replied as she rubbed her face with the back of her palm. "I am just starving, and I want to go out."

A tear ran down her cheek.

"Is that why you are crying?" Angela asked in surprise.

"I am not crying. The tears won't just stop falling from my face," she said as more tears fell. "I guess it's because I miss my husband, or maybe I'm just hungry."

Angela tried to conceal the laughter that was building up inside of her. It was the mood swings pregnant women experienced. "Alright, my lady, it's okay." She moved close and wiped away Justina's tears. "What do you want me to get for you? I'll do it right away."

Lady Justina was quiet for a while and then finally broke the silence. "I want to get the bread in town."

"The bread in town?" Angela asked in surprise. There were different flavors of bread in the castle and the special one she used to make with her husband. "There are—"

"I know, Angela, I don't want those. They all taste the same."

Angela opened her mouth to laugh. There was flavored bread; the special olive and buttered flavor, amongst others. "Alright, my lady, I'll send a servant to get it for you in the

market. I can't leave you all by yourself."

"No, no. I want to go get them myself. My legs are swollen a bit and are killing me." Lady Justina gently put her leg up for Angela to see.

"I see, my lady. You can take a walk around the castle or in the garden—"

"No, Angela, I don't want to walk around the castle or anywhere here. It's boring. I walked there today."

"It's three o'clock, and the sun is up and dazzling," Angela complained. "And besides, the Prince strictly warned me not to allow you to do anything strenuous or anything that could hurt you."

"I am not walking to the market, Angela, and besides, when did walking become something that could hurt?" Lady Justina laughed. "I'll be in the carriage, but I'll walk when I get to town."

Angela shook her head in disapproval. It was not safe for Lady Justina to walk around far from the castle. She could fall into labor, and it would be quite a distance to get the court physician to help.

"But…" She hesitated. "You know, I would always want to look out for you. I don't want you to get hurt."

"Angela…" She looked into her eyes in a way Angela could no longer resist. "I'll be fine. I promise. I am grateful for your help. You have been much more to me, and I am sorry for making you uncomfortable."

"Don't say that. You've done so much for me, for us. Even while you were working for us back then." She smiled. "Alright, my lady. We leave before it gets too late. I don't want us heading back to the castle late at night." She said firmly but softly. "I'll be back in a few minutes to get you prepared." She headed for the door.

Lady Justina went to the balcony for some air. She had a warm bath prepared for her, so she freshened up before she went on her expedition. She felt heavy as her legs ached with each step; it was going to be a big and healthy baby.

"Ohhh." She chuckled as she felt a slight kick. "You are eager to go out with me, right? Yes, I am, too." She rubbed her belly gently. "I can't wait to see you. We'll see so many lovely places together." She smiled.

Angela came back some minutes later, and they got into the carriage to town. She had packed some things they would need in case anything happened. She had some neatly folded clothes Lady Justina could change into if she vomited. Angela could count the number of times she had had to change the bedspread because she suddenly said she didn't like it or it was making her nauseous.

The court physician had said walking would help her joints be less stiff and ease the pain she usually felt in her thighs. The town was glad to have her visiting as they gave her gifts to take back to the castle for her and the baby. After eating what she wanted, Lady Justina retired back to the castle.

The moon shone in the night sky and a cool breeze blew the curtains as if in a dance parade. Lady Justina walked to the balcony, hands on her protruded belly. She missed her husband very much. How she wished he was there to keep her company. Angela was doing her best, but she desired Vlad's warmth. His manly hands held her and on his shoulder, she could rest her head.

She would write to him. She needed him.

~~~

Days turned into weeks and as time passed slowly and steadily, the time drew closer for Justina's child to be born. According to the court physician, she had a little over two months to go. In her letter to her husband, Justina reiterated the physician's words. She wanted him to be there when their baby was born, and thankfully she wasn't the only one with such a sentiment.

"For you, my lord." The armored man bowed as he presented him with a beautifully embroidered wrap. Vlad knew what it was: a letter from his wife. He took it and nodded to the man, who left. Gently opening the kerchief and bringing out a paper, he smiled.

Immediately, he got to his chair and began writing. He was fine; he had to be, for his unborn child, his wife, and his lands.

~~

To the best woman in the world,

I received your letter with so much happiness and I can't wait to be there with you to watch my precious one arrive in the world. I say to you I am safe and alive, as I have been just for you.

I will be home soon to wrap you in my arms. I miss you even more than you know, my love, for you are the best gift nothing can compare to.

See you soon, my love.

~~

Vlad Tepes' reply came within a week. Lady Justina was delighted. He was safe and alive; that was one of the most important things she wanted to know. Her friends made good company, as they assisted her in every way they could.

She ate a lot and had a constant craving to sniff the flowers in the garden. She would spend hours sitting amidst the flowers and enjoying their beauty.

She was large and uncomfortable and the physician worried that the baby should be here already and tried to find out what was wrong by touching around and feeling for any abnormality. The baby was where it was supposed to be and other than that, she was emotional because it was the day before Vlad would arrive. She had counted on a reason other than just having people gathered; she was feeling great. Angela, Nicolae, Helen, and Esme were there with her to keep her company and Esme tried to talk to her about birthing and give her some advice. Later that day, after lunch and making plans to walk a bit around the castle with her friends, she started having pains in her abdomen and it felt as if the baby was moving in her stomach.

Her back burned and her legs ached to carry her weight. The physician was called, and he urgently attended to Justina, asking Esme to slowly rub her back as she was going into labor. Fright gripped Justina and she begged that she didn't want to go into Labor until Vlad was present. The physician tried to calm her down, and he told her that since it was her first time, it would take hours before the baby arrived.

This relieved Justina a bit as she had already informed Vlad of the expected day and if all was right, he should be on his way back and would hopefully arrive before the hours have gone by. The pains increased, and she was moved into the bath bowl as she tried to stay calm and delay the process.

* * *

Vlad Tepes kept to his word.

"Welcome, Your Grace." The guard at the entrance bowed to him.

Nodding in acknowledgment, he took off his armor. "Where is my wife?"

"She is in her chamber. The baby is coming."

Vlad ran as fast as he could to meet her, his heart thumping in his chest.

Some servants were gathered at the doorway, some with their hands clasped in prayer and some with their ears glued to the door. They tried to stop him from going in but he insisted. The servants started in fear. He didn't say a word, nor did he chase them, but grabbed the knob slowly and gulped before pushing the door in.

Pain that dominated Justina's entire being came with every baby movement that she experienced. In those times, during those seconds that seemed to go on forever, there was nothing else happening at all. She may want to listen to the sounds of the servants coming into and out of the room, but she didn't make a single sound the entire time. When the ache stopped, it became most effective for about a minute, and whilst she breathed, she did it with her eyes closed because she became unwilling to re-engage with existence beyond the boundaries of her own frame. She could not articulate or put her finger on the specific emotions that she experienced over time. Her veins were filled with anxious anticipation. Unlike when the labor had started, now she was eager for this to be over with so she could check on her newborn baby. She has been moved back to her bed from the bath bowl. The room may as well have been empty for all the awareness that she had, and when they conversed, contact, and grab her attention, she determined it was so difficult to pay attention to what they were saying. For her to respond, she had to extricate herself from the most private part of her thoughts and force herself to move ahead so that she could speak and open her eyes.

She screamed, grabbing the ropes tied on the four corners of the bed hard for support. A midwife was present now and was staring at Justina like a mother hen would do her chick.

"Do not push yet. You are almost there."

Sweat trickled down her body like the rain drenched her. Her hair was sticking to her back. She couldn't and didn't care about how she looked.

"My husband!" she said. "Where…?"

"He is here. He will join you soon," the midwife cooed gently as another patted her head, trying to keep her calm.

Vlad walked in, slowly closing the door behind him as the servants continued to eavesdrop from the door. Seeing the state of his wife, he pitied her and was grateful he was there. He couldn't stand the sight. He felt like rushing to the chamber pot and throwing up. Dizziness assaulted him. He wasn't tired, it wasn't a sign of fatigue, but he was scared. A life coming out of another.

How he wished he could ease the pain, but he had to be strong. His heart was beating faster; he had never felt that way before, not even when he impaled his enemies.

He walked up to his wife and gently knelt by her side, holding her hands in his delicately.

She gripped his hand tight, making him wince as she continued in labor. The pain was more than she could handle, but she was glad her husband was there. A wave of strength crashed into her as she felt the baby close.

"You push when I tell you to, my lady," the midwife said, and she replied by nodding aggressively as if wanting to throw the pain away somewhere.

As much as she wanted to see her baby, his face, and touch him, she wanted the pain to end. It was indescribable, more than anything she has ever felt.

Vlad ran his hand through her hair and she impatiently pushed it away. He couldn't watch. It was more of a sight he couldn't behold, one he had never seen before or experienced until now.

"It's going to be okay, my darling. You'll be fine," he said as he tried to maintain his unwavering facade of strength.

The midwife eventually informed her it was time to push on the baby. She performed it with a rumbling sound, and then she was told to stop because it was only allowed one time. She felt the baby crowning and the recent stretching of the flesh, and she held her breath the entire time. The physician handed the baby over to the midwife with no further effort being made on either party's part. After that, when her baby was born, it became as if the greatest sunshine existed on the earth. It turned as if the entire world was ushered into peace, and the moments of terrible pain had long been forgotten. She looked into those fresh eyes, which revealed a brand spanking new awareness, one that was ideal and seeking her love. In that instant, she realized she would do anything to protect her child and that her love had grown to be as massive as the universe but as unyielding as a rock. She gave birth to a child and may always continue to do so. There was elation, a boy at last, and in a matter of seconds he turned into there, innocent, fledgling eyes opening, and a tongue digging for milk.

The noise of the door squeaking awakened her from her sleep. When she looked up, she saw her husband carrying their child while it was wrapped in a fabric that had silver lace on it. A blue blanket was draped over the front of the cot. At that very moment, she realized it would be a boy child. The happiness was clear in Vlad's eyes, and he simply couldn't contain his grin. He lifted him out of the cot and brought him to sit in his hands at the same time while still holding him still. The servants and maidservants gathered, chatting happily and giggling. Vlad sat on the chair next to his wife and held him out on his legs so they could all have a good view. As she turned to look at them over a corner of the big bed, she could see a little head with not very much hair. When she sat up on the bed so she could sit beside her husband, she just stared at the baby. He turned into such a charming little creature; his little eyelids crinkled shut, and he had these teeny eyelashes that looked very adorable. His nostril shrunk to where it looked like a button, and the flush of color that spread across his cheeks made them look like plums picked straight from the tree. It appeared as though he had puckered up his lips, and that they were pink and had a great deal of shape to them. Vlad moved his face close to his to give him a head kiss. He had the most alluring and refreshing aroma. The moment Vlad laid eyes on Justina, he couldn't help but break into a grin. He could not stop the tears from streaming down his face. Lady Justina felt an overwhelming sense of joy at the prospect of welcoming a new child into her life. At that one instant, nothing else meant anything at all. The mother, Justina, had eyes that glowed with boundless compassion and unending love for her child.

Breastfeeding was hard at first. There was pain and bleeding. At first, she had blocked ducts, and when they burst, it was bloody raw. She was a first-time mother and it all felt new to her. There was more pain and discomfort for a few days or more. Even though she had people around to help her, one day blended into the next in a tired blur. But after that, it was easy and pleasurable. She liked it that her little one searched for her breast and the look on his face when he finally found it. Within a short time, her baby was fed and got fatter and healthier. She loved him and named him after his father. He was Vlad Călugărul.

Their first son was a beautiful, pink bundle of joy, and he brought delight to everyone, even his gruff, distant second cousin, the king. Vlad Tepes sent a message to King Matthias, and he sent a congratulatory message, along with lots of gifts, and a promise to pay them a visit in Transylvania to see the newborn, but he never visited.

And that was when the Prince and Princess suspected there might be some cracks in their alliance. Ok.

CHAPTER THIRTY ONE

YEARS LATER...

The Ottomans were a sickening thorn in the flesh. It was hard to be rid of them. No matter how much they were exterminated or pushed back, they would lie low for a while, strategizing and planning to make a return, and when they did, it would cause more havoc and destruction. Vlad Tepes fought endlessly against the Ottomans' encroachment on Transylvania throughout his lifetime, and he became a respected leader among his people for that.

The Ottoman Sultan, Mehmed II, has been a grievous and insatiable ruler, always looking for territories to capture. He eyed the seat of the Voivode of Wallachia. He requested Vlad Tepes pay homage to him personally, but Vlad had a better idea and impaled the Sultan's envoy, sending out a loud and clear message to the sultan. The strife between Vlad Tepes and Sultan Mehmed lingered on for years, with both alternating between offense and defense.

Sultan Mehmed was not to be underestimated either, as he was calculative and scheming. Trying as much as he could to get Vlad out of the way. He posed a serious threat to him anyway, defeating most of his men by impaling them most cruelly ever, although he perfected it by every means possible. Vlad defeated them all by strategizing small ambushes.

The sultan heard about Vlad Tepes' wedding, and thereafter the birth of his child, and decided the Voivode must party and waste away time, being merry that he must have gotten so lax and weak, so he decided that that was the perfect time to strike and claim Transylvania for himself.

Vlad Tepes was a smart man, however, and knew not to allow any room for his enemies to prevail. He had watchtowers built around the city and soldiers on patrol around the kingdom so that with an attack, the news would get to the castle and they would be prepared. His pre-imposed security system paid off one evening when a message arrived from the outlands. Vlad Tepes was on the rooftop of the castle, enjoying the quiet evening breeze with his princess, who was already expecting another child when a guard came to announce a soldier from the outpost.

Vlad could perceive from the guard's expression that some- thing serious was going on and left at once for the courtroom to grant the soldier an audience. He was not the only one, however, to read the atmosphere. Lady Justina noticed the grave expression on the guard who came to announce the unexpected visitor and she did not have a good feeling about it. She left for the courtroom, trailing behind Vlad. Part of the reason that endeared Vlad to her was that he treated her as a person and he filled her in on every activity of the kingdom. He trusted her to the extent of giving her charge of state affairs when he was away. That was not something she could hope for her cousin to do.

She followed closely behind to the courtroom but did not enter, but she listened in and found out the reason for the unscheduled visit— the Ottomans. She gritted her teeth when she heard that name. She was tired of hearing about their constant brawls and sneaky attacks. She had heard so many stories about them, some told by Vlad Tepes himself of how he defeated them, and yet, they never stayed defeated.

"My lord," the soldier said to Vlad while Justina listened in, hidden in the shadows. "He has gathered an army of mercenaries, outcasts, and estranged soldiers... he even made allies of kingdoms that fear you, promoting exaggerated stories of your... your..." The words stopped flowing as the soldier tried to think of a better word to use. He would love to keep his head on his shoulders and still brash at a time such as this would mean the exact opposite.

"Cruelty?" Vlad Tepes said, urging him to keep speaking. The soldier nodded and bowed reverently.

"Hmm, I see." Vlad Tepes replied. Those were the last words out of his mouth, and they signaled the abrupt end of the discussion.

Vlad got up without warning and disappeared into the dark. Lady Justina followed. She suspected where he was headed and was not surprised when he went to the armory.

"What are you doing?" she asked, stepping out of the shadows and blowing her cover.

He gave a dry laugh when he saw her. "Ah! My lady, what do I do with you? I should have known that you followed." He turned to face her. "You're getting better at this." He winked. Lady Justina scoffed. It was so like him to make light of a situation like this. She took a deep breath and tried to come up with a solution. Vlad Tepes was just as stubborn as her cousin was and trying to force him not to do something would only serve as motivation to make him want to do it, so she tried a softer approach, triggering her womanly appeal. She coaxed.

"My Lord, why don't you stay for the night? Invite your guest in and let him get some rest, and by first light, you both can ride out tomorrow. I mean, he must be worn out from traveling such a long distance in such a short time."

Her goal was to buy her time that night so that she could think and come up with a better strategy. Vlad Tepes, however, was not easily dissuaded. In the end, she resigned and accepted the fact he would not change his mind.

"If you insist on leaving, then please, how about you ask my cousin for help? You have an alliance and his Black Army is the most feared in the kingdoms. At least that should be a good match for the Ottomans, even better."

"I will, my lady," Vlad Tepes assured her, then kissed her on the lips and stomach. "Take care of my little ones until I return, my love." And then, with a mischievous grin, added, "and we can make some more little ones when I return."

It was a joke, and Lady Justina understood it as one, but she was too afraid to laugh. She had a bad feeling about this fight.

CHAPTER THIRTY TWO

The Ottomans were slowly advancing towards Castle Bran, at the heart of Transylvania. Justina heard a report about the battle between Vlad Tepes' army and the Ottomans, and it was a long, tiring, back-and-forth fight. Vlad's army had driven out the Ottomans from their regions, sending them far away from the land, but the Ottomans had been better prepared and another troop marched straight for Transylvania to lay claim to the kingdom while the Voivode was out fighting.

Vlad got news of the Ottomans' plan to attack Transylvania and traveled back home just in time. He arrived in the city just as the Ottoman forces were trying to push back the city walls and invade. There, outside the city gates, he laid waste to the lot of them with his soldiers. Swords clashed aggressively and heads rolled on the ground, guts were spilled, and limbs were cut.

Vlad's sword clashed with that of a man who seemed to be the leader of the ottomans and he smirked bitterly, knowing this would be the end for the unlucky fellow. "Prepare to meet your gods."

"It'll be you meeting your gods Tepes!" He yelled, leaping off his feet and swinging his sword violently which Vlad easily countered with his sword blocking it off.

Vlad smiled knowing he had already won because whoever attacked so angrily never lasted in the fight long enough. With one hand behind him, he fought off the leader and backed off, dodging and jumping to avoid the sword swings. Just when his opponent caught his breath, Vlad swung his sword so hard against the man that even though he countered, the force was enough to send him to the ground.

His eyes went wide, fear flashing in them and Vlad swiftly threw his sword, getting him right in his neck, piercing right through, and sending a rush of blood out. He died on the spot and so did the Ottomans' will to continue fighting.

Some others tried to escape and were captured and brought back to the kingdom. Filled with rage at the thought that they would dare invade his city and the unimaginable thoughts of what could have been done to his wife and children, he ordered them to be impaled.

It was going to be a sign to the world, daring them never to cross him.

He was a just and fair ruler. Living up to his reputation as a strong and great ruler. He only punished those who did him wrong, and those who were a threat to him and his kingdom. There were several rumors about him, some calling him a cruel and heartless ruler. But he knew who he was himself, a man of dignity, honor, and respect. As much as he never cared about what happened to his enemies, beneath the strength and power was a soft man at heart who cared so much for his family. He could become a beast, or rather, he was a beast if anybody tried to kill or harm them.

Vlad stayed back in Transylvania for a while until he was sure that there was peace and the kingdom was not in danger.

Standing next to the row of books in the library with a book in his hand, he heard a soft knock.

"Enter."

Lady Justina walked in with a tray in her hand; she smiled at him. She had instructed the servants not to touch anything as she wanted to prepare her husband's favorite. He had been in the library and studying without coming out, and he only went out to attend meetings.

"My love," he said, closing the book in his hands and smiling back at her as he went to assist her with the door.

"Thank you." She smiled cheekily, showing her beautiful set of teeth. "I made this for you, and I want you to try it." She settled the tray on the table and opened the plate of delicious delicacies; honey cakes and flavored bread.

"Oh… I…" Vlad salivated. "I can't wait to taste this. I know it would taste as delicious as you." He grabbed a spoon and scooped the food into his mouth, closing his eyes.

Lady Justina blushed as she found a seat and sat, enjoying the look on her husband's face as he devoured the food.

"How did you know I needed this so much?" He didn't stop munching. "This is so heavenly, my darling, that I could devour you right away."

"That would be wonderful, my love." She giggled like a child. "You haven't been out of the study for days, so I made you this and some tea to help you relax."

He sipped his wine, his lips laced gorgeously on the lid of the cup. "And this tastes perfectly good. Just as I love it."

"I made all of this," she boasted. She wasn't allowed to cook while she was at the castle back in Hungary, but she had taken some lessons from Esme. "And I am sure you'll love it, Your Grace."

Vlad stopped eating and looked at his wife. "I can't trade you for anything in this world. Your cooking is the best in all the land. Better than any other renowned cook in the kingdom." Lady Justina couldn't hide the blush on her face. She was red with excitement and flattery.

She loved her husband too much. "How are things? Have you written to King Matthias?" "Yes, I have. I need his support as soon as possible and hope he lends me."

"I'm sure he will. He wouldn't want to turn his back on you." At least he has something to gain.

"Yes. I presume so."

"I can request an audience with him if that will help. I can talk to him."

"No, my love, there is no need for you to stress at all. I expect his reply soon."

"Alright, let me know if you need my help. I am going to back you up in whatever decision you make," she said, her eyes full of compassion.

She was a great wife, caring and understanding. Vlad knew from the first time he met her she was the right one for him. Maybe fate had strung them together, for him to be wrongfully accused and locked up in King Matthias' castle so he could see her and meet her and for her to have gone through all she had so she could be ready for all of this. He couldn't get enough of her and he never would, she was unique and mysterious.

Nobody could believe such a woman who looked humble, kind, and simple had so much more wisdom than you could imagine. Vlad smiled to himself as he watched her, appreciating her beauty and never taking his eyes off her.

She packed the used plates in the tray neatly and put them aside.

Vlad wiped his lips with the napkin and sighed in satisfac- tion. He enjoyed the food and the unwavering support his wife had given him.

"And thank you, my lady. For this sumptuous meal that made my stomach merry."

Lady Justina smiled and sat back in her seat, embarrassed at the constant flush she felt on her cheeks. Although she needed not to, he was her husband and could compliment her in whatever way he wanted, but every time he mentioned or appreciated her beauty, it felt as when they met for the first time. Every single moment of it was unique and special. Her heart thumped hard in her chest in excitement and butterflies fluttered in her stomach.

He had written to King Matthias, informing him of the ongoing conflict between himself and the Ottoman Sultan, Mehmed II. He beseeched the king to send him help and come to his aid in driving out the attackers from his lands. He planned to conduct a raid in all his kingdoms until he had driven out and laid waste to every one of the Ottoman camps within his territory.

King Matthias replied to Vlad's message more promptly than he had ever done before. He was furious at the Ottomans' audacity and promised to send out his troops to fight alongside Vlad Tepes and his men. Encouraged by the strength of the king's promise to him, Vlad Tepes set off with his men to pursue the Ottomans.

He was in for a rude awakening.

She saw him, his back turned against her, and she tried to   call him. He was standing in the middle of a field, green with fresh plants and colorful flowers. Happiness flushed through Justina, her husband was back from the fight, but something was odd. The other soldiers he went to battle with weren't there.

"Vlad! You're back!" she said eagerly, but he didn't reply. He was odd; his stance wasn't as gallant as it used to be. She moved closer to him, trying to get him to face her, so she called his name.

"Vlad!" she called out, but there was no response. She stretched her hand to touch him but he faded away.

Confused and scared, she looked around to find him. Suddenly, the green field she was standing in was no longer blossoming and beautiful. It was now an arid land with dried leaves and the gushing sound of the harsh dust.

"Vlad! Vlad! Where are you?"

She looked around frantically, but he wasn't there.

"My darling," he said softly, love and regret showing in his eyes, walking towards her and cupping her face in his palm. "How I've missed you!"

"Vlad," she sank into his warmth, tears pouring down her face. "I've missed you too, my love."

His eyes were warm. "My darling," he said again.

"When will you be home? I have made your favorite. Little Vlad is expecting you."

His eyes went down in sadness.

"What is wrong, my love?" she asked, fear in her voice.

He smiled and cupped her face once again. Words refused to come even when he tried to speak. He was sorry to leave her all alone by herself. He was sorry for not staying with her forever, as he had promised.

Talk to me," she said. She lifted her hands to wipe his tears, but he melted away slowly.

"Vlad!" she called out in horror, but he was gone, leaving her in the vast, dry, arid land.

She jumped awake sweating profusely, her heart hammering and her head aching. She checked her bedside, and it was empty.

Wrapping her robe around herself tightly, she walked to the balcony. It was midnight, and the crescent moon reflected its light on the earth. The breeze blew her hair, drying her of the sweat that stuck on her body.

Sitting in the bath, with her neck resting on the tip of the round tub, she closed her eyes, reminiscing about the night- mare she had. She saw fragments of him again. Something was wrong with her husband, and she had gotten a sign.

After her bath, she slipped on her robe and headed back to the balcony.

An owl flew past and rested on the tree branch a few meters away. It stared at her for a while, their gazes meeting each other, then hooted.

An odd sign. She was uneasy. There was something she didn't know.

Justina went back to bed, but still could not sleep. She stared at the ceiling, her thoughts troubling her and the dream lingering in her mind.

"Come back to me, husband," she whispered as she slowly went to sleep.

After several weeks without news, Lady Justina inquired about the raids and found out it was not going according to plan. Vlad Tepes had lost a good number of his men; his retinue had been ambushed, and the enemy had captured him.

CHAPTER THIRTY THREE

Lady Justina requested for a fast carriage to be prepared and journeyed to Hungary to see her cousin. On arrival, she was shocked to notice that not just the king but all of his finest fighters had stayed back in Hungary. It appeared none of them even had left to fight alongside her husband. Blinded by rage, she dashed into the king's courtroom. The king was alone with Sebastian, poring over state matters.

"How could you?" she said, dashing in. The royal guard at the door was on her tail and bowed apologetically before the king. The king dismissed the guard, and Lord Sebastian excused himself from the king's presence.

"Ah! Dear cousin, I must say, you have grown. You look so big..." His voice trailed off, and a thought dropped in his head. Suddenly, his face lit up with a smile. "Is that...? Wow! You're pregnant!"

"Stop the pretense, cousin."

King Matthias's eyes flared, and he rebuked her. "I am your king, and you will address me as such."

She glared at him, pulsing with rage at his supposed calm- ness. Memories of how he had used her in the past to acquire more power and lands flooded her, and she realized that once again, she had been used to acquire Vlad Tepes' territory. Her cousin had manipulated her husband's love for her into a tool to acquire more kingdoms.

"You… You're not human. You started the alliance, and when he needed you, what did you do? You hide here, in this suffocating castle, playing king and using everyone else as pawns in your wicked scheme."

"Guards!" the king said, and at once, royal guards trooped into the courtroom. The king's request was clear enough, but they hesitated. They wanted to be certain that the king meant for them to arrest her.

How dare she accuse him? The guards were confused, looking at the king and Justina. They didn't know what to do. The king's eyes were fixated on Justina, who returned the fixed look in anger.

"Don't just stand there," the king said, and the guards moved into action, one person on either side of her, holding on to her arms.

"I'm sorry, my lady," the guard on her left muttered.

She barely heard him. She was ready for whatever fate she met here. She felt betrayed, used, and hated him as much as she hated herself for ever believing there was good in him. She walked forward, the guards unsure of what to do or how to handle her.

"Don't bother locking me up, cousin. I dare you to pull that sword by your waist and slit my throat here. Who knows? Death might bring relief." As she said that, her hand subconsciously went over her stomach protectively.

She clenched her jaw tight. Her fists clenched so tightly that her nails almost pierced her palms. She was filled with rage that she couldn't contain.

He had no empathy. How could he use her like that? With no sense of remorse or care for how much damage he had done to her?

This was not the first time it had happened that he had used her for his selfish gain and under the pretense that he put her best interests at heart.

"You won't talk to me like that," he said now, his gaze fixed upon her. She knew he could see it all, how hurt, angry, and damaged she was. It wasn't his fault, and there was nothing to blame him for. Vlad Tepes was a strong man, and a great ally also, but he couldn't risk himself or his position for a threat from a stronger force. His cousin was the perfect candidate for all of his schemes. She had been a great asset to him, but politics was politics, a game played by dirty people.

You had to be. If you were not, you would be swept away like the dust of the earth. Justina had to understand that, too. Justina's eyes were red. She tried to press down on the tears building in her eyes. She would have to stand up to him one day, tell him his years of puppeteering her were over, and everything seemed to make sense to her now.

During her wedding to Vlad Tepes, his countenance had looked rather satisfactory. He didn't want to be too involved in anything after the alliance had been sealed with the marriage. She didn't notice, and neither did Vlad. He didn't stay long at their wedding, either, to even congratulate them on their bliss, and afterward, they heard nothing from him as he didn't interfere.

The next was when she had her child. He sent only a letter and gifts but didn't come to see if she gave birth to a human or a centaur. The puzzles became clear to her as she pieced them together.

And when her husband needed his help, his response was rather too hasty, and he was willing. Her cousin was rather not too willing to do anything that would not benefit him. Unlike his letter when she had her child that came later, his reply was fast, as if he knew his plan was working out.

The king flicked his hand at the guards, and they released their grip on Justina. He dismissed them and they saluted and marched out of his presence, leaving them alone.

His voice was calm when he spoke, circling his cousin as he did. Justina eyed him, still fuming.

"You will find out, Justina, that I have your best interests at heart. I always do."

Justina's eyes flared again. How selfish he was. Thoughts ran through her head wildly as they rang in anger. King Matthias sat back, rubbing his palms together and then reaching out for a drink.

He could still drink. Justina didn't keep her gaze off him. With each piercing look that was like needles in his body, the king was no longer comfortable. He requested for a guard to come and escort her back to her carriage and back to Transylvania. She had said her piece, so she did not resist, but on her way out, the king called her name and said, "My deepest condolences," raising a goblet to her.

His words struck her, and she sighed in defeat. "No, my condolences," she said quickly in reply, and those words haunted the king for a long time.

A smile forming on her face, she turned to leave, never looking back or letting her step falter. She felt free now. The freedom she had always wanted, free from his grasp, his schemes, and selfish interests. King Matthias could not stop thinking about what she said to him. She was nothing; just someone who bluffed but could be terrifyingly cruel when she meant to be.

"What could she possibly do? …With what army?" He thought to himself.

He chuckled at the thought of his own cousin waging war against him. He knew he might have crossed the line, but to him, that was just how politics worked. He needed to have a strong heart to have a strong hand. He would do anything to protect his people.

The night was suddenly cold. He missed Esme. He had sent Esme far away to bear his son. It was hard for him at first but he soon got used to it. He visited them often, and they came over on the weekends to spend some time with him, but it was never enough for him. The castle had now felt empty most of the time.

He had fallen in love with Babara so much that no other maiden could satisfy him.

Now his sister was threatening him.

Of course, he had to take Vlad out smartly, it's not like he dug a hole in his chest, someone else did, and even cut his head off. Why was she channeling her anger toward him?

He was going to take everything Transylvania had. Along with Vlad and his wife's titles. Lady Justina was supposed to be grateful to him for that opportunity she had because now Vlad is dead and she could never be a Princess. He owned that power and he would do anything to keep it.

Lady Justina was filled with so much hate, like never. She swore to avenge her husband's death. She swore to protect Transylvania from her evil and selfish cousin.

There was nothing left for her to do with him again. The next thing on her mind was securing her position as the head of her home. To defend her children and her people and make sure nobody dared threaten her or anybody she cared about.

Justina's story will continue…

EPILOGUE

The news of Vlad Tepes' death arrived in Transylvania before Lady Justina returned from her visit to Hungary. She heard how he was brutally beheaded and his head delivered to Sultan Mehmed II, in Constantinople, in a barrel of honey to preserve it. Grief clouded her sight, and she wept bitterly, mourning him for a long time.

She wished she had stopped him, but no, she didn't see this coming.

Whenever she closed her eyes, it was like he was there. It hurt her deeply when she realized how hard it'll be when her sons ask her where daddy was. They were going to grow up without a father. She cried.

He took three of her lovers away from her in a snap. Her cousin had to be the worst man who ever lived.

She ordered her guards to enforce tight security all around Transylvania. They were to kill any trespasser!

She chuckled at the thought of her past self. She had been so naïve.

She tried not to think of what would have been done to his body, but the thought plagued her still. She imagined they would hang his head on a pole as a trophy, and it was indeed what happened. Vlad

Tepes' head on a pole was the grand treasure of Sultan Mehmed, Leader of the Ottomans.

Lady Justina held a burial for her late husband. She had planned for it to be a small affair, but the people also wanted to commemorate their leader, who died trying to keep their land safe and everyone gathered to pay their final respects to him.

After she had concluded the burial rite, Lady Justina decided it was time to avenge her husband, and her first call was to make sure none of the power-hungry traitors who had taken part in his death would ever get the throne of Transylvania.

She was the Princess Consort of Wallachia, and she claimed the seat in the name of her late husband and her young sons. The people validated her decision and swore their allegiance to her.

The story was just beginning...

Dedication

I would like to dedicate this book to my mother Floarea Stancu, who turned 60 this year. I love you more than words can describe. Thank you for being such a good mother to us.

Have you liked Petronella Pearson on Facebook?

Be the first to know about Petronella's latest books, access exclusive competition and stay in touch with news about Petronella.

Made in the USA
Middletown, DE
30 November 2023